# O'HALLORAN'S LUCK

## and Other Short Stories by

## STEPHEN VINCENT BENÉT

British Library Cataloguing-in-Publication Data
A catalogue record for this book is available from the
British Library

# Stephen Vincent Benét

Stephen Vincent Benét was born on 22nd July 1898 in Bethlehem, Pennsylvania, United States.

Benét was sent to the Hitchcock Military Academy at the age of ten and then continued his education at The Albany Academy in New York. He also attended Yale University where he received his M.A. in English.

Benét was an accomplished writer at an early age, having had his first book published at 17 and submitting his third volume of poetry in lieu of a thesis for his degree. During his time at Yale, he was an influential figure at the 'Yale Lit' literary magazine, and a fellow member of the Elizabethan Club. Benét was also a part-time contributor for the early Time Magazine.

Benét's involvement with the University literary scene led to a decade-long judgeship of the Yale Series of Younger Poets Competition. He is also responsible for publishing the first volumes of work by authors such as James Agee, Muriel Rukeyser, Jeremy Ingalls, and Margaret Walker. In 1931, he was elected as a fellow of the American Academy of Arts ad Sciences.

Benét's best known works are the book-length narrative poem *American Civil War, John Brown's Body* (1928), for which he won a Pulitzer Prize in 1929, and two short stories, *The Devil and Daniel Webster* (1936) and *By the Waters of Babylon* (1937). Benét won a second Pulitzer Prize posthumously for his unfinished poem *Western Star* in 1944.

Stephen Vincent Benét died of a heart attack in New York City, on 13th March, 1943, and is buried in Evergreen Cemetery, Stonington, Conneticut.

# CONTENTS

# O'HALLORAN'S LUCK

## AND OTHER SHORT STORIES

# O'HALLORAN'S LUCK

They were strong men built the Big Road, in the early days of America, and it was the Irish did it.

My grandfather, Tim O'Halloran, was a young man then, and wild. He could swing a pick all day and dance all night, if there was a fiddler handy; and if there was a girl to be pleased he pleased her, for he had the tongue and the eye. Likewise, if there was a man to be stretched, he could stretch him with the one blow.

I saw him later on in years when he was thin and white-headed, but in his youth he was not so. A thin, white-headed man would have had little chance, and they driving the Road to the West. It was two-fisted men cleared the plains and bored through the mountains. They came in the thousands to do it from every county in Ireland; and now the names are not known. But it's over their graves you pass, when you ride in the Pullmans. And Tim O'Halloran was one of them, six feet high and solid as the Rock of Cashel when he stripped to the skin.

He needed to be all of that, for it was not easy labor. 'Twas a time of great booms and expansions in the railroad line, and they drove the tracks north and south, east and west, as if the devil was driving behind. For this they must have the boys with shovel and pick, and every immigrant ship from Ireland was crowded with bold young men. They left famine and England's rule behind them —and it was the thought of many they'd pick up gold for the asking in the free States of America, though it's little gold that most of them ever saw. They found themselves up to their necks in the water of the canals, and burnt

1

black by the suns of the prairie—and that was a great surprise to them. They saw their sisters and their mothers
made servants that had not been servants in Ireland, and
that was a strange change too. Eh, the death and the
broken hopes it takes to make a country! But those with
the heart and the tongue kept the tongue and the heart.

Tim O'Halloran came from Clonmelly, and he was the
fool of the family and the one who listened to tales. His
brother Ignatius went for a priest and his brother James
for a sailor, but they knew he could not do those things.
He was strong and biddable and he had the O'Halloran
tongue; but there came a time of famine, when the
younger mouths cried for bread and there was little room
in the nest. He was not entirely wishful to emigrate, and
yet, when he thought of it, he was wishful. 'Tis often
enough that way, with a younger son. Perhaps he was
the more wishful because of Kitty Malone.

'Tis a quiet place, Clonmelly, and she'd been the light
of it to him. But now the Malones had gone to the States
of America—and it was well known that Kitty had a po-
sition there the like of which was not to be found in all
Dublin Castle. They called her a hired girl, to be sure,
but did not she eat from gold plates, like all the citizens
of America? And when she stirred her tea, was not the
spoon made of gold? Tim O'Halloran thought of this,
and of the chances and adventures that a bold young man
might find, and at last he went to the boat. There were
many from Clonmelly on that boat, but he kept himself
to himself and dreamed his own dreams.

The more disillusion it was to him, when the boat
landed him in Boston and he found Kitty Malone there,
scrubbing the stairs of an American house with a pail
and brush by her side. But that did not matter, after the
first, for her cheeks still had the rose in them and she
looked at him in the same way. 'Tis true there was an
Orangeman courting her—conductor he was on the horsecars, and Tim did not like that. But after Tim had seen

her, he felt himself the equal of giants; and when the call came for strong men to work in the wilds of the West, he was one of the first to offer. They broke a sixpence between them before he left—it was an English sixpence, but that did not matter greatly to them. And Tim O'Halloran was going to make his fortune, and Kitty Malone to wait for him, though her family liked the Orangeman best.

Still and all, it was cruel work in the West, as such work must be, and Tim O'Halloran was young. He liked the strength and the wildness of it—he'd drink with the thirstiest and fight with the wildest—and that he knew how to do. It was all meat and drink to him—the bare tracks pushing ahead across the bare prairie and the fussy cough of the wood-burning locomotives and the cold blind eyes of a murdered man, looking up at the prairie stars. And then there was the cholera and the malaria—and the strong man you'd worked on the grade beside, all of a sudden gripping his belly with the fear of death on his face and his shovel falling to the ground.

Next day he would not be there and they'd scratch a name from the pay roll. Tim O'Halloran saw it all.

He saw it all and it changed his boyhood and hardened it. But, for all that, there were times when the black fit came upon him, as it does to the Irish, and he knew he was alone in a strange land. Well, that's a hard hour to get through, and he was young. There were times when he'd have given all the gold of the Americas for a smell of Clonmelly air or a glimpse of Clonmelly sky. Then he'd drink or dance or fight or put a black word on the foreman, just to take the aching out of his mind. It did not help him with his work and it wasted his pay; but it was stronger than he, and not even the thought of Kitty Malone could stop it. 'Tis like that, sometimes.

Well, it happened one night he was coming back from the place where they sold the potheen, and perhaps he'd had a trifle more of it than was advisable. Yet he had not drunk it for that, but to keep the queer thoughts from his mind. And yet, the more that he drank, the queerer were the thoughts in his head. For he kept thinking of the Luck of the O'Hallorans and the tales his granda had told about it in the old country—the tales about pookas and banshees and leprechauns with long white beards.

"And that's a queer thing to be thinking and myself at labor with a shovel on the open prairies of America," he said to himself. "Sure, creatures like that might live and thrive in the old country—and I'd be the last to deny it—but 'tis obvious they could not live here. The first sight of Western America would scare them into conniptions. And as for the Luck of the O'Hallorans, 'tis little good I've had of it, and me not even able to rise to foreman and marry Kitty Malone. They called me the fool of the family in Clonmelly, and I misdoubt but they were right. Tim O'Halloran, you're a worthless man, for all your strong back and arms." It was with such black, bitter thoughts as these that he went striding over the prairie. And it was just then that he heard the cry in the grass.

'Twas a strange little piping cry, and only the half of it human. But Tim O'Halloran ran to it, for in truth he was spoiling for a fight. "Now this will be a beautiful young lady," he said to himself as he ran, "and I will save her from robbers; and her father, the rich man, will ask me—but, wirra, 'tis not her I wish to marry, 'tis Kitty Malone. Well, he'll set me up in business, out of friendship and gratitude, and then I will send for Kitty—"

But by then he was out of breath, and by the time he had reached the place where the cry came from he could see that it was not so. It was only a pair of young wolf cubs, and they chasing something small and helpless and playing with it as a cat plays with a mouse. Where the wolf cub is the old wolves are not far, but Tim O'Halloran felt as bold as a lion. "Be off with you!" he cried and he threw a stick and a stone. They ran away into the night, and he could hear them howling—a lonesome sound. But he knew the camp was near, so he paid small attention to that but looked for the thing they'd been chasing.

It scuttled in the grass but he could not see it. Then he stooped down and picked something up, and when he had it in his hand he stared at it unbelieving. For it was a tiny shoe, no bigger than a child's. And more than that, it was not the kind of shoe that is made in America. Tim O'Halloran stared and stared at it—and at the silver buckle upon it—and still he could not believe.

"If I'd found this in the old country," he said to himself, half aloud, "I'd have sworn that it was a leprechaun's and looked for the pot of gold. But here, there's no chance of that—"

"I'll trouble you for the shoe," said a small voice close by his feet.

Tim O'Halloran stared round him wildly. "By the piper that played before Moses!" he said. "Am I drunk beyond comprehension? Or am I mad? For I thought that I heard a voice."

"So you did, silly man," said the voice again, but irritated, "and I'll trouble you for my shoe, for it's cold in the dewy grass."

"Honey," said Tim O'Halloran, beginning to believe his ears, "honey dear, if you'll but show yourself—"

"I'll do that and gladly," said the voice; and with that the grasses parted, and a little old man with a long white beard stepped out. He was perhaps the size of a well-grown child, as O'Halloran could see clearly by the moonlight on the prairie; moreover, he was dressed in the clothes of antiquity, and he carried cobbler's tools in the belt at his side.

"By faith and belief, but it *is* a leprechaun!" cried O'Halloran, and with that he made a grab for the apparition. For you must know, in case you've been ill brought up, that a leprechaun is a sort of cobbler fairy and each one knows the whereabouts of a pot of gold. Or it's so they say in the old country. For they say you can tell a leprechaun by his long white beard and his cobbler's tools; and once you have the possession of him, he must tell you where his gold is hid.

The little old man skipped out of reach as nimbly as a cricket. "Is this Clonmelly courtesy?" he said with a shake in his voice, and Tim O'Halloran felt ashamed.

"Sure, I didn't mean to hurt your worship at all," he said, "but if you're what you seem to be, well, then, there's the little matter of a pot of gold—"

"Pot of gold!" said the leprechaun, and his voice was hollow and full of scorn. "And would I be here today if I had that same? Sure, it all went to pay my sea passage, as you might expect."

"Well," said Tim O'Halloran, scratching his head, for that sounded reasonable enough, "that may be so or again it may not be so. But—"

"Oh, 'tis bitter hard," said the leprechaun, and his voice was weeping, "to come to the waste, wild prairies all alone, just for the love of Clonmelly folk—and then to be disbelieved by the first that speaks to me! If it had been an Ulsterman now, I might have expected it. But the O'Hallorans wear the green."

"So they do," said Tim O'Halloran, "and it shall not be said of an O'Halloran that he denied succor to the friendless. I'll not touch you."

"Do you swear it?" said the leprechaun.

"I swear it," said Tim O'Halloran.

"Then I'll just creep under your coat," said the leprechaun, "for I'm near destroyed by the chills and damps of the prairie. Oh, this weary emigrating!" he said, with a sigh like a furnace. " 'Tis not what it's cracked up to be."

Tim O'Halloran took off his own coat and wrapped it around him. Then he could see him closer—and it could not be denied that the leprechaun was a pathetic sight. He'd a queer little boyish face, under the long white beard, but his clothes were all torn and ragged and his cheeks looked hollow with hunger.

"Cheer up!" said Tim O'Halloran and patted him on

the back. "It's a bad day that beats the Irish. But tell me first how you came here—for that still sticks in my throat."

"And would I be staying behind with half Clonmelly on the water?" said the leprechaun stoutly. "By the bones of Finn, what sort of a man do you think I am?"

"That's well said," said Tim O'Halloran. "And yet I never heard of the Good People emigrating before."

"True for you," said the leprechaun. "The climate here's not good for most of us and that's a fact. There's a boggart or so that came over with the English, but then the Puritan ministers got after them and they had to take to the woods. And I had a word or two, on my way West, with a banshee that lives by Lake Superior—a decent woman she was, but you could see she'd come down in the world. For even the bits of children wouldn't believe in her; and when she let out a screech, sure they thought it was a steamboat. I misdoubt she's died since then—she was not in good health when I left her.

"And as for the native spirits—well, you can say what you like, but they're not very comfortable people. I was captive to some of them a week and they treated me well enough, but they whooped and danced too much for a quiet man, and I did not like the long, sharp knives on them. Oh, I've had the adventures on my way here," he said, "but they're over now, praises be, for I've found a protector at last," and he snuggled closer under O'Halloran's coat.

"Well," said O'Halloran, somewhat taken aback, "I did not think this would be the way of it when I found O'Halloran's Luck that I'd dreamed of so long. For, first I save your life from the wolves; and now, it seems, I must be protecting you further. But in the tales it's always the other way round."

"And is the company and conversation of an ancient and experienced creature like myself nothing to you?" said the leprechaun fiercely. "Me that had my own castle at Clonmelly and saw O'Sheen in his pride? Then St. Patrick came—wirra, wirra!—and there was an end to it all. For some of us—the Old Folk of Ireland—he baptized, and some of us he chained with the demons of hell. But I was Lazy Brian, betwixt and between, and all I wanted was peace and a quiet life. So he changed me to what you see—me that had six tall harpers to harp me awake in the morning—and laid a doom upon me for being betwixt and between. I'm to serve Clonmelly folk and follow them wherever they go till I serve the servants of servants in a land at the world's end. And then, perhaps, I'll be given a Christian soul and can follow my own inclinations."

"Serve the servants of servants?" said O'Halloran. "Well, that's a hard riddle to read."

"It is that," said the leprechaun, "for I never once met the servant of a servant in Clonmelly, all the time I've been looking. I doubt but that was in St. Patrick's mind."

"If it's criticizing the good saint you are, I'll leave you here on the prairie," said Tim O'Halloran.

"I'm not criticizing him," said the leprechaun with a sigh, "but I could wish he'd been less hasty. Or more specific. And now, what do we do?"

"Well," said O'Halloran, and he sighed, too, " 'tis a great responsibility, and one I never thought to shoulder. But since you've asked for help, you must have it. Only there's just this to be said. There's little money in my pocket."

"Sure, 'tis not for your money I've come to you," said the leprechaun joyously. "And I'll stick closer than a brother."

"I've no doubt of that," said O'Halloran with a wry laugh. "Well, clothes and food I can get for you—but if you stick with me, you must work as well. And perhaps the best way would be for you to be my young nephew, Rory, run away from home to work on the railroad."

"And how would I be your young nephew, Rory, and me with a long white beard?"

"Well," said Tim O'Halloran with a grin, "as it happens, I've got a razor in my pocket."

And with that you should have heard the leprechaun.
He stamped and he swore and he pled—but it was no use
at all. If he was to follow Tim O'Halloran, he must do it
on Tim O'Halloran's terms and no two ways about it.
So O'Halloran shaved him at last, by the light of the
moon, to the leprechaun's great horror, and when he got
him back to the construction camp and fitted him out in
some old duds of his own—well, it wasn't exactly a boy he
looked, but it was more like a boy than anything else.
Tim took him up to the foreman the next day and got
him signed on for a water boy, and it was a beautiful tale
he told the foreman. As well, too, that he had the O'Halloran tongue to tell it with, for when the foreman first
looked at young Rory you could see him gulp like a man
that's seen a ghost.

"And now what do we do?" said the leprechaun to Tim
when the interview was over.

"Why, you work," said Tim with a great laugh, "and
Sundays you wash your shirt."

"Thank you for nothing," said the leprechaun with an
angry gleam in his eye. "It was not for that I came here
from Clonmelly."

"Oh, we've all come here for great fortune," said Tim,
"but it's hard to find that same. Would you rather be with
the wolves?"

"Oh, no," said the leprechaun.

"Then drill, ye tarrier, drill!" said Tim O'Halloran
and shouldered his shovel, while the leprechaun trailed
behind.

At the end of the day the leprechaun came to him.

"I've never done mortal work before," he said, "and
there's no bone in my body that's not a pain and an
anguish to me."

"You'll feel better after supper," said O'Halloran.
"And the night's made for sleep."

"But where will I sleep?" said the leprechaun.

"In the half of my blanket," said Tim, "for are you
not young Rory, my nephew?"

It was not what he could have wished, but he saw he could do no otherwise. Once you start a tale, you must play up to the tale.

But that was only the beginning, as Tim O'Halloran soon found out. For Tim O'Halloran had tasted many things before, but not responsibility, and now responsibility was like a bit in his mouth. It was not so bad the first week, while the leprechaun was still ailing. But when, what with the food and the exercise, he began to recover his strength, 'twas a wonder Tim O'Halloran's hair did not turn gray overnight. He was not a bad creature, the leprechaun, but he had all the natural mischief of a boy of twelve and, added to that, the craft and knowledge of generations.

There was the three pipes and the pound of shag the leprechaun stole from McGinnis—and the dead frog he slipped in the foreman's tea—and the bottle of potheen he got hold of one night when Tim had to hold his head in a bucket of water to sober him up. A fortunate thing it was that St. Patrick had left him no great powers, but at that he had enough to put the jumping rheumatism on Shaun Kelly for two days—and it wasn't till Tim threatened to deny him the use of his razor entirely that he took off the spell.

That brought Rory to terms, for by now he'd come to take a queer pleasure in playing the part of a boy and he did not wish to have it altered.

Well, things went on like this for some time, and Tim O'Halloran's savings grew; for whenever the drink was running he took no part in it, for fear of mislaying his wits when it came to deal with young Rory. And as it was with the drink, so was it with other things—till Tim O'Halloran began to be known as a steady man. And then, as it happened one morning, Tim O'Halloran woke up early. The leprechaun had finished his shaving and was sitting cross-legged, chuckling to himself.

"And what's your source of amusement so early in the day?" said Tim sleepily.

"Oh," said the leprechaun, "I'm just thinking of the rare hard work we'll have when the line's ten miles farther on."

"And why should it be harder there than it is here?" said Tim.

"Oh, nothing," said the leprechaun, "but those fools of surveyors have laid out the line where there's hidden springs of water. And when we start digging, there'll be the devil to pay."

"Do you know that for a fact?" said Tim.

"And why wouldn't I know it?" said the leprechaun. "Me that can hear the waters run underground."

"Then what should we do?" said Tim.

"Shift the line half a mile to the west and you'd have a firm roadbed," said the leprechaun.

Tim O'Halloran said no more at the time. But for all that, he managed to get to the assistant engineer in charge of construction at the noon hour. He could not have done it before, but now he was known as a steady man. Nor did he tell where he got the information—he put it on having seen a similar thing in Clonmelly.

Well, the engineer listened to him and had a test made —and sure enough, they struck the hidden spring. "That's clever work, O'Halloran," said the engineer. "You've saved us time and money. And now how would you like to be foreman of a gang?"

"I'd like it well," said Tim O'Halloran.

"Then you boss Gang Five from this day forward," said the engineer. "And I'll keep my eye on you. I like a man that uses his head."

"Can my nephew come with me," said Tim, "for, 'troth, he's my responsibility?"

"He can," said the engineer, who had children of his own.

So Tim got promoted and the leprechaun along with him. And the first day on the new work, young Rory stole the gold watch from the engineer's pocket, because he liked the tick of it, and Tim had to threaten him with fire and sword before he'd put it back.

Well, things went on like this for another while, till finally Tim woke up early on another morning and heard the leprechaun laughing.

"And what are you laughing at?" he said.

"Oh, the more I see of mortal work, the less reason there is to it," said the leprechaun. "For I've been watching the way they get the rails up to us on the line. And they do it thus and so. But if they did it so and thus, they could do it in half the time with half the work."

"Is that so indeed?" said Tim O'Halloran, and he made him explain it clearly. Then, after he'd swallowed his breakfast, he was off to his friend the engineer.

"That's a clever idea, O'Halloran," said the engineer. "We'll try it." And a week after that, Tim O'Halloran found himself with a hundred men under him and more responsibility than he'd ever had in his life. But it seemed little to him beside the responsibility of the leprechaun, and now the engineer began to lend him books to study and he studied them at nights while the leprechaun snored in its blanket.

A man could rise rapidly in those days—and it was then Tim O'Halloran got the start that was to carry him far. But he did not know he was getting it, for his heart was near broken at the time over Kitty Malone. She'd written him a letter or two when he first came West, but now there were no more of them and at last he got a word from her family telling him he should not be disturbing Kitty with letters from a laboring man. That was bitter for Tim O'Halloran, and he'd think about Kitty and the Orangeman in the watches of the night and groan. And then, one morning, he woke up after such a night and heard the leprechaun laughing.

"And what are you laughing at now?" he said sourly. "For my heart's near burst with its pain."

"I'm laughing at a man that would let a cold letter keep

him from his love, and him with pay in his pocket and the contract ending the first," said the leprechaun.

Tim O'Halloran struck one hand in the palm of the other.

"By the piper, but you've the right of it, you queer little creature!" he said. "'Tis back to Boston we go when this job's over."

It was laborer Tim O'Halloran that had come to the West, but it was Railroadman Tim O'Halloran that rode back East in the cars like a gentleman, with a free pass in his pocket and the promise of a job on the railroad that was fitting a married man. The leprechaun, I may say, gave some trouble in the cars, more particularly when he bit a fat woman that called him a dear little boy; but what with giving him peanuts all the way, Tim O'Halloran managed to keep him fairly quieted.

When they got to Boston he fitted them both out in new clothes from top to toe. Then he gave the leprechaun some money and told him to amuse himself for an hour or so while he went to see Kitty Malone.

He walked into the Malones' flat as bold as brass, and there sure enough, in the front room, were Kitty Malone and the Orangeman. He was trying to squeeze her hand, and she refusing, and it made Tim O'Halloran's blood boil to see that. But when Kitty saw Tim O'Halloran she let out a scream.

"Oh, Tim!" she said. "Tim! And they told me you were dead in the plains of the West!"

"And a great pity that he was not," said the Orangeman, blowing out his chest with the brass buttons on it, "but a bad penny always turns up."

"Bad penny is it, you brass-buttoned son of iniquity," said Tim O'Halloran. "I have but the one question to put you. Will you stand or will you run?"

"I'll stand as we stood at Boyne Water," said the Orangeman, grinning ugly. "And whose backs did we see that day?"

"Oh, is that the tune?" said Tim O'Halloran. "Well,

I'll give you a tune to match it. Who fears to speak of Ninety-Eight?"

With that he was through the Orangeman's guard and stretched him at the one blow, to the great consternation of the Malones. The old woman started to screech and Pat Malone to talk of policemen, but Tim O'Halloran silenced the both of them.

"Would you be giving your daughter to an Orangeman that works on the horsecars, when she might be marrying a future railroad president?" he said. And with that he pulled his savings out of his pocket and the letter that promised the job for a married man. That quieted the Malones a little and, once they got a good look at Tim O'Halloran, they began to change their tune. So, after they'd got the Orangeman out of the house—and he did not go willing, but he went as a whipped man must—Tim O'Halloran recounted all of his adventures.

The tale did not lose in the telling, though he did not speak of the leprechaun, for he thought that had better be left to a later day; and at the end Pat Malone was offering him a cigar. "But I find I have none upon me," said he with a wink at Tim, "so I'll just run down to the corner."

"And I'll go with you," said Kitty's mother, "for if Mr. O'Halloran stays to supper—and he's welcome—there's a bit of shopping to be done."

So the old folks left Tim O'Halloran and his Kitty alone. But just as they were in the middle of their planning and contriving for the future, there came a knock on the door.

"What's that?" said Kitty, but Tim O'Halloran knew well enough and his heart sank within him. He opened the door—and sure enough, it was the leprechaun.

"Well, Uncle Tim," said the creature, grinning, "I'm here."

Tim O'Halloran took a look at him as if he saw him for the first time. He was dressed in new clothes, to be sure, but there was soot on his face and his collar had thumbmarks on it already. But that wasn't what made the difference. New clothes or old, if you looked at him for the first time, you could see he was an unchancy thing, and not like Christian souls.

"Kitty," he said, "Kitty darlint, I had not told you. But this is my young nephew, Rory, that lives with me."

Well, Kitty welcomed the boy with her prettiest manners, though Tim O'Halloran could see her giving him a side look now and then. All the same, she gave him a slice of cake, and he tore it apart with his fingers; but in the middle of it he pointed to Kitty Malone.

"Have you made up your mind to marry my Uncle Tim?" he said. "Faith, you'd better, for he's a grand catch."

"Hold your tongue, young Rory," said Tim O'Halloran angrily, and Kitty blushed red. But then she took the next words out of his mouth.

"Let the gossoon be, Tim O'Halloran," she said bravely. "Why shouldn't he speak his mind? Yes, Roryeen—it's I that will be your aunt in the days to come—and a proud woman too."

"Well, that's good," said the leprechaun, cramming the last of the cake in his mouth, "for I'm thinking you'll make a good home for us, once you're used to my ways."

"Is that to be the way of it, Tim?" said Kitty Malone very quietly, but Tim O'Halloran looked at her and knew what was in her mind. And he had the greatest impulse in the world to deny the leprechaun and send him about his business. And yet, when he thought of it, he knew that he could not do it, not even if it meant the losing of Kitty Malone.

"I'm afraid that must be the way of it, Kitty," he said with a groan.

"Then I honor you for it," said Kitty, with her eyes like stars. She went up to the leprechaun and took his hard little hand. "Will you live with us, young Rory?" she said. "For we'd be glad to have you."

"Thank you kindly, Kitty Malone—O'Halloran to be," said the leprechaun. "And you're lucky, Tim O'Halloran

—lucky yourself and lucky in your wife. For if you had denied me then, your luck would have left you—and if she had denied me then, 'twould be but half luck for you both. But now the luck will stick to you the rest of your lives. And I'm wanting another piece of cake," said he.

"Well, it's a queer lad you are," said Kitty Malone, but she went for the cake. The leprechaun swung his legs and looked at Tim O'Halloran. "I wonder what keeps my hands off you," said the latter with a groan.

"Fie!" said the leprechaun, grinning, "and would you be lifting the hand to your one nephew? But tell me one thing, Tim O'Halloran, was this wife you're to take ever in domestic service?"

"And what if she was?" said Tim O'Halloran, firing up. "Who thinks the worse of her for that?"

"Not I," said the leprechaun, "for I've learned about mortal labor since I came to this country—and it's an honest thing. But tell me one thing more. Do you mean to serve this wife of yours and honor her through the days of your wedded life?"

"Such is my intention," said Tim, "though what business it is of—"

"Never mind," said the leprechaun. "Your shoelace is undone, bold man. Command me to tie it up."

"Tie up my shoe, you black-hearted, villainous little anatomy!" thundered Tim O'Halloran, and the leprechaun did so. Then he jumped to his feet and skipped about the room.

"Free! Free!" he piped. "Free at last! For I've served the servants of servants and the doom has no power on me longer. Free, Tim O'Halloran! O'Halloran's Luck is free!"

Tim O'Halloran stared at him, dumb; and even as he stared, the creature seemed to change. He was small, to be sure, and boyish—but you sould see the unchancy look leave him and the Christian soul come into his eyes. That was a queer thing to be seen, and a great one too.

"Well," said Tim O'Halloran in a sober voice, "I'm

glad for you, Rory. For now you'll be going back to Clonmelly, no doubt—and faith, you've earned the right."

The leprechaun shook his head.

"Clonmelly's a fine, quiet place," said he, "but this country's bolder. I misdoubt it's something in the air—you will not have noticed it, but I've grown two inches and a half since first I met you, and I feel myself growing still. No, it's off to the mines of the West I am, to follow my natural vocation—for they say there are mines out there you could mislay all Dublin Castle in—and wouldn't I like to try! But speaking of that, Tim O'Halloran," he said, "I was not quite honest with you about the pot of gold. You'll find your share behind the door when I've gone. And now good day and long life to you!"

"But, man dear," said Tim O'Halloran, " 'tis not good-by!" For it was then he realized the affection that was in him for the queer little creature.

"No, 'tis not good-by," said the leprechaun. "When you christen your first son, I'll be at his cradle, though you may not see me—and so with your sons' sons and their sons, for O'Halloran's luck's just begun. But we'll part for the present now. For now I'm a Christian soul, I've work to do in the world."

"Wait a minute," said Tim O'Halloran. "For you would not know, no doubt, and you such a new soul. And no doubt you'll be seeing the priest—but a layman can do it in an emergency and I think this is one. I dare not have you leave me—and you not even baptized."

And with that he made the sign of the cross and baptized the leprechaun. He named him Rory Patrick.

" 'Tis not done with all the formalities," he said at the end, "but I'll defend the intention."

"I'm grateful to you," said the leprechaun. "And if there was a debt to be paid, you've paid it back and more."

And with that he was gone somehow, and Tim O'Halloran was alone in the room. He rubbed his eyes. But there was a little sack behind the door, where the leprechaun had left it—and Kitty was coming in with a slice of cake on a plate.

"Well, Tim," she said, "and where's that young nephew of yours?"

So he took her into his arms and told her the whole story. And how much of it she believed, I do not know. But there's one remarkable circumstance. Ever since then, there's always been one Rory O'Halloran in the family, and that one luckier than the lave. And when Tim O'Halloran got to be a railroad president, why, didn't he call his private car "The Leprechaun"? For that matter, they said, when he took his business trips there'd be a small boyish-looking fellow would be with him now and again. He'd turn up from nowhere, at some odd stop or other, and he'd be let in at once, while the great of the railroad world were kept waiting in the vestibule. And after a while, there'd be singing from inside the car.

# JACOB AND THE INDIANS

It goes back to the early days—may God profit all who lived then—and the ancestors.

Well, America, you understand, in those days was different. It was a nice place, but you wouldn't believe it if you saw it today. Without busses, without trains, without states, without Presidents, nothing!

With nothing but colonists and Indians and wild woods all over the country and wild animals to live in the wild woods. Imagine such a place! In these days, you children don't even think about it; you read about it in the schoolbooks, but what is that? And I put in a call to my daughter, in California, and in three minutes I am saying "Hello, Rosie," and there it is Rosie and she is telling me about the weather, as if I wanted to know! But things were not always that way. I remember my own days, and they were different. And in the times of my grandfather's grandfather, they were different still. Listen to the story.

My grandfather's grandfather was Jacob Stein, and he came from Rettelsheim, in Germany. To Philadelphia he came, an orphan in a sailing ship, but not a common man. He had learning—he had been to the *chedar*—he could have been a scholar among the scholars. Well, that is the way things happen in this bad world. There was a plague and a new grand duke—things are always so. He would say little of it afterward—they had left his teeth in his mouth, but he would say little of it. He did not have to say—we are children of the Dispersion—we know a black day when it comes.

Yet imagine—a young man with fine dreams and learning, a scholar with a pale face and narrow shoulders, set down in those early days in such a new country. Well, he must work, and he did. It was very fine, his learning, but it did not fill his mouth. He must carry a pack on his back and go from door to door with it. That was no disgrace; it was so that many began. But it was not expounding the Law, and at first he was very homesick. He would sit in his room at night, with the one candle, and read the preacher Koheleth, till the bitterness of the preacher rose in his mouth. Myself, I am sure that Koheleth was a great preacher, but if he had had a good wife he would have been a more cheerful man. They had too many wives in those old days—it confused them. But Jacob was young.

As for the new country where he had come, it was to him a place of exile, large and frightening. He was glad to be out of the ship, but, at first, that was all. And when he saw his first real Indian in the street—well, that was a day! But the Indian, a tame one, bought a ribbon from him by signs, and after that he felt better. Nevertheless, it seemed to him at times that the straps of the pack cut into his very soul, and he longed for the smell of the *chedar* and the quiet streets of Rettelsheim and the good smoked goose-breast pious housewives keep for the scholar. But there is no going back—there is never any going back.

All the same, he was a polite young man, and a hard-working. And soon he had a stroke of luck—or at first it seemed so. It was from Simon Ettelsohn that he got the trinkets for his pack, and one day he found Simon Ettelsohn arguing a point of the Law with a friend, for Simon was a pious man and well thought of in the Congregation Mikveh Israel. Our grandfather's grandfather stood by very modestly at first—he had come to replenish his pack and Simon was his employer. But finally his heart moved within him, for both men were wrong, and he spoke and told them where they erred. For half an hour he spoke, with his pack still upon his shoulders, and never has a text been expounded with more complexity, not even by the great Reb Samuel. Till, in the end, Simon Ettelsohn threw up his hands and called him a young David and a candle of learning. Also, he allowed him a more profitable route of trade. But, best of all, he invited young Jacob to his house, and there Jacob ate well for the first time since he had come to Philadelphia. Also he laid eyes upon Miriam Ettelsohn for the first time, and she was Simon's youngest daughter and a rose of Sharon.

After that, things went better for Jacob, for the protection of the strong is like a rock and a well. But yet things did not go altogether as he wished. For, at first, Simon Ettelsohn made much of him, and there was stuffed fish and raisin wine for the young scholar, though he was a peddler. But there is a look in a man's eyes that says "H'm? Son-in-law?" and that look Jacob did not see. He was modest—he did not expect to win the maiden overnight, though he longed for her. But gradually it was borne in upon him what he was in the Ettelsohn house— a young scholar to be shown before Simon's friends, but a scholar whose learning did not fill his mouth. He did not blame Simon for it, but it was not what he had intended. He began to wonder if he would ever get on in the world at all, and that is not good for any man.

Nevertheless, he could have borne it, and the aches and pains of his love, had it not been for Meyer Kappelhuist. Now, there was a pushing man! I speak no ill of anyone, not even of your Aunt Cora, and she can keep the De Groot silver if she finds it in her heart to do so; who lies down in the straw with a dog, gets up with fleas. But this Meyer Kappelhuist! A big, red-faced fellow from Holland with shoulders the size of a barn door and red hair on the backs of his hands. A big mouth for eating and drinking and telling schnorrer stories—and he talked about the Kappelhuists, in Holland, till you'd think they were made of gold. The crane says, "I am really a peacock—at least on my mother's side." And yet, a thriving man—that could not be denied. He had started with a pack, like our grandfather's grandfather, and now he was trading with the Indians and making money hand over fist. It seemed to Jacob that he could never go to the Ettelsohn house without meeting Meyer and hearing about those Indians. And it dried the words in Jacob's mouth and made his heart burn.

For, no sooner would our grandfather's grandfather begin to expound a text or a proverb, than he would see Meyer Kappelhuist looking at the maiden. And when Jacob had finished his expounding, and there should have been a silence, Meyer Kappelhuist would take it upon himself to thank him, but always in a tone that said: "The Law is the Law and the Prophets are the Prophets, but prime beaver is also prime beaver, my little scholar!" It took the pleasure from Jacob's learning and the joy of the maiden from his heart. Then he would sit silent and burning, while Meyer told a great tale of Indians, slapping his hands on his knees. And in the end he was always careful to ask Jacob how many needles and pins he had sold that day; and when Jacob told him, he would smile and say very smoothly that all things had small beginnings, till the maiden herself could not keep from a little smile. Then, desperately, Jacob would rack his brains for more interesting matter. He would tell of the wars of the Maccabees and the glory of the Temple. But even as he told them, he felt they were far away. Whereas Meyer and his accursed Indians were there, and the maiden's eyes shone at his words.

Finally he took his courage in both hands and went to Simon Ettelsohn. It took much for him to do it, for he had not been brought up to strive with men, but with words. But it seemed to him now that everywhere he went he heard of nothing but Meyer Kappelhuist and his trading with the Indians, till he thought it would drive him mad. So he went to Simon Ettelsohn in his shop.

"I am weary of this narrow trading in pins and needles," he said, without more words.

Simon Ettelsohn looked at him keenly; for while he was an ambitious man, he was kindly as well.

"*Nu,*" he said. "A nice little trade you have and the people like you. I myself started in with less. What would you have more?"

"I would have much more," said our grandfather's grandfather stiffly. "I would have a wife and a home in this new country. But how shall I keep a wife? On needles and pins?"

"*Nu,* it has been done," said Simon Ettelsohn, smiling a little. "You are a good boy, Jacob, and we take an interest in you. Now, if it is a question of marriage, there are many worthy maidens. Asher Levy, the baker, has a daughter. It is true that she squints a little, but her heart is of gold." He folded his hands and smiled.

"It is not of Asher Levy's daughter I am thinking," said Jacob, taken aback. Simon Ettelsohn nodded his head and his face grew grave.

"*Nu,* Jacob," he said. "I see what is in your heart. Well, you are a good boy, Jacob, and a fine scholar. And if it were in the old country, I am not saying. But here, I have one daughter married to a Seixas and one to a Da Silva. You must see that makes a difference." And he smiled the smile of a man well pleased with his world.

"And if I were such a one as Meyer Kappelhuist?" said Jacob bitterly.

"Now—well, that is a little different," said Simon Ettelsohn sensibly. "For Meyer trades with the Indians. It is true, he is a little rough. But he will die a rich man."

"I will trade with the Indians too," said Jacob, and trembled.

Simon Ettelsohn looked at him as if he had gone out of his mind. He looked at his narrow shoulders and his scholar's hands.

"Now, Jacob," he said soothingly, "do not be foolish. A scholar you are, and learned, not an Indian trader. Perhaps in a store you would do better. I can speak to Aaron Copras. And sooner or later we will find you a nice maiden. But to trade with Indians—well, that takes a different sort of man. Leave that to Meyer Kappelhuist."

"And your daughter, that rose of Sharon? Shall I leave her, too, to Meyer Kappelhuist?" cried Jacob.

Simon Ettelsohn looked uncomfortable.

"*Nu*, Jacob," he said. "Well, it is not settled, of course. But—"

"I will go forth against him as David went against Goliath," said our grandfather's grandfather wildly. "I will go forth into the wilderness. And God should judge the better man!"

Then he flung his pack on the floor and strode from the shop. Simon Ettelsohn called out after him, but he did not stop for that. Nor was it in his heart to go and seek the maiden. Instead, when he was in the street, he counted the money he had. It was not much. He had meant to buy his trading goods on credit from Simon Ettelsohn, but now he could not do that. He stood in the sunlit street of Philadelphia, like a man bereft of hope.

Nevertheless, he was stubborn—though how stubborn he did not yet know. And though he was bereft of hope, he found his feet taking him to the house of Raphael Sanchez.

Now, Raphael Sanchez could have bought and sold Simon Ettelsohn twice over. An arrogant old man he was, with fierce black eyes and a beard that was whiter than snow. He lived apart, in his big house with his granddaughter, and men said he was very learned, but also very disdainful, and that to him a Jew was not a Jew who did not come of the pure sephardic strain.

Jacob had seen him, in the Congregation Mikveh Israel, and to Jacob he had looked like an eagle, and fierce as an eagle. Yet now, in his need, he found himself knocking at that man's door.

It was Raphael Sanchez himself who opened. "And what is for sale today, peddler?" he said, looking scornfully at Jacob's jacket where the pack straps had worn it.

"A scholar of the Law is for sale," said Jacob in his bitterness, and he did not speak in the tongue he had learned in this country, but in Hebrew.

The old man stared at him a moment.

"Now am I rebuked," he said. "For you have the tongue. Enter, my guest," and Jacob touched the scroll by the doorpost and went in.

They shared the noon meal at Raphael Sanchez's table. It was made of dark, glowing mahogany, and the light sank into it as sunlight sinks into a pool. There were many precious things in that room, but Jacob had no eyes for them. When the meal was over and the blessing said, he opened his heart and spoke, and Raphael Sanchez listened, stroking his beard with one hand. When the young man had finished, he spoke.

"So, Scholar," he said, though mildly, "you have crossed an ocean that you might live and not die, and yet all you see is a girl's face."

"Did not Jacob serve seven years for Rachel?" said our grandfather's grandfather.

"Twice seven, Scholar," said Raphael Sanchez dryly, "but that was in the blessed days." He stroked his beard again. "Do you know why I came to this country?" he said.

"No," said Jacob Stein.

"It was not for the trading," said Raphael Sanchez. "My house has lent money to kings. A little fish, a few furs —what are they to my house? No, it was for the promise— the promise of Penn—that this land should be an habitation and a refuge, not only for the Gentiles. Well, we know Christian promises. But so far, it has been kept. Are you spat upon in the street here, Scholar of the Law?"

"No," said Jacob. "They call me Jew, now and then. But the Friends, though Gentile, are kind."

"It is not so in all countries," said Raphael Sanchez, with a terrible smile.

"No," said Jacob quietly, "it is not."

The old man nodded. "Yes, one does not forget that," he said. "The spittle wipes off the cloth, but one does not forget. One does not forget the persecutor or the persecuted. That is why they think me mad, in the Congregation Mikveh Israel, when I speak what is in my mind. For, look you"—and he pulled a map from a drawer—"here is what we know of these colonies, and here and here our people make a new beginning, in another air. But here is New France—see it?—and down the great river come the French traders and their Indians."

"Well?" said Jacob in puzzlement.

"Well?" said Raphael Sanchez. "Are you blind? I do not trust the King of France—the king before him drove out the Huguenots, and who knows what he may do? And if they hold the great rivers against us, we shall never go westward."

"We?" said Jacob in bewilderment.

"We," said Raphael Sanchez. He struck his hand on the map. "Oh, they cannot see it in Europe—not even their lords in parliament and their ministers of state," he said. "They think this is a mine, to be worked as the Spaniards worked Potosi, but it is not a mine. It is something beginning to live, and it is faceless and nameless yet. But it is our lot to be part of it—remember that in the wilderness, my young scholar of the Law. You think you are going there for a girl's face, and that is well enough. But you may find something there you did not expect to find."

He paused and his eyes had a different look.

"You see, it is the trader first," he said. "Always the trader, before the settled man. The Gentiles will forget that, and some of our own folk too. But one pays for the land of Canaan; one pays in blood and sweat."

Then he told Jacob what he would do for him and dismissed him, and Jacob went home to his room with his head buzzing strangely. For at times it seemed to him that the Congregation Mikveh Israel was right in thinking Raphael Sanchez half mad. And at other times it seemed to him that the old man's words were a veil, and behind them moved and stirred some huge and unguessed shape. But chiefly he thought of the rosy cheeks of Miriam Ettelsohn.

It was with the Scotchman, McCampbell, that Jacob made his first trading journey. A strange man was McCampbell, with grim features and cold blue eyes, but strong and kindly, though silent, except when he talked of the Ten Lost Tribes of Israel. For it was his contention that they were the Indians beyond the Western Mountains, and on this subject he would talk endlessly.

Indeed, they had much profitable conversation, McCampbell quoting the doctrines of a rabbi called John Calvin, and our grandfather's grandfather replying with Talmud and Torah till McCampbell would almost weep that such a honey-mouthed scholar should be destined to eternal damnation. Yet he did not treat our grandfather's grandfather as one destined to eternal damnation, but as a man, and he, too, spoke of cities of refuge as a man speaks of realities, for his people had also been persecuted.

First they left the city, behind them, and then the outlying towns and, soon enough, they were in the wilderness. It was very strange to Jacob Stein. At first he would wake at night and lie awake listening, while his heart pounded, and each rustle in the forest was the step of a wild Indian, and each screech of an owl in the forest the whoop before the attack. But gradually this passed. He began to notice how silently the big man, McCampbell, moved in the woods; he began to imitate him. He began to learn many things that even a scholar of the Law, for all his wisdom, does not know—the girthing of a packsaddle and the making of fires, the look of dawn in the forest and the look of evening. It was all very new to him, and sometimes he thought he would die of it, for his flesh weakened. Yet always he kept on.

When he saw his first Indians—in the woods, not in the town—his knees knocked together. They were there as he had dreamt of them in dreams, and he thought of the spirit, Iggereth-beth-Mathlan, and her seventy-eight dancing demons, for they were painted and in skins. But he could not let his knees knock together, before heathens and a Gentile, and the first fear passed. Then he found they were grave men, very ceremonious and silent at first, and then when the silence had been broken, full of curiosity. They knew McCampbell, but him they did not know, and they discussed him and his garments with the frankness of children, till Jacob felt naked before them, and yet not afraid. One of them pointed to the bag that hung at Jacob's neck—the bag in which, for safety's sake, he carried his phylactery—then McCampbell said something and the brown hand dropped quickly, but there was a buzz of talk.

Later on, McCampbell explained to him that they, too, wore little bags of deerskin and inside them sacred objects—and they thought, seeing his, that he must be a person of some note. It made him wonder. It made him wonder more to eat deer meat with them, by a fire.

It was a green world and a dark one that he had fallen in—dark with the shadow of the forest, green with its green. Through it ran trails and paths that were not yet roads or highways—that did not have the dust and smell of the cities of men, but another scent, another look. These paths Jacob noted carefully, making a map, for that was one of the instructions of Raphael Sanchez. It seemed a great labor and difficult and for no purpose; yet, as he had promised, so he did. And as they sank deeper and deeper into the depths of the forest, and he saw pleasant streams and wide glades, untenanted but by the deer, strange thoughts came over him. It seemed to him that the Germany he had left was very small and crowded together; it seemed to him that he had not known there was so much width to the world.

Now and then he would dream back—dream back to the quiet fields around Rettelsheim and the red-brick houses of Philadelphia, to the stuffed fish and the raisin wine, the chanting in the *chedar* and the white twisted loaves of calm Sabbath, under the white cloth. They would seem very close for the moment, then they would seem very far away. He was eating deer's meat in a forest and sleeping beside embers in the open night. It was so that Israel must have slept in the wilderness. He had not thought of it as so, but it was so.

Now and then he would look at his hands—they seemed tougher and very brown, as if they did not belong to him any more. Now and then he would catch a glimpse of his own face, as he drank at a stream. He had a beard, but it was not the beard of a scholar—it was wild and black. Moreover, he was dressed in skins, now; it seemed strange to be dressed in skins at first, and then not strange.

Now all this time, when he went to sleep at night, he would think of Miriam Ettelsohn. But, queerly enough, the harder he tried to summon up her face in his thoughts, the vaguer it became.

He lost track of time—there was only his map and the trading and the journey. Now it seemed to him that they should surely turn back, for their packs were full. He spoke of it to McCampbell, but McCampbell shook his head. There was a light in the Scotchman's eyes now—a light that seemed strange to our grandfather's grandfather —and he would pray long at night, sometimes too loudly. So they came to the banks of the great river, brown and great, and saw it, and the country beyond it, like a view across Jordan. There was no end to the country—it stretched to the limits of the sky and Jacob saw it with his eyes. He was almost afraid at first, and then he was not afraid.

It was there that the strong man, McCampbell, fell sick, and there that he died and was buried. Jacob buried him on a bluff overlooking the river and faced the grave to the west. In his death sickness, McCampbell raved of the Ten Lost Tribes again and swore they were just across the river and he would go to them. It took all Jacob's strength to hold him—if it had been at the beginning of the journey, he would not have had the strength. Then he turned back, for he, too, had seen a Promised Land, not for his seed only, but for nations yet to come.

· Nevertheless, he was taken by the Shawnees, in a season of bitter cold, with his last horse dead. At first, when misfortune began to fall upon him, he had wept for the loss .of the horses and the good beaver. But, when the Shawnees took him, he no longer wept; for it seemed to him that he was no longer himself, but a man he did not know.

He was not concerned when they tied him to the stake and piled the wood around him, for it seemed to him still that it must be happening to another man. Nevertheless he prayed, as was fitting, chanting loudly; for Zion in the wilderness he prayed. He could smell the smell of the *chedar* and hear the voices that he knew—Reb Moses and Reb Nathan, and through them the curious voice of Raphael Sanchez, speaking in riddles. Then the smoke took him and he coughed. His throat was hot. He called for drink, and though they could not understand his words, all men know the sign of thirst, and they brought him a bowl filled. He put it to his lips eagerly and drank, but the stuff in the bowl was scorching hot and burned his mouth. Very angry then was our grandfather's grandfather, and without so much as a cry he took the bowl in both hands and flung it straight in the face of the man who had brought it, scalding him. Then there was a cry and a murmur from the Shawnees and, after some moments, he felt himself unbound and knew that he lived.

It was flinging the bowl at the man while yet he stood at the stake that saved him, for there is an etiquette about such matters. One does not burn a madman, among the Indians; and to the Shawnees, Jacob's flinging the bowl proved that he was mad, for a sane man would not have done so. Or so it was explained to him later, though he was never quite sure that they had not been playing cat-and-mouse with him, to test him. Also they were much concerned by his chanting his death song in an unknown tongue and by the phylactery that he had taken from its bag and bound upon brow and arm for his death hour, for these they thought strong medicine and uncertain. But in any case they released him, though they would not give him back his beaver, and that winter he passed in the lodges of the Shawnees, treated sometimes like a servant and sometimes like a guest, but always on the edge of peril. For he was strange to them, and they could not quite make up their minds about him, though the man with the scalded face had his own opinion, as Jacob could see.

Yet when the winter was milder and the hunting better than it had been in some seasons, it was he who got the credit of it, and the holy phylactery also; and by the end of the winter he was talking to them of trade, though diffidently at first. Ah, our grandfather's grandfather, *selig,* what woes he had! And yet it was not all woe, for he learned much woodcraft from the Shawnees and began to speak in their tongue.

Yet he did not trust them entirely; and when spring came and he could travel, he escaped. He was no longer a scholar then, but a hunter. He tried to think what day it was by the calendar, but he could only remember the Bee Moon and the Berry Moon. Yet when he thought of a feast he tried to keep it, and always he prayed for Zion. But when he thought of Zion, it was not as he had thought of it before—a white city set on a hill—but a great and open landscape, ready for nations. He could not have said why his thought had changed, but it had.

I shall not tell all, for who knows all? I shall not tell of the trading post he found deserted and the hundred and forty French louis in the dead man's money belt. I shall not tell of the half-grown boy, McGillvray, that he found on the fringes of settlement—the boy who was to be his partner in the days to come—and how they traded again with the Shawnees and got much beaver. Only this remains to be told, for this is true.

It was a long time since he had even thought of Meyer Kappelhuist—the big pushing man with red hairs on the backs of his hands. But now they were turning back toward Philadelphia, he and McGillvray, their packhorses and their beaver; and as the paths began to grow familiar, old thoughts came into his mind. Moreover, he would hear now and then, in the outposts of the wilderness, of a red-haired trader. So when he met the man himself, not thirty miles from Lancaster, he was not surprised.

Now, Meyer Kappelhuist had always seemed a big man to our grandfather's grandfather. But he did not seem such a big man, met in the wilderness by chance, and at that Jacob was amazed. Yet the greater surprise was Meyer Kappelhuist's, for he stared at our grandfather's grandfather long and puzzledly before he cried out, "But it's the little scholar!" and clapped his hand on his knee. Then they greeted each other civilly and Meyer Kappelhuist drank liquor because of the meeting, but Jacob drank nothing. For, all the time they were talking, he could see Meyer Kappelhuist's eyes fixed greedily upon his packs of beaver, and he did not like that. Nor did he like the looks of the three tame Indians who traveled with Meyer Kappelhuist and, though he was a man of peace, he kept his hand on his arms, and the boy, McGillvray, did the same.

Meyer Kappelhuist was anxious that they should travel on together, but Jacob refused, for, as I say, he did not like the look in the red-haired man's eyes. So he said he was taking another road and left it at that.

"And the news you have of Simon Ettelsohn and his family—it is good, no doubt, for I know you are close to them," said Jacob, before they parted.

"Close to them?" said Meyer Kappelhuist, and he looked black as thunder. Then he laughed a forced laugh. "Oh, I see them no more," he said. "The old rascal has promised his daughter to a cousin of the Seixas, a greeny, just come over, but rich, they say. But to tell you the truth, I think we are well out of it, Scholar—she was always a little too skinny for my taste," and he laughed coarsely.

"She was a rose of Sharon and a lily of the valley," said Jacob respectfully, and yet not with the pang he would have expected at such news, though it made him more determined than ever not to travel with Meyer Kappelhuist. And with that they parted and Meyer Kappelhuist went his way. Then Jacob took a fork in the trail that McGillvray knew of and that was as well for him. For when he got to Lancaster, there was news of the killing of a trader by the Indians who traveled with him; and when Jacob asked for details, they showed him something dried on a willow hoop. Jacob looked at the thing and saw the hairs upon it were red.

"Sculped all right, but we got it back," said the frontiersman, with satisfaction. "The red devil had it on him when we caught him. Should have buried it, too, I guess, but we'd buried him already and it didn't seem feasible. Thought I might take it to Philadelphy, sometime— might make an impression on the governor. Say, if you're going there, you might—after all, that's where he come from. Be a sort of memento to his folks."

"And it might have been mine, if I had traveled with him," said Jacob. He stared at the thing again, and his heart rose against touching it. Yet it was well the city people should know what happened to men in the wilderness, and the price of blood. "Yes, I will take it," he said.

Jacob stood before the door of Raphael Sanchez, in Philadelphia. He knocked at the door with his knuckles, and the old man himself peered out at him.

"And what is your business with me, Frontiersman?" said the old man, peering.

"The price of blood for a country," said Jacob Stein. He did not raise his voice, but there was a note in it that had not been there when he first knocked at Raphael Sanchez's door.

The old man stared at him soberly. "Enter, my son," he said at last, and Jacob touched the scroll by the doorpost and went in.

He walked through the halls as a man walks in a dream. At last he was sitting by the dark mahogany table. There was nothing changed in the room—he wondered greatly that nothing in it had changed.

"And what have you seen, my son?" said Raphael Sanchez.

"I have seen the land of Canaan, flowing with milk and honey," said Jacob, Scholar of the Law. "I have brought back grapes from Eshcol, and other things that are terrible to behold," he cried, and even as he cried he felt the sob rise in his throat. He choked it down. "Also there are eighteen packs of prime beaver at the warehouse and a boy named McGillvray, a Gentile, but very trusty," he said. "The beaver is very good and the boy under my protection. And McCampbell died by the great river, but he had seen the land and I think he rests well. The map is not made as I would have it, but it shows new things. And we must trade with the Shawnees. There are three posts to be established—I have marked them on the map —and later, more. And beyond the great river there is country that stretches to the end of the world. That is where my friend McCampbell lies, with his face turned west. But what is the use of talking? You would not understand."

He put his head on his arms, for the room was too quiet and peaceful, and he was very tired. Raphael Sanchez moved around the table and touched him on the shoulder.

"Did I not say, my son, that there was more than a girl's face to be found in the wilderness?" he said.

"A girl's face?" said Jacob. "Why, she is to be married and, I hope, will be happy, for she was a rose of Sharon. But what are girls' faces beside this?" and he flung something on the table. It rattled dryly on the table, like a cast snakeskin, but the hairs upon it were red.

"It was Meyer Kappelhuist," said Jacob childishly, "and he was a strong man. And I am not strong, but a scholar. But I have seen what I have seen. And we must say Kaddish for him."

"Yes, yes," said Raphael Sanchez. "It will be done. I will see to it."

"But you do not understand," said Jacob. "I have eaten

deer's meat in the wilderness and forgotten the month and the year. I have been a servant to the heathen and held the scalp of my enemy in my hand. I will never be the same man."

"Oh, you will be the same," said Sanchez. "And no worse a scholar, perhaps. But this is a new country."

"It must be for all," said Jacob. "For my friend Mc-Campbell died also, and he was a Gentile."

"Let us hope," said Raphael Sanchez and touched him again upon the shoulder. Then Jacob lifted his head and he saw that the light had declined and the evening was upon him. And even as he looked, Raphael Sanchez's granddaughter came in to light the candles for Sabbath. And Jacob looked upon her, and she was a dove, with dove's eyes.

# THE SOBBIN' WOMEN

They came over the Pass one day in one big wagon—all ten of them—man and woman and hired girl and seven big boy children, from the nine-year-old who walked by the team to the baby in arms. Or so the story runs—it was in the early days of settlement and the town had never heard of the Sobbin' Women then. But it opened its eyes one day, and there were the Pontipees.

They were there but they didn't stay long—just time enough to buy meal and get a new shoe for the lead horse. You couldn't call them unsociable, exactly—they seemed to be sociable enough among themselves. But you could tell, somehow, from the look of them, that they weren't going to settle on ground other people had cleared. They were all high-colored and dark-haired— handsome with a wilderness handsomeness—and when you got them all together, they looked more like a tribe or a nation than an ordinary family. I don't know how they gave folks that feeling, but they did. Yes, even the baby, when the town women tried to handle him. He was a fine, healthy baby, but they said it was like trying to pet a young raccoon.

Well, that was all there was to it, at the start. They paid for what they bought in good money and drove on up into Sobbin' Women Valley—only it wasn't called Sobbin' Women Valley then. And pretty soon, there was smoke from a chimney there that hadn't been there before. But you know what town gossip is when it gets started. The Pontipees were willing enough to let other folks alone— in fact, that was what they wanted. But, because it was

37

what they wanted, the town couldn't see why they wanted it. Towns get that way, sometimes.

So, it was mostly cross questions and crooked answers when the Pontipees came into town, to trade off their pelts and such and buy at the store. There wasn't much actual trouble—not after two loafers at the tavern made fun of Pa Pontipee's fur cap and Pa Pontipee stretched them both before you could say "Jack Robinson." But there wasn't a neighborly feeling—yes, you could say that. The women would tell their children about the terrible Pontipees and the men would wag their heads. And when they came in to church—which they did once a year—there'd be a sort of rustle in the congregation, though they always took a back pew and listened perfectly respectful. But the minister never seemed to be able to preach as good a sermon as usual that Sunday—and naturally, he blamed the Pontipees for that. Till, finally, they got to be a sort of legend in the community—the wild folks who lived up the valley like bears in the woods—and, indeed, some said they turned into bears in the winter time, which just shows you what people will say. And, though the boys were well set up, they might as well have been deaf-mutes for all the notice the town-girls took of them—except to squeak and run to the other side of the road when the Pontipees came marching along.

While, as for the Pontipees—nobody knew what they made of it all, for they weren't much on talking. If one of them said "It's a fine day" and another admitted it was, that was conversation that would last them a long while. Besides, they had work enough and to spare, in their own valley, to keep them busy; and, if Ma Pontipee would have liked more society, she never let on. She did her duty by the boys and tried to give them some manners, in spite of their backwoods raising; and that was enough for any woman to do.

But things never stand still in this world, and soon enough, the boys weren't boys any more, they were men. And when the fall of a tree took Pa Pontipee, his wife didn't linger long after him. There was a terrible fuss about the funerals too—for the Pontipee boys got the minister, but they wouldn't let the burials take place in town. They said Pa and Ma wouldn't feel comfortable, all crowded up among strangers in the churchyard, so they laid them to rest in the Valley where they'd lived, and the town found that queerer than ever. But there's worse places to lie than looking out over the fields you've cleared.

After that, though, the town thought some of the boys, at least, would move in from the Valley and get more sociable. They figured they'd have to—they figured with their Pa and Ma gone, the boys would fight amongst themselves—they figured a dozen things. But none of the things they figured happened at all. The Pontipee boys stayed out in the Valley, and when they came to the town, they walked through it as proud as Lucifer, and when they came to the church, they put just the same money in the collection-plate they had when Ma and Pa Pontipee were alive. Some thought it was because they were stupid to count, but I don't think it was that.

They went on just the same, as I say, but things didn't go quite the same for them. For one thing, the hired girl couldn't keep the place the way Ma Pontipee kept it. And besides, she was getting old herself. Well, pretty soon, she up and died. They gave her as good a funeral as they knew how—she'd always been part of the family. But, after that, though the farm went ahead as well as ever, things in the house began to go from bad to worse.

Menlike, they didn't notice what was wrong at first, except there was a lot of dust around and things didn't get put away. But, after each one of them had tried a week of cooking for the others and all the others had cursed out the one who was cooking something proper, they decided something had to be done about it. It took them a long time to decide that—they were slow thinkers as well as slow talkers, the Pontipees. But, when they decided about a thing, it got done.

"The flapjacks are greasy again," said Harry Pontipee, one evening—Harry was the oldest. "You know what we've got to get, brothers? We've got to get a woman to take care of this place. I can lay a tree within two inches of where I want it to fall. I can shoot the eye out of a grey squirrel in a treetop. I can do all a man should do. But I can't cook and make it taste human."

"You're right, brother," said Hob Pontipee—Hob was the youngest. "I can tan deerskin better than an Injun squaw. I can wrastle underholt and overholt and throw any man in this county. I can play on a boxwood fiddle—but I can't sweep dust so it stays swept. It takes a woman to do that, for there seems to be a trick about it. We've got to get a woman."

Then they all joined in saying what they could do—and it was plenty—but they couldn't cook and they couldn't dust and they couldn't make a house comfortable because that was woman's business, and there seemed to be a trick about it. So they had to get a woman to keep house for them. But where were they going to get her?

"We could get a hired girl, maybe," said Hosea Pontipee—the middle one—but, even as he spoke, there wasn't much hope in his voice.

"That hired girl we had was the last one left in the East," said Harry Pontipee. "Some may have growed up, since her time, but I don't want to go back across the Pass on the chance of an out-and-out miracle."

"Well then," said Hob Pontipee, practical, "there's just one thing to do. One of us has to get married. And I think it ought to be Harry—he's the eldest."

Well, that remark nearly caused a break-up in the family. Harry kicked like a cow in fly-time at the bare idea of getting married, and tried to put it on to Halbert, who was next in line. And Halbert passed it on to Harvey, but Harvey said women was snares and delusions, or so he'd heard, and he wouldn't have a strange woman around him for a brand-new plow.

So it went on down to Hob and he wouldn't hear of

it—and it wasn't till a couple of chairs had been broken and Hob had a black eye that the ruckus quieted at all. But, gradually, they came to see that one of 'em would have to get married, as a matter of family duty, or they'd all be eating spoiled flapjacks for the rest of their lives. Only then the question came up as to who it was to be, and that started a bigger disturbance than ever.

Finally, they agreed that the only fair way was drawing straws. So Hob held the straws and they drew—and, sure enough, Harry got the long one. Sick enough he looked about it—but there it was. The others started congratulating him and making jokes—especially Hob.

"You'll have to slick up, tomorrow," said Hob, glad it wasn't him. "You'll have to cut your hair and brush your clothes and act pretty, if you're going to be a bridegroom!"

Next morning they got him down and cut his hair and put bear's grease on it and dressed him up in the best clothes they had and sent him into town to look for a wife.

It was all right when he started out from the Valley. He even took a look at himself in a spring and was kind of surprised at the young man who looked back at him. But the nearer he got to town, the queerer and tremblier he felt, and the less able to go about doing what he'd promised.

He tried to remember how it had been when his Pa and Ma had been courting. But, naturally, as he hadn't been born then, he didn't know. Then he tried to think of various girls in the village, but the more he thought of them, the more they mixed in his mind—till, finally, all he could think of was a high, wild bank of rhododendron flowers that mixed and shimmered and laughed at you the closer you came to it.

"Oh, Lordy! It's a heavy responsibility to lay on a man!" he said and mopped his forehead with his sleeve.

Finally, however, he made up his mind. "I'll ask the first woman I see, pretty or ugly!" he said to himself, with the perspiration fairly rolling down his face, though it was a cold March day. And he gave his horse a lick.

But, when he got into town, the first woman he saw was the storekeeper's wife. The second he saw was a little girl in a pinafore—and the third was the minister's daughter. He was all set up to speak to her—but she squeaked and ran to the other side of the street as soon as she saw him and left him standing there with his hat in his hand. That sort of took the courage out of him.

"By the whiskers of Moses!" he said to himself, "this marryin' job is a harder job than I bargained for. I guess I'll go over to the tavern and get me a drink—maybe that will put some ideas in my head."

It was there he saw her—feeding the chickens out in the poultry-yard. Her name was Milly and she was a bound girl, as they had in those days. Next door to a slave she was, for all she'd come of good stock and had some education. She was young and thin, with a sharp little thoughtful face and ragged clothes, but she walked as straight as an Indian as she went about the yard. Harry Pontipee couldn't have said if she were pretty or plain, but, as he watched her through the window, feeding the chickens, something seemed to tell him that he might have better luck with her than he'd had with the others.

Well, he drank his drink and went out.

"Hello, girl," he said, in one of those big voices men use when they're pretending not to be embarrassed.

She looked up at him straight. "Hello, backwoodsman!" she said, friendly enough. She didn't look a bit scared of him and that put him off.

"It's a nice morning," said Harry, louder, trying to lead up to his point.

"It is for some," said the girl, perfectly polite but going on feeding the chickens.

Harry swallowed hard at that. "It'd be a nice morning to get married, they tell me," he said, with the perspiration breaking out all over him again. He'd meant to say something else, but when it came to the point, he couldn't.

Well, she didn't say anything to that so he had to start all over again.

"My name's Harry Pontipee," he said. "I've got a good farm up the Valley."

"Have you?" said the girl.

"Yes," he said. "It's a right good farm. And some folks seem to think I'd make a good husband."

"Do they?" said the girl. I guess she was smiling by now but Harry couldn't see it—she had her head turned.

"Yes they do," said Harry, kind of desperate, his voice getting louder and louder. "What do you think about it?"

"I couldn't tell on such short acquaintance," said the girl.

"Will you marry me and find out?" said Harry, in a perfect bellow, shaking all over.

"Yes, I will, if you don't ask me quite so loud," she said, very prim—and even Harry could see she was smiling now.

Well, they made a queer pair when they went up to the minister—the girl still in her chicken-feed clothes, for she didn't have any others, and Harry in his backwoods finery. He'd had to buy out her time from the innkeeper for twelve beaver pelts and a hunting knife.

But when the wedding service was over, "Well, we're woman now, and what's fit for a chicken-girl isn't fit for a married woman."

"Oh, no we won't," said she. "We're going to the store first and buy me some cloth for a decent dress—for landless I may be and dowryless I may be, but I'm a married woman now, and what's for a chicken-girl isn't fit for a married woman."

In a sort of daze, he saw her lay out the price of twelve more beaver pelts in cloth and woman's fixings, and beat down the storekeeper on the price, too.

He only asked her a question about one thing—a little pair of slippers she bought. They were fancy slippers, with embroidery on them. "I thought you had a pair of shoes," he said. She turned to him, with a cocky sort of look on her face. "Silly," she said. "How could anyone tell your wife had pretty feet in the shoes I had?"

Well, he thought that over, and, after a while, something in the way she said it and the cocky look on her face made him feel pleased, and he began to laugh. He wasn't used to laughing in front of a girl, but he could see it might have its points.

Then they rode back to the Valley, her riding pillion, with her bundles in the saddlebags. And all the way back, she was trying him and testing him and trying to find out, by one little remark or another, just what kind of a man he was. She was a spunky little girl, and she had more education than she let on. And long ago, she'd made up her mind to get out of being a bound girl the first way that offered. But, all the same, marrying Harry Pontipee was a leap in the dark.

But the more she tried and tested Harry, the better bargain she seemed to think she'd made. And that took courage to admit—for the way was a wild one and a lonesome, and, naturally, she'd heard stories of Pontipee Valley. She couldn't quite believe they lived with bears, up there, but she didn't know.

And finally, they came to the house, and there were dark things moving outside it. "Bears!" thought Milly, kind of hopeless, and her heart went into her throat, but she didn't let on.

"W-what's that, Harry dear?" she said, holding on tight.

"Oh, that's just my brothers," said Harry, kind of careless, and with that those six hungry six-footers moved into the light.

"Oh!" said Milly, "you didn't tell me you had six brothers." But her voice wasn't reproachful, just sort of soft and quiet.

"I guess it was the wedding kind of knocked it out of

my mind," said Harry. "But, there—you'll see enough of
'em anyhow, because we all live together."

"Oh," said Milly again, kind of soft. "I see." And the
brothers came up, one by one, and shook hands. They'd
intended to cut quite a few jokes on Harry if he did come
home with a wife, but, somehow, when they looked at
Milly, they forgot about that.

Well, they brought her into the house. It was a handsome house, for the times, with genuine windowglass. But
Milly rubbed her finger along a window sill and saw it
come off black and then she wrote her name in the dust
on the mantelpiece.

"What a lovely big house!" she said, coughing a little
with the dust she'd raised.

"It's mebbe a little dusty now," said Harry. "But now
you're here——"

"Yes," said Milly and passed on to the kitchen. Well,
the kitchen was certainly a sight. But Milly didn't seem
to notice.

Presently, "What a great big jar of flapjack batter!" she
said. "And what a big tub of salt pork!"

"That's for tonight," said Harry. "Me and my brothers
is hearty eaters. We haven't been eating so well since we
had to cook for ourselves, but now you're here——"

"Yes," said Milly and passed on to the laundry. The
laundry was half full of huckaback shirts and such that
needed washing—piles and piles of them.

"What a lot of wash!" said Milly.

"That's so," said Harry, kind of pleased. "Me and my
brothers is kind of hard on our clothes—all seven of us—
so there's lots of washing and mending, but now you're
here——"

"Yes," said Milly, swallowing a little. "And now all you
men clear out of my kitchen while I get supper. Clear
out!" she said, smiling at them, though she didn't feel
much like smiling.

I don't know what she said to herself when they'd left
her alone. I know what a man would have said and I

guess she said that, too. I know she thought at least once of the money in her stocking and how far it was back to town. And then her eye happened to fall on that great big jar of flapjack batter—and, all of a sudden the whole thing struck her as funny, and she laughed till she cried.

But then she found a clean handkerchief and blew her nose and straightened her hair and set about her work.

Those boys hadn't had a supper like that in months and they treated it respectful. And Milly didn't say a word to them about manners then, though, later on, she said plenty. She just sat and watched them, with a curious light in her eyes.

When it was over finally, and they were stuffed, "Mrs. Harry," said Howard. "You're a wonder, Mrs. Harry!" and "You're sure a wonder, Mrs. Harry!" chorused all the rest of them, down to Hob. She could see they meant it, too.

"Thanks," she said, very polite and gracious. "Thank you, Howard, and you, Hosea, and all my brothers."

At the end of three months, there wasn't one of those boys that wouldn't have laid down his life for Milly, and, as for Harry, he just worshipped the ground she walked on. With all that work to do, naturally, she got thinner and thinner and peakeder and peakeder, but she didn't complain. She knew what she wanted and how she was going to get it—and she waited her chance.

Finally Harry noticed how thin she was getting and he spoke to her about it.

"Can't you ever sit down and rest, Milly?" he said one day, watching her fly around the kitchen, doing six things at once.

But she just laughed at him and said, "I'm cooking for you and your six brothers, and that makes work, you know."

Well, he thought that over, inside him, but he didn't say anything, then. But he came up to her in the laundry another time, and when she was dusting the house another time—she was looking peakeder each day—and asked her if she couldn't rest a spell. The last time, he brought his fist down on the table with a bang.

"This has got to stop!" he said. "Me and my six brothers is wearing you to skin and bone with our victuals and our shirts and the dust we track in the house, and I won't have it no more! It's got to stop!"

"Well, Harry," she said, sort of quiet, "if it's got to stop, it's got to—and pretty soon, Harry. Because, I'm expecting, and a woman that's expecting can't work like a woman in her usual health."

Well, after he got his sense back, after hearing that, he called the whole family into consultation that evening and put it to them plain. They'd do anything for Milly by then.

She led the conversation where she wanted it to go, though she didn't seem to, and finally they decided it was up to Halbert, the second oldest, to get married, so his wife could take some of the work off Milly's hands. So next day, Halbert spruced up and went to town to look for a wife. But when he came home, he was alone and all dejected.

"They won't have me," he said, very mournful. "They won't none of 'em have me—and I asked fourteen of 'em."

"Why, what's the matter?" said Milly.

"Well," said Halbert, "it seems they've heard about the seven of us and the lot of victuals we eat and the wash and all—and they say only a fool would marry into a family like that and they don't see how you stand it, Milly."

"Oh, that's what they say, is it?" said Milly, with her eyes as bright as candles. "Well, your turn next, Harvey."

So Harvey tried it and Hosea tried it and all of them tried it. But none of them had any luck. And then, finally, Milly let loose at them, good and proper.

"You great big lumps of men!" she said, with the cocky look on her face. "There's more ways of killing a cat than choking it with cream. If they won't marry you after you've asked 'em—why don't you marry 'em first and ask 'em afterwards?"

"But how can we do that?" said Harvey, who was the stupidest.

"Well," said Milly—and here's where her education came in that I've made such a point of—"I read in a history book once about a bunch of people called Romans who were just in your fix." And she went on to tell them about the Romans—how they were settled in a country that was unfriendly to them, just like the Pontipees, and how they all needed wives, just like the Pontipees, and how, when they couldn't get them in the ordinary way from the other people of the country who were called the Sobbin's or the Sabbin's or some such name, they raided the Sobbin' town one night and carried off a lot of the Sobbin' women and married them.

"And, if you can't do as well for yourselves as a lot of old dead Romans," she ended, "you're no brothers of mine and you can cook your own suppers the rest of your lives."

They all sat around dumbfounded for a while. Finally Hob spoke up.

"That sounds all right, in history," he said, "but this is different. Supposing these women just cry and pine away when we've carried them off—supposing that?"

"Listen to me," said Milly. "I know what I'm talking about. Every one of those girls is crazy to get married— and there's not half enough men in town to go round. They think a lot of you boys, too, for I've heard them talk about you; but they're scared of your being backwoodsmen, and scared of the work, and each one is scared of being the first to leave the others. I'll answer for them, once you've married them. Is there anybody around here who can marry people, except the regular minister?"

"There's a sort of hedge-parson just come to town," said Hob. "I reckon he can tie a knot as tight as any preacher in the county."

"All right," said Milly. "That settles it."

It was the evening of the big sociable that it happened. They held it once a year, around Thanksgiving time, and those who had rifles and weapons left them at the door. The Pontipee boys had never attended before—so there was a good deal of stir when they marched in, all seven of them, with Milly in the middle. The brothers were shaved and clean and dressed up spick and span and Milly never looked better, in a dress she'd made out of store cloth and her embroidered slippers.

There was quite a bit of giggling from the town girls, as the Pontipees entered, and a buzz around the hall, but then the fiddler struck up and people began to dance and play games and enjoy themselves, and pretty soon they forgot the Pontipees were there at all, except that the Pontipee boys acted very polite to everybody—Milly'd taught 'em that—and, I guess, before the evening was over, some of the town girls were wondering why they'd turned down boys like that just because they lived in the back-woods.

But they didn't get much chance to think about it, at that. Because, just as they were all going to sit down to supper—"Ready, boys?" called Milly, in a voice that cut through all the talk and commotion. Everybody turned to look at her. And then there was a gasp and a cry, for "Ready!" chorused the six bachelor Pontipees; and suddenly, each one had one hand on a rifle and the other holding a girl, while Harry and Milly trained a couple more rifles on the rest of the community to keep them quiet. It happened so sudden, half the folks didn't even know it was happening—till the Pontipee boys had their girls outside in the street, and the big doors locked and bolted behind them.

Then there was Cain to raise for fair in the meeting-hall, and people started to beat and kick at the doors—but they built solid, in those days. There wasn't any use in trying to shoot the locks off, because the Pontipee boys had tied up the guard over the weapons and dumped him and them outside in a shed.

It wasn't till pretty near dawn that the doors gave way —and when they did, the townspeople took one look outside and groaned. For it was snowing, lickety split, till you couldn't see your hand before your face—and when it snows, in our part of the country, it certainly snows. The blizzard didn't let up for four days, either, and by that time, the pass through the hills to Pontipee Valley was blocked solid, and nothing to do but wait for Spring and the thaw.

And, meanwhile, Milly had her work cut out for her. It wasn't an easy job, convoying three sleigh-loads full of hysterics all that long, cold ride. But she let them hysteric away, and by the time they got to the Pontipee house, the stolen brides were so tuckered out that they'd quieted down a good deal.

Still, at first, they swore they wouldn't take bite or sup till they were restored to their grieving families. But Milly had some tea ready for them, in a jiffy—and a woman will usually take tea, no matter how mad she is. Well, Milly let them get warm and a little cozy, and then, when they were on their second cups, she made her little speech.

"Ladies," she said, "this affair makes me mighty sad—to see fine girls like you stole away by a lot of uncouth backwoodsmen. And I'd never have lent a hand to it if I'd known the truth of the matter. But, you and me, we'll turn the tables on them yet. You can't get back to your families till the blizzard lets up, but, while you've got to stay here, I'll see you're treated respectful. And just to prove that"—and she took a bunch of keys from her pocket—"I'll lock this house up tight, with us inside it; and, as for those backwoods Pontipees, they can sleep and eat in the stable with the livestock. That'll teach them they can't fool us!"

Well, that little speech—and the tea—cheered the girls up quite a bit. And by the time Milly showed them to their rooms—nice-looking rooms, too—and let them bolt themselves in, they were pretty well convinced that Milly was their friend.

So a week or so went by like that—the girls keeping

house for themselves and never seeing hide nor hair of a Pontipee.

At first, it was a regular picnic for the girls. They allowed as how they'd always wanted to live without any men around, and, now they were, it was even better than they'd thought. And Milly agreed with them as hard as she could agree. She made them little speeches about the worthlessness of men in general and husbands in particular that would have raised the hair off any man's head. And, at first, the other girls listened to her and chimed in, and then they listened, but you could see they were being polite. And, by the end of the week, it was awful hard for her to get a real audience.

So, when she began to catch them looking out of windows when they should have been dusting, and peeking from behind curtains to try and get a sight of the terrible Pontipees, she knew it was time for the next step. For things got duller and duller in the house and little spats and quarrels began to break out among the girls. So, one afternoon, she suggested, tactfully, just to break the monotony, that they all go up and rummage in the garret.

They rummaged around and had quite a bit of fun, until finally the minister's daughter opened a long box and gave a little squeal of joy.

"What a lovely wedding-dress—whose was it?" she said, and pulled out the long white veil and the dress itself, while the rest stood round and admired.

"Oh, shucks, that's just an old wedding-dress those backwoodsmen made me make when they thought you were going to marry 'em," said Milly, in a very disgusted voice. "Put it back!" But the girls weren't paying attention.

"Will it fit me, I wonder?" said the minister's daughter.

"It's bad luck, trying on wedding-dresses, if you're not going to have a wedding!" said Milly. "Let's go downstairs and have tea." But the minister's daughter was stepping out of her regular clothes already. The other girls helped fix her up—and then they oh-ed and ah-ed, for, I must say, she made a handsome-looking bride.

"That Pontipee boy named Hob's got curly hair," said the minister's daughter, trailing out her veil. "I always did have a liking for curly hair."

"Hob's not nearly as good-looking as Halbert," said the lawyer's niece, quite violent, and another one said, "Handsome is as handsome does—the one they call Harvey isn't so handsome, maybe, but he certainly has nice eyes."

"There's something about a man around the house that brisks things up remarkable," said a fourth one. "Not that I want to get married, but Howard's a nice name, even if Pontipee is hitched to it and——"

"Girls, girls—are you crazy, girls?" said Milly, shocked and horrified. But the minute she started to reprove them, they all turned on her, most ungratefully, and there was a regular revolt. So, at last, she had to give in and admit that there were five more wedding-dresses in the garret—and that if anybody was thinking of getting married, there just happened to be a hedge-parson, spending the winter with the Pontipees. But one thing she was firm about.

"Get married if you like," she said. "I can't stop you. But I'm responsible for you to your families—and, after the ceremony's ended, your husbands go back to the stable and stay there, till I know your families approve of them." She looked very fierce about it, and she made them promise. The hedge-parson married them all—all six in their wedding-dresses—and then the boys went back to the stable. And, at dinner that night, the minister's daughter burst out crying.

"I hate men just as much as ever!" she wailed. "But it's terrible to be lawful married to a man you can't even see, except now and then out of a window!"

So Milly saw she had to make some new rules and she did. Three afternoons a week, the boys were allowed to call on their new wives, and once in a while, for a great treat, they could stay to supper. But, always with Milly to chaperon.

Well, at first, the husbands and wives were mighty stiff and formal with each other, but, gradually, they got better and better acquainted. Till, pretty soon, the minister's daughter was letting Hob hold her hand, when she thought Milly wasn't looking, and the lawyer's niece was asking permission to sew a button on Halbert's coat—and there was a general atmosphere of courting around the Pontipee place that'd make an old bachelor sick.

Milly took it all in but she never stopped chaperoning.

Well, finally, it was one day along in January. Milly woke up in the morning—and she knew she was near her time. But, first thing in the morning, as always, she reached underneath her pillow for her keys—and then she smiled. For somebody must have stolen them while she was sleeping—and when she got up, and went to the window in her wrapper, the door of the house was wide open. And there was Hob and his wife, helping each other shovel snow from the doorstep, and Halbert and his wife were throwing snowballs at Harvey and his, and Howard was kissing the doctor's eldest behind the kitchen door. "Praise be!" said Milly. "I can have my baby in peace"—and she went down to congratulate them all.

Only then, there were the families and the relatives still to fix. But Milly had a plan for that—she had plans for everything. When they stole the girls away, they left a letter she drew up, signed by all the boys and expressing all the honorable intentions you could put a name to. But she was afraid that wouldn't cool down the townspeople much, even when they thought it over, and it didn't.

One day when the first thaws had come and Milly's baby was about six weeks old, Hob came running in from his lookout post.

"They're coming, Milly!" he said. "The whole dum town! They've got rifles and scythes and ropes and they look mighty wild and bloodthirsty! What'll we do?"

"Do?" said Milly, perfectly calm. "You get the boys

together and keep out of sight—and tell the girls to come here. For it's women's work, now, that'll save us, if anything will."

When she got the girls together, she gave them their orders. I guess they were a bit white-faced, but they obeyed. Then she looked out of the window—and there was the town, marching up the road, slow and steady. She'd have liked it better if they'd shouted or cried, but they didn't shout nor cry. The minister was in the lead, with his lips shut, and a six-foot rifle in his hand, and his face like an iron mask.

She saw them come up to the gate of the Pontipee place. The gate was wide open and nobody there to hinder. She could see them take that in—and the little waver in the crowd. Because that made them feel queer.

Then they caught themselves and came tramping along toward the house, the minister still in the lead. Milly caught her breath, for they still looked awful mad. She knew what they'd expect when they got near the house— every window barred and every door bolted and red-hot bullets spitting through the loop-holes in the walls.

But the windows were open—you could see white curtains in them; there were plants on some of the sills. The door of the house stood ajar and Milly's cat was asleep on the doorstone, there in the sun.

They stood outside that door for quite a little bit, just milling around and staring. It was very quiet; they could hear their own breath breathe and their own hearts knock. Finally the minister brushed his face, as if he were brushing a cobweb away from it, and he gripped his gun and went up on the porch and knocked at the open door. He'd intended to stomp up those steps like a charge of cavalry, but he walked soft, instead. He couldn't have told you why.

He knocked once and he knocked again—and then Milly was standing in the door, with her baby in her arms.

Somebody at the back of the crowd dropped the scythe he was carrying, and another one coughed in his hand.

"You're just in time to christen my child, your reverence," said Milly. "Have you brought that rifle to help you christen my child?"

The minister's eyes dropped, after a minute, and he lowered his rifle but he still held it in the crook of his arm.

"Your child?" he said, and his voice was as low as Milly's, but there was a fierceness in it. "What about my child?"

"Listen!" said Milly, raising her hand, and the whole crowd fell dead still. Then from somewhere in the house came the hum of a spinning-wheel, low and steady, and a woman's voice, humming with the wheel.

"That's your child you hear, your reverence," said Milly. "Does she sound hurt, your reverence, or does she sound content?"

The minister hesitated for a moment and the crowd fell dead still again. Then they all heard the hum of the wheel and the hum of the woman's voice, humming back and forth to each other, as they did their work in the world.

"She sounds content—heaven help me!" said the minister, and a twist went over his face. But then there was a sudden outburst of cries and questions from the others. "My child, what about my child?" "Where's Mary?" "Is Susy safe?"

"Listen!" said Milly again, and they all fell silent once more. And, from somewhere, there came the splash of a churn and the voice of a woman talking to the butter to make it come; and the rattling of pans in a kitchen and a woman singing at her work; and the slap of clothes on a laundry board and the little clatter a woman makes setting table.

"There's your children," said Milly. "Hear 'em? Don't

they sound all right? And—dinner will be ready in about half an hour—and you're all staying, I hope."

Then the daughters came out and their folks rushed to them; and, after all the crying and conniptions were over, Milly introduced the parents to their sons-in-law.

# DOC MELLHORN AND THE PEARLY GATES

Doc Mellhorn had never expected to go anywhere at all when he died. So, when he found himself on the road again, it surprised him. But perhaps I'd better explain a little about Doc Mellhorn first. He was seventy-odd when he left our town; but when he came, he was as young as Bates or Filsinger or any of the boys at the hospital. Only there wasn't any hospital when he came. He came with a young man's beard and a brand-new bag and a lot of newfangled ideas about medicine that we didn't take to much. And he left, forty-odd years later, with a first-class county health record and a lot of people alive that wouldn't have been alive if he hadn't been there. Yes, a country doctor. And nobody ever called him a man in white or a death grappler that I know of, though they did think of giving him a degree at Pewauket College once. But then the board met again and decided they needed a new gymnasium, so they gave the degree to J. Prentiss Parmalee instead.

They say he was a thin young man when he first came, a thin young man with an Eastern accent who'd wanted to study in Vienna. But most of us remember him chunky and solid, with white hair and a little bald spot that always got burned bright red in the first hot weather. He had about four card tricks that he'd do for you, if you were a youngster—they were always the same ones—and now and then, if he felt like it, he'd take a silver half dollar out of the back of your neck. And that worked as well with the youngsters who were going to build rocket ships as it had with the youngsters who were going to be railway engineers. It always worked. I guess it was Doc Mellhorn more than the trick.

But there wasn't anything unusual about him, except maybe the card tricks. Or, anyway, he didn't think so. He was just a good doctor and he knew us inside out. I've heard people call him a pigheaded, obstinate old mule— that was in the fight about the water supply. And I've heard a weepy old lady call him a saint. I took the tale to him once, and he looked at me over his glasses and said, "Well, I've always respected a mule. Got ten times the sense of a—horse." Then he took a silver half dollar out of my ear.

Well, how do you describe a man like that? You don't —you call him up at three in the morning. And when he sends in his bill, you think it's a little steep.

All the same, when it came to it, there were people who drove a hundred and fifty miles to the funeral. And the Masons came down from Bluff City, and the Poles came from across the tracks, with a wreath the size of a house, and you saw cars in town that you didn't often see there. But it was after the funeral that the queer things began for Doc Mellhorn.

The last thing he remembered, he'd been lying in bed, feeling pretty sick, on the whole, but glad for the rest. And now he was driving his Model T down a long straight road between rolling, misty prairies that seemed to go from nowhere to nowhere.

It didn't seem funny to him to be driving the Model T again. That was the car he'd learned on, and he kept to it till his family made him change. And it didn't seem funny to him not to be sick any more. He hadn't had much time to be sick in his life—the patients usually attended to that. He looked around for his bag, first thing, but it was there on the seat beside him. It was the old bag, not the presentation one they'd given him at the hospital, but that was all right too. It meant he was out on a call and, if he couldn't quite recollect at the moment just where the call was, it was certain to come to him. He'd wakened up often enough in his buggy, in the old days, and found the horse was taking him home, without his doing much about it. A doctor gets used to things like that.

All the same, when he'd driven and driven for some time without raising so much as a traffic light, just the same rolling prairies on either hand, he began to get a little suspicious. He thought, for a while, of stopping the car and getting out, just to take a look around, but he'd always hated to lose time on a call. Then he noticed something else. He was driving without his glasses. And yet he hadn't driven without his glasses in fifteen years.

"H'm," said Doc Mellhorn. "I'm crazy as a June bug. Or else—Well, it might be so, I suppose."

But this time he did stop the car. He opened his bag and looked inside it, but everything seemed to be in order. He opened his wallet and looked at that, but there were his own initials, half rubbed away, and he recognized them. He took his pulse, but it felt perfectly steady.

"H'm," said Doc Mellhorn. "Well."

Then, just to prove that everything was perfectly normal, he took a silver half dollar out of the steering wheel of the car.

"Never did it smoother," said Doc Mellhorn. "Well, all the same, if this is the new highway, it's longer than I remember it."

But just then a motorcycle came roaring down the road and stopped with a flourish, the way motor cops do.

"Any trouble?" said the motor cop. Doc Mellhorn couldn't see his face for his goggles, but the goggles looked normal.

"I am a physician," said Doc Mellhorn, as he'd said a thousand times before to all sorts of people, "on my way to an urgent case." He passed his hand across his forehead. "Is this the right road?" he said.

"Straight ahead to the traffic light," said the cop. "They're expecting you, Doctor Mellhorn. Shall I give you an escort?"

"No; thanks all the same," said Doc Mellhorn, and the
motor cop roared away. The Model T ground as Doc
Mellhorn gassed her. "Well, they've got a new breed of
traffic cop," said Doc Mellhorn, "or else—"

But when he got to the light, it was just like any light
at a crossroads. He waited till it changed and the officer
waved him on. There seemed to be a good deal of traffic
going the other way, but he didn't get a chance to notice
it much, because Lizzie bucked a little, as she usually did
when you kept her waiting. Still, the sight of traffic re-
lieved him, though he hadn't passed anybody on his own
road yet.

Pretty soon he noticed the look of the country had
changed. It was parkway now and very nicely landscaped.
There was dogwood in bloom on the little hills, white
and pink against the green; though, as Doc Mellhorn
remembered it, it had been August when he left his house.
And every now and then there'd be a nice little white-
painted sign that said TO THE GATES.

"H'm," said Doc Mellhorn. "New State Parkway, I
guess. Well, they've fixed it up pretty. But I wonder where
they got the dogwood. Haven't seen it bloom like that
since I was East."

Then he drove along in a sort of dream for a while,
for the dogwood reminded him of the days when he was
a young man in an Eastern college. He remembered the
look of that college and the girls who'd come to dances,
the girls who wore white gloves and had rolls of hair.
They were pretty girls, too, and he wondered what had
become of them. "Had babies, I guess," thought Doc
Mellhorn. "Or some of them, anyway." But he liked to
think of them as the way they had been when they were
just pretty, and excited at being at a dance.

He remembered other things too—the hacked desks
in the lecture rooms, and the trees on the campus, and
the first pipe he'd ever broken in, and a fellow called
Paisley Grew that he hadn't thought of in years—a raw-

boned fellow with a gift for tall stories and playing the jew's-harp.

"Ought to have looked up Paisley," he said. "Yes, I ought. Didn't amount to a hill of beans, I guess, but I always liked him. I wonder if he still plays the jew's-harp. Pshaw, I know he's been dead twenty years."

He was passing other cars now and other cars were passing him, but he didn't pay much attention, except when he happened to notice a license you didn't often see in the state, like Rhode Island or Mississippi. He was too full of his own thoughts. There were foot passengers, too, plenty of them—and once he passed a man driving a load of hay. He wondered what the man would do with the hay when he got to the Gates. But probably there were arrangements for that.

"Not that I believe a word of it," he said, "but it'll surprise Father Kelly. Or maybe it won't. I used to have some handsome arguments with that man, but I always knew I could count on him, in spite of me being a heretic."

Then he saw the Wall and the Gates, right across the valley. He saw them, and they reached to the top of the sky. He rubbed his eyes for a while, but they kept on being there.

"Quite a sight," said Doc Mellhorn.

No one told him just where to go or how to act, but it seemed to him that he knew. If he'd thought about it, he'd have said that you waited in line, but there wasn't any waiting in line. He just went where he was expected to go and the reception clerk knew his name right away.

"Yes, Doctor Mellhorn," he said. "And now, what would you like to do first?"

"I think I'd like to sit down," said Doc Mellhorn. So he sat, and it was a comfortable chair. He even bounced the springs of it once or twice, till he caught the reception clerk's eye on him.

"Is there anything I can get you?" said the reception clerk. He was young and brisk and neat as a pin, and you could see he aimed to give service and studied about it. Doc Mellhorn thought, "He's the kind that wipes off your windshield no matter how clean it is."

"No," said Doc Mellhorn. "You see, I don't believe this. I don't believe any of it. I'm sorry if that sounds cranky, but I don't."

"That's quite all right, sir," said the reception clerk. "It often takes a while." And he smiled as if Doc Mellhorn had done him a favor.

"Young man, I'm a physician," said Doc Mellhorn, "and do you mean to tell me—"

Then he stopped, for he suddenly saw there was no use arguing. He was either there or he wasn't. And it felt as if he were there.

"Well," said Doc Mellhorn, with a sigh, "how do I begin?"

"That's entirely at your own volition, sir," said the reception clerk briskly. "Any meetings with relatives, of course. Or if you would prefer to get yourself settled first. Or take a tour, alone or conducted. Perhaps these will offer suggestions," and he started to hand over a handful of leaflets. But Doc Mellhorn put them aside.

"Wait a minute," he said. "I want to think. Well, naturally, there's Mother and Dad. But I couldn't see them just yet. I wouldn't believe it. And Grandma—well, now, if I saw Grandma—and me older than she is—was—used to be—well, I don't know what it would do to me. You've got to let me get my breath. Well, of course, there's Uncle Frank—he'd be easier." He paused. "Is he here?" he said.

The reception clerk looked in a file. "I am happy to say that Mr. Francis V. Mellhorn arrived July 12, 1907," he said. He smiled winningly.

"Well!" said Doc Mellhorn. "Uncle Frank! Well, I'll be—well! But it must have been a great consolation to Mother. We heard—well, never mind what we heard—I guess it wasn't so. . . . No, don't reach for that phone just yet, or whatever it is. I'm still thinking."

"We sometimes find," said the reception clerk eagerly,

"that a person not a relative may be the best introduction. Even a stranger sometimes—a distinguished stranger connected with one's own profession—"

"Well, now, that's an idea," said Doc Mellhorn heartily, trying to keep his mind off how much he disliked the reception clerk. He couldn't just say why he disliked him, but he knew he did.

It reminded him of the time he'd had to have his gall bladder out in the city hospital and the young, brisk interns had come to see him and called him "Doctor" every other word.

"Yes, that's an idea," he said. He reflected. "Well, of course, I'd like to see Koch," he said. "And Semmelweiss. Not to speak of Walter Reed. But, shucks, they'd be busy men. But there is one fellow—only he lived pretty far back—"

"Hippocrates, please," said the reception clerk into the telephone or whatever it was. *"H for horse—"*

"No!" said Doc Mellhorn quite violently. "Excuse me, but you just wait a minute. I mean if you can wait. I mean, if Hippocrates wants to come, I've no objection. But I never took much of a fancy to him, in spite of his oath. It's Aesculapius I'm thinking about. George W. Oh, glory!" he said. "But he won't talk English. I forgot."

"I shall be happy to act as interpreter," said the reception clerk, smiling brilliantly.

"I haven't a doubt," said Doc Mellhorn. "But just wait a shake." In a minute, by the way the clerk was acting, he was going to be talking to Aesculapius. "And what in time am I going to say to the man?" he thought. "It's too much." He gazed wildly around the neat reception room—distempered, as he noticed, in a warm shade of golden tan. Then his eyes fell on the worn black bag at his feet and a sudden warm wave of relief flooded over him.

"Wait a minute," he said, and his voice gathered force and authority. "Where's my patient?"

"Patient?" said the reception clerk, looking puzzled for the first time.

"Patient," said Doc Mellhorn. "*P* for phlebitis." He tapped his bag.

"I'm afraid you don't quite understand, sir," said the reception clerk.

"I understand this," said Doc Mellhorn. "I was called here. And if I wasn't called professionally, why have I got my bag?"

"But, my dear Doctor Mellhorn—" said the reception clerk.

"I'm not your dear doctor," said Doc Mellhorn. "I was called here, I tell you. I'm sorry not to give you the patient's name, but the call must have come in my absence and the girl doesn't spell very well. But in any well-regulated hospital—"

"But I tell you," said the reception clerk, and his hair wasn't slick any more, "nobody's ill here. Nobody can be ill. If they could, it wouldn't be He—"

"Humph," said Doc Mellhorn. He thought it over, and felt worse. "Then what does a fellow like Koch do?" he said. "Or Pasteur?" He raised a hand. "Oh, don't tell me," he said. "I can see they'd be busy. Yes, I guess it'd be all right for a research man. But I never was . . . Oh, well, shucks, I've published a few papers. And there's that clamp of mine—always meant to do something about it. But they've got better ones now. Mean to say there isn't so much as a case of mumps in the whole place?"

"I assure you," said the reception clerk, in a weary voice. "And now, once you see Doctor Aesculapius—"

"Funny," said Doc Mellhorn. "Lord knows there's plenty of times you'd be glad to be quit of the whole thing. And don't talk to me about the healer's art or grateful patients. Well, I've known a few . . . a few. But I've known others. All the same, it's different, being told there isn't any need for what you can do."

"*A* for Ararát," said the reception clerk into his instrument. "*E* for Eden."

"Should think you'd have a dial," said Doc Mellhorn desperately. "We've got 'em down below." He thought hard and frantically. "Wait a shake. It's coming back to me," he said. "Got anybody named Grew here? Paisley Grew?"

"*S* for serpent . . ." said the reception clerk. "What was that?"

"Fellow that called me," said Doc Mellhorn. "G-r-e-w. First name, Paisley."

"I will consult the index," said the reception clerk. He did so, and Doc Mellhorn waited, hoping against hope.

"We have 94,183 Grews, including 83 Prescotts and one Penobscot," the reception clerk said at last. "But I fail to find Paisley Grew. Are you quite sure of the name?"

"Of course," said Doc Mellhorn briskly. "Paisley Grew. Chronic indigestion. Might be appendix—can't say—have to see. But anyhow, he's called." He picked up his bag. "Well, thanks for the information," he said, liking the reception clerk better than he had yet. "Not your fault, anyway."

"But—but where are you going?" said the reception clerk.

"Well, there's another establishment, isn't there?" said Doc Mellhorn. "Always heard there was. Call probably came from there. Crossed wires, I expect."

"But you can't go there!" said the reception clerk. "I mean—"

"Can't go?" said Doc Mellhorn. "I'm a physician. A patient's called me."

"But if you'll only wait and see Aesculapius!" said the reception clerk, running his hands wildly through his hair. "He'll be here almost any moment."

"Please give him my apologies," said Doc Mellhorn. "He's a doctor. He'll understand. And if any messages come for me, just stick them on the spike. Do I need a road map? Noticed the road I came was all one way."

"There is, I believe, a back road in rather bad repair,"

said the reception clerk icily. "I can call Information if you wish."

"Oh, don't bother," said Doc Mellhorn. "I'll find it. And I never saw a road beat Lizzie yet." He took a silver half dollar from the doorknob of the door. "See that?" he said. "Slick as a whistle. Well, good-by, young man."

But it wasn't till he'd cranked up Lizzie and was on his way that Doc Mellhorn really felt safe. He found the back road and it was all the reception clerk had said it was and more. But he didn't mind—in fact, after one particularly bad rut, he grinned.

"I suppose I ought to have seen the folks," he said. "Yes, I know I ought. But—not so much as a case of mumps in the whole abiding dominion! Well, it's lucky I took a chance on Paisley Grew."

After another mile or so, he grinned again.

"And I'd like to see old Aesculapius' face. Probably rang him in the middle of dinner—they always do. But shucks, it's happened to all of us."

Well, the road got worse and worse and the sky above it darker and darker, and what with one thing and another, Doc Mellhorn was glad enough when he got to the other gates. They were pretty impressive gates, too, though of course in a different way, and reminded Doc Mellhorn a little of the furnaces outside Steeltown, where he'd practiced for a year when he was young.

This time Doc Mellhorn wasn't going to take any advice from reception clerks and he had his story all ready. All the same, he wasn't either registered or expected, so there was a little fuss. Finally they tried to scare him by saying he came at his own risk and that there were some pretty tough characters about. But Doc Mellhorn remarked that he'd practiced in Steeltown. So, after he'd told them what seemed to him a million times that he was a physician on a case, they finally let him in and directed him to Paisley Grew. Paisley was on Level 346 in Pit 68,953, and Doc Mellhorn recognized him the minute he saw him. He even had the jew's-harp, stuck in the back of his overalls.

"Well, Doc," said Paisley finally, when the first greetings were over, "you certainly are a sight for sore eyes! Though, of course, I'm sorry to see you here," and he grinned.

"Well, I can't see that it's so different from a lot of places," said Doc Mellhorn, wiping his forehead. "Warm-ish, though."

"It's the humidity, really," said Paisley Grew. "That's what it really is."

"Yes, I know," said Doc Mellhorn. "And now tell me, Paisley; how's that indigestion of yours?"

"Well, I'll tell you, Doc," said Paisley. "When I first came here, I thought the climate was doing it good. I did for a fact. But now I'm not so sure. I've tried all sorts of things for it—I've even tried being transferred to the boiling asphalt lakes. But it just seems to hang on, and every now and then, when I least expect it, it catches me. Take last night. I didn't have a thing to eat that I don't generally eat—well, maybe I did have one little snort of hot sulphur, but it wasn't the sulphur that did it. All the same, I woke up at four, and it was just like a knife. Now . . ."

He went on from there and it took him some time. And Doc Mellhorn listened, happy as a clam. He never thought he'd be glad to listen to a hypochondriac, but he was. And when Paisley was all through, he examined him and prescribed for him. It was just a little soda bicarb and pepsin, but Paisley said it took hold something wonderful. And they had a fine time that evening, talking over the old days.

Finally, of course, the talk got around to how Paisley liked it where he was. And Paisley was honest enough about that.

"Well, Doc," he said, "of course this isn't the place for you, and I can see you're just visiting. But I haven't many real complaints. It's hot, to be sure, and they work you, and some of the boys here are rough. But they've had some pretty interesting experiences, too, when you get them talking—yes, sir. And anyhow, it isn't Peabodyville, New Jersey," he said with vehemence. "I spent five years in Peabodyville, trying to work up in the leather business. After that I bust out, and I guess that's what landed me here. But it's an improvement on Peabodyville." He looked at Doc Mellhorn sidewise. "Say, Doc," he said, "I know this is a vacation for you, but all the same there's a couple of the boys—nothing really wrong with them of course—but—well, if you could just look them over—"

"I was thinking the office hours would be nine to one," said Doc Mellhorn.

So Paisley took him around and they found a nice little place for an office in one of the abandoned mine galleries, and Doc Mellhorn hung out his shingle. And right away patients started coming around. They didn't get many doctors there, in the first place, and the ones they did get weren't exactly the cream of the profession, so Doc Mellhorn had it all to himself. It was mostly sprains, fractures, bruises and dislocations, of course, with occasional burns and scalds—and, on the whole, it reminded Doc Mellhorn a good deal of his practice in Steeltown, especially when it came to foreign bodies in the eye. Now and then Doc Mellhorn ran into a more unusual case—for instance, there was one of the guards that got part of himself pretty badly damaged in a rock slide. Well, Doc Mellhorn had never set a tail before, but he managed it all right, and got a beautiful primary union, too, in spite of the fact that he had no X-ray facilities. He thought of writing up the case for the State Medical Journal, but then he couldn't figure out any way to send it to them, so he had to let it slide. And then there was an advanced carcinoma of the liver—a Greek named Papadoupolous or Prometheus or something. Doc Mellhorn couldn't do much for him, considering the circumstances, but he did what he could, and he and the Greek used to have long conversations. The rest was just everyday practice—run of the mine—but he enjoyed it.

Now and then it would cross his mind that he ought to get out Lizzie and run back to the other place for a visit with the folks. But that was just like going back East had been on earth—he'd think he had everything pretty well cleared up, and then a new flock of patients would come in. And it wasn't that he didn't miss his wife and children and grandchildren—he did. But there wasn't any way to get back to them, and he knew it. And there was the work in front of him and the office crowded every day. So he just went along, hardly noticing the time.

Now and then, to be sure, he'd get a suspicion that he wasn't too popular with the authorities of the place. But he was used to not being popular with authorities and he didn't pay much attention. But finally they sent an inspector around. The minute Doc Mellhorn saw him, he knew there was going to be trouble.

Not that the inspector was uncivil. In fact, he was a pretty high-up official—you could tell by his antlers. And Doc Mellhorn was just as polite, showing him around. He showed him the free dispensary and the clinic and the nurse—Scotch girl named Smith, she was—and the dental chair he'd rigged up with the help of a fellow named Ferguson, who used to be an engineer before he was sentenced. And the inspector looked them all over, and finally he came back to Doc Mellhorn's office. The girl named Smith had put up curtains in the office, and with that and a couple of potted gas plants it looked more homelike than it had. The inspector looked around it and sighed.

"I'm sorry, Doctor Mellhorn," he said at last, "but you can see for yourself, it won't do."

"What won't do?" said Doc Mellhorn, stoutly. But, all the same, he felt afraid.

"Any of it," said the inspector. "We could overlook the alleviation of minor suffering—I'd be inclined to do so myself—though these people are here to suffer, and there's no changing that. But you're playing merry Hades with the whole system."

"I'm a physician in practice," said Doc Mellhorn.

"Yes," said the inspector. "That's just the trouble. Now, take these reports you've been sending," and he took out a sheaf of papers. "What have you to say about that?"

"Well, seeing as there's no county health officer, or at least I couldn't find one—" said Doc Mellhorn.

"Precisely," said the inspector. "And what have you done? You've condemned fourteen levels of this pit as unsanitary nuisances. You've recommended 2136 lost souls for special diet, remedial exercise, hospitalization—Well—I won't go through the list."

"I'll stand back of every one of those recommendations," said Doc Mellhorn. "And now we've got the chair working, we can handle most of the dental work on the spot. Only Ferguson needs more amalgam."

"I know," said the inspector patiently, "but the money has to come from somewhere—you must realize that. We're not a rich community, in spite of what people think. And these unauthorized requests—oh, we fill them, of course, but—"

"Ferguson needs more amalgam," said Doc Mellhorn. "And that last batch wasn't standard. I wouldn't use it on a dog."

"He's always needing more amalgam!" said the inspector bitterly, making a note. "Is he going to fill every tooth in Hades? By the way, my wife tells me I need a little work done myself—but we won't go into that. We'll take just one thing—your entirely unauthorized employment of Miss Smith. Miss Smith has no business working for you. She's supposed to be gnawed by a never-dying worm every Monday, Wednesday and Friday."

"Sounds silly to me," said Doc Mellhorn.

"I don't care how silly it sounds," said the inspector. "It's regulations. And, besides, she isn't even a registered nurse."

"She's a practical one," said Doc Mellhorn. "Of course, back on earth a lot of her patients died. But that was because when she didn't like a patient, she poisoned him. Well, she can't poison anybody here and I've kind of got her out of the notion of it anyway. She's been doing A-1 work for me and I'd like to recommend her for—"

"Please!" said the inspector. "Please! And as if that wasn't enough, you've even been meddling with the staff. I've a note here on young Asmodeus—Asmodeus XIV—"

"Oh, you mean Mickey!" said Doc Mellhorn, with a chuckle. "Short for Mickey Mouse. We call him that in the clinic. And he's a young imp if I ever saw one."

"The original Asmodeus is one of our most prominent citizens," said the inspector severely. "How do you suppose he felt when we got your report that his fourteenth great-grandson had rickets?"

"Well," said Doc Mellhorn, "I know rickets. And he had 'em. And you're going to have rickets in these youngsters as long as you keep feeding 'em low-grade coke. I put Mickey on the best Pennsylvania anthracite and look at him now!"

"I admit the success of your treatment," said the inspector, "but, naturally—well, since then we've been deluged with demands for anthracite from as far south as Sheol. We'll have to float a new bond issue. And what will the taxpayers say?"

"He was just cutting his first horns when he came to us," said Doc Mellhorn reminiscently, "and they were coming in crooked. Now, I ask you, did you ever see a straighter pair? Of course, if I'd had cod liver oil—My gracious, you ought to have somebody here that can fill a prescription; I can't do it all."

The inspector shut his papers together with a snap. "I'm sorry, Doctor Mellhorn," he said, "but this is final. You have no right here, in the first place; no local license to practice in the second—"

"Yes, that's a little irregular," said Doc Mellhorn, "but I'm a registered member of four different medical associations—you might take that into account. And I'll take any examination that's required."

"No," said the inspector violently. "No, no, no! You can't stay here! You've got to go away! It isn't possible!"

Doc Mellhorn drew a long breath. "Well," he said, "there wasn't any work for me at the other place. And here you won't let me practice. So what's a man to do?"

The inspector was silent.

"Tell me," said Doc Mellhorn presently. "Suppose you do throw me out? What happens to Miss Smith and Paisley and the rest of them?"

"Oh, what's done is done," said the inspector impatiently, "here as well as anywhere else. We'll have to keep on with the anthracite and the rest of it. And Hades only knows what'll happen in the future. If it's any satisfaction to you, you've started something."

"Well, I guess Smith and Ferguson between them can handle the practice," said Doc Mellhorn. "But that's got to be a promise."

"It's a promise," said the inspector.

"Then there's Mickey—I mean Asmodeus," said Doc Mellhorn. "He's a smart youngster—smart as a whip—if he is a hellion. Well, you know how a youngster gets. Well, it seems he wants to be a doctor. But I don't know what sort of training he'd get—"

"He'll get it," said the inspector feverishly. "We'll found the finest medical college you ever saw, right here in West Baal. We'll build a hospital that'll knock your eye out. You'll be satisfied. But now, if you don't mind—"

"All right," said Doc Mellhorn, and rose.

The inspector looked surprised. "But don't you want to—" he said. "I mean my instructions are we're to give you a banquet, if necessary—after all, the community appreciates—"

"Thanks," said Doc Mellhorn, with a shudder, "but if I've got to go, I'd rather get out of town. You hang around and announce your retirement, and pretty soon folks start thinking they ought to give you a testimonial. And I never did like testimonials."

All the same, before he left he took a silver half dollar out of Mickey Asmodeus' chin.

When he was back on the road again and the lights of the gates had faded into a low ruddy glow behind him, Doc Mellhorn felt alone for the first time. He'd been lonely at times during his life, but he'd never felt alone like this before. Because, as far as he could see, there was only him and Lizzie now.

"Now, maybe if I'd talked to Aesculapius—" he said. "But pshaw, I always was pigheaded."

He didn't pay much attention to the way he was driving and it seemed to him that the road wasn't quite the same. But he felt tired for a wonder—bone-tired and beaten—and he didn't much care about the road. He hadn't felt tired since he left earth, but now the loneliness tired him.

"Active—always been active," he said to himself. "I can't just lay down on the job. But what's a man to do?"

"What's a man to do?" he said. "I'm a doctor. I can't work miracles."

Then the black fit came over him and he remembered all the times he'd been wrong and all the people he couldn't do anything for. "Never was much of a doctor, I guess," he said. "Maybe, if I'd gone to Vienna. Well, the right kind of man would have gone. And about that Bigelow kid," he said. "How was I to know he'd hemorrhage? But I should have known.

"I've diagnosed walking typhoid as appendicitis. Just the once, but that's enough. And I still don't know what held me back when I was all ready to operate. I used to wake up in a sweat, six months afterward, thinking I had.

"I could have saved those premature twins, if I'd known as much then as I do now. I guess that guy Dafoe would have done it anyway—look at what he had to work with. But I didn't. And that finished the Gorhams' hav·

ing children. That's a dandy doctor, isn't it? Makes you feel fine.

"I could have pulled Old Man Halsey through. And Edna Biggs. And the little Lauriat girl. No. I couldn't have done it with her. That was before insulin. I couldn't have cured Ted Allen. No, I'm clear on that. But I've never been satisfied about the Collins woman. Bates is all right—good as they come. But I knew her, inside and out—ought to, too—she was the biggest nuisance that ever came into the office. And if I hadn't been down with the flu . . .

"Then there's the flu epidemic. I didn't take my clothes off, four days and nights. But what's the good of that, when you lose them? Oh, sure, the statistics looked good. You can have the statistics.

"Should have started raising hell about the water supply two years before I did.

"Oh, yes, it makes you feel fine, pulling babies into the world. Makes you feel you're doing something. And just fine when you see a few of them, twenty-thirty years later, not worth two toots on a cow's horn. Can't say I ever delivered a Dillinger. But there's one or two in state's prison. And more that ought to be. Don't mind even that so much as a few of the fools. Makes you wonder.

"And then, there's incurable cancer. That's a daisy. What can you do about it, Doctor? Well, Doctor, we can alleviate the pain in the last stages. Some. Ever been in a cancer ward, Doctor? Yes, Doctor, I have.

"What do you do for the common cold, Doctor? Two dozen clean linen handkerchiefs. Yes, it's a good joke— I'll laugh. And what do you do for a boy when you know he's dying, Doctor? Take a silver half dollar out of his ear. But it kept the Lane kid quiet and his fever went down that night. I took the credit, but I don't know why it went down.

"I've only got one brain. And one pair of hands.

"I could have saved. I could have done. I could have.

"Guess it's just as well you can't live forever. You make

fewer mistakes. And sometimes I'd see Bates looking at me as if he wondered why I ever thought I could practice.

"Pigheaded, opinionated, ineffective old imbecile! And yet, Lord, Lord, I'd do it all over again."

He lifted his eyes from the pattern of the road in front of him. There were white markers on it now and Lizzie seemed to be bouncing down a residential street. There were trees in the street and it reminded him of town. He rubbed his eyes for a second and Lizzie rolled on by herself—she often did. It didn't seem strange to him to stop at the right house.

"Well, Mother," he said rather gruffly to the group on the lawn. "Well, Dad. . . . Well, Uncle Frank." He beheld a small, stern figure advancing, hands outstretched. "Well, Grandma," he said meekly.

Later on he was walking up and down in the grape arbor with Uncle Frank. Now and then he picked a grape and ate it. They'd always been good grapes, those Catawbas, as he remembered them.

"What beats me," he said, not for the first time, "is why I didn't notice the Gates. The second time, I mean."

"Oh, that Gate," said Uncle Frank, with the easy, unctuous roll in his voice that Doc Mellhorn so well remembered. He smoothed his handle-bar mustaches. "That Gate, my dear Edward—well, of course it has to be there in the first place. Literature, you know. And then, it's a choice," he said richly.

"I'll draw cards," said Doc Mellhorn. He ate another grape.

"Fact is," said Uncle Frank, "that Gate's for one kind of person. You pass it and then you can rest for all eternity. Just fold your hands. It suits some."

"I can see that it would," said Doc Mellhorn.

"Yes," said Uncle Frank, "but it wouldn't suit a Mellhorn. I'm happy to say that very few of our family remain permanently on that side. I spent some time there myself." He said, rather self-consciously, "Well, my last years had been somewhat stormy. So few people cared for

refined impersonations of our feathered songsters, including lightning sketches. I felt that I'd earned a rest.
But after a while—well, I got tired of being at liberty."

"And what happens when you get tired?" said Doc
Mellhorn.

"You find out what you want to do," said Uncle Frank.

"My kind of work?" said Doc Mellhorn.

"Your kind of work," said his uncle. "Been busy,
haven't you?"

"Well," said Doc Mellhorn. "But here. If there isn't
so much as a case of mumps in—"

"Would it have to be mumps?" said his uncle. "Of
course, if you're aching for mumps, I guess it could be
arranged. But how many new souls do you suppose we
get here a day?"

"Sizable lot, I expect."

"And how many of them get here in first-class condition?" said Uncle Frank triumphantly. "Why, I've seen
Doctor Rush—Benjamin Rush—come back so tired from
a day's round he could hardly flap one pinion against
the other. Oh, if it's work you want—And then, of course,
there's the earth."

"Hold on," said Doc Mellhorn. "I'm not going to ap-
pear to any young intern in wings and a harp. Not at my
time of life. And anyway, he'd laugh himself sick."

" 'Tain't that," said Uncle Frank. "Look here. You've
left children and grandchildren behind you, haven't you?
And they're going on?"

"Yes," said Doc Mellhorn.

"Same with what you did," said Uncle Frank. "I mean
the inside part of it—that stays. I don't mean any funny
business—voices in your ear and all that. But haven't you
ever got clean tuckered out, and been able to draw on
something you didn't know was there?"

"Pshaw, any man's done that," said Doc Mellhorn. "But
you take the adrenal—"

"Take anything you like," said Uncle Frank placidly.
"I'm not going to argue with you. Not my department.

But you'll find it isn't all adrenalin. Like it here?" he said abruptly. "Feel satisfied?"

"Why, yes," said Doc Mellhorn surprisedly, "I do." He looked around the grape arbor and suddenly realized that he felt happy.

"No, they wouldn't all arrive in first-class shape," he said to himself. "So there'd be a place." He turned to Uncle Frank. "By the way," he said diffidently, "I mean, I got back so quick—there wouldn't be a chance of my visiting the other establishment now and then? Where I just came from? Smith and Ferguson are all right, but I'd like to keep in touch."

"Well," said Uncle Frank, "you can take that up with the delegation." He arranged the handkerchief in his breast pocket. "They ought to be along any minute now," he said. "Sister's been in a stew about it all day. She says there won't be enough chairs, but she always says that."

"Delegation?" said Doc Mellhorn. "But—"

"You don't realize," said Uncle Frank, with his rich chuckle. "You're a famous man. You've broken pretty near every regulation except the fire laws, and refused the Gate first crack. They've got to do something about it."

"But—" said Doc Mellhorn, looking wildly around for a place of escape.

"Sh-h!" hissed Uncle Frank. "Hold up your head and look as though money were bid for you. It won't take long—just a welcome." He shaded his eyes with his hand. "My," he said with frank admiration, "you've certainly brought them out. There's Rush, by the way."

"Where?" said Doc Mellhorn.

"Second from the left, third row, in a wig," said Uncle Frank. "And there's—"

Then he stopped, and stepped aside. A tall grave figure was advancing down the grape arbor—a bearded man with a wise, majestic face who wore robes as if they belonged to him, not as Doc Mellhorn had seen them worn in college commencements. There was a small fillet of gold about his head and in his left hand, Doc Mellhorn noticed without astonishment, was a winged staff entwined with two fangless serpents. Behind him were many others. Doc Mellhorn stood straighter.

The bearded figure stopped in front of Doc Mellhorn. "Welcome, Brother," said Aesculapius.

"It's an honor to meet you, Doctor," said Doc Mellhorn. He shook the outstretched hand. Then he took a silver half dollar from the mouth of the left-hand snake.

# INTO EGYPT

It had finally been decided to let them go and now, for three days, they had been passing. The dust on the road to the frontier had not settled for three days or nights. But the strictest orders had been given and there were very few incidents. There could easily have been more.

Even the concentration camps had been swept clean, for this thing was to be final. After it, the State could say "How fearless we are—we let even known conspirators depart." It is true that, in the case of those in the concentration camps, there had been a preliminary rectification—a weeding, so to speak. But the news of that would not be officially published for some time and the numbers could always be disputed. If you kill a few people, they remain persons with names and identities, but, if you kill in the hundreds, there is simply a number for most of those who read the newspapers. And, once you start arguing about numbers, you begin to wonder if the thing ever happened at all. This too had been foreseen.

In fact, everything had been foreseen—and with great acuteness. There had been the usual diplomatic tension, solved, finally, by the usual firm stand. At the last moment, the other Powers had decided to co-operate. They had done so unwillingly, grudgingly, and with many representations, but they had done so. It was another great victory. And everywhere the trains rolled and the dust rose on the roads, for, at last and at length, the Accursed People were going. Every one of them, man, woman and child, to the third and the fourth generation —every one of them with a drop of that blood in his veins. And this was the end of it all and, by sunset on the third

79

day, the land would know them no more. It was another great victory—perhaps the greatest. There would be a week of celebration after it, with appropriate ceremonies and speeches, and the date would be marked in the new calendar, with the date of the founding of the State and other dates.

Nevertheless, and even with the noteworthy efficiency of which the State was so proud, any mass evacuation is bound to be a complicated and fatiguing affair. The lieutenant stationed at the crossroads found it so—he was young and in the best of health but the strain was beginning to tell on him, though he would never have admitted it. He had been a little nervous at first —a little nervous and exceedingly anxious that everything should go according to plan. After all, it was an important post, the last crossroads before the frontier. A minor road, of course—they'd be busier on the main highways and at the ports of embarkation—but a last crossroads, nevertheless. He couldn't flatter himself it was worth a decoration— the bigwigs would get those. But, all the same, he was expected to evacuate so many thousands—he knew the figures by heart. Easy enough to say one had only to follow the plan! That might do for civilians—an officer was an officer. Would he show himself enough of an officer, would he make a fool of himself in front of his men? Would he even, perhaps, by some horrible, unforeseen mischance, get his road clogged with fleeing humanity till they had to send somebody over from Staff to straighten the tangle out? The thought was appalling.

He could see it happening in his mind—as a boy, he had been imaginative. He could hear the staff officer's words while he stood at attention, eyes front. One's first real command and a black mark on one's record! Yes, even if it was only police work—that didn't matter—a citizen of the state, a member of the Party must be held to an unflinching standard. If one failed to meet that standard there was nothing left in life. His throat had been dry and his movements a little jerky as he made his last dispositions and saw the first black specks begin to straggle toward the crossroads.

He could afford to laugh at that now, if he had had time. He could even afford to remember old Franz, his orderly, trying to put the brandy in his coffee, that first morning "It's a chilly morning, Lieutenant," but there had been a question in Franz's eyes. He'd refused the brandy, of course, and told Franz off properly, too. The new State did not depend on Dutch courage but on the racial valor of its citizens. And the telling-off had helped —it had made his own voice firmer and given a little fillip of anger to his pulse. But Franz was an old soldier and imperturbable. What was it he had said, later? "The lieutenant must not worry. Civilians are always sheep—it is merely a matter of herding them." An improper remark, of course, to one's lieutenant, but it had helped settle his mind and make it cooler. Yes, an orderly like Franz was worth something, once one learned the knack of keeping him in his place.

Then they had begun to come, slowly, stragglingly, not like soldiers. He couldn't remember who had been the first. It was strange but he could not—he had been sure that he would remember. Perhaps a plodding family, with the scared children looking at him—perhaps one of the old men with long beards and burning eyes. But, after three days, they all mixed, the individual faces. As Franz had said, they became civilian sheep—sheep that one must herd and keep moving, keep moving always through day and night, moving on to the frontier. As they went, they wailed. When the wailing grew too loud, one took measures; but, sooner or later it always began again. It would break out down the road, die down as it came toward the post. It seemed to come out of their mouths without their knowledge—the sound of broken wood, of wheat ground between stones. He had tried to stop it completely at first, now he no longer bothered. And yet there were many— a great many—who did not wail.

At first, it had been interesting to see how many different types there were. He had not thought to find such variety among the Accursed People—one had one's own mental picture, reinforced by the pictures in the news-papers. But, seeing them was different. They were not all like the picture. They were tall and short, plump and lean, black-haired, yellow-haired, red-haired. It was ob-vious, even under the film of dust, that some had been rich, others poor, some thoughtful, others active. Indeed, it was often hard to tell them, by the looks. But that was not his affair—his affair was to keep them moving. All the same, it gave you a shock, sometimes, at first.

Perhaps the queerest thing was that they all looked so ordinary, so much a part of everyday. That was because one had been used to seeing them—it could be no more than that. But, under the film of dust and heat, one would look at a face. And then one would think, unconsciously, "Why, what is that fellow doing, so far from where he lives? Why, for heaven's sake, is he straggling along this road? He doesn't look happy." Then the mind would resume control and one would remember. But the thought would come, now and then, without orders from the mind.

He had seen very few that he knew. That was natural —he came from the South. He had seen Willi Schneider, to be sure—that had been the second day and it was very dusty. When he was a little boy, very young, he had played in Willi's garden with Willi, in the summers, and, as they had played, there had come to them, through the open window, the ripple of a piano and the clear, rip-pling flow of Willi's mother's voice. It was not a great voice—not a Brunhild voice—but beautiful in *lieder* and beautifully sure. She had sung at their own house; that was odd to remember. Of course, her husband had not been one of them—a councilor, in fact. Needless to say, that had been long before the discovery that even the faintest trace of that blood tainted. As for Willi and him-self, they had been friends—yes, even through the first year or so at school. Both of them had meant to run away and be cowboys, and they had had a secret password. Naturally, things had changed, later on.

For a horrible moment, he had thought that Willi would speak to him—recall the warm air of summer and the smell of linden and those young, unmanly days. But Willi did not. Their eyes met, for an instant, then both had looked away. Willi was helping an old woman along, an old woman who muttered fretfully as she walked, like a cat with sore paws. They were both of them covered with dust and the old woman went slowly. Willi's mother had walked with a quick step and her voice had not been cracked or fretful. After play, she had given them both cream buns, laughing and moving her hands, in a bright green dress. It was not permitted to think further of Willi Schneider.

That was the only real acquaintance but there were other, recognizable faces. There was the woman who had kept the newsstand, the brisk little waiter at the summer hotel, the taxi chauffeur with the squint and the heart specialist. Then there was the former scientist—one could still tell him from his pictures—and the actor one had often seen. That was all that one knew and not all on the same day. That was enough. He had not imagined the taxi chauffeur with a wife and children and that the youngest child should be lame. That had surprised him —surprised him almost as much as seeing the heart specialist walking along the road like any man. It had surprised him, also, to see the scientist led along between two others and to recognize the fact that he was mad.

But that also mixed with the dust—the endless, stifling cloud of the dust, the endless, moving current. The dust got in one's throat and one's eyes—it was hard to cut, even with brandy, from one's throat. It lay on the endless bundles people carried; queer bundles, bulging out at the ends, with here a ticking clock, and there a green bunch of carrots. It lay on the handcarts a few of them pushed— the handcarts bearing the sort of goods that one would snatch, haphazard, from a burning house. It rose and whirled and penetrated—it was never still. At night, slashed by the efficient searchlights that made the night bright as day, it was still a mist above the road. As for sleep—well, one slept when one could, for a couple of hours after midnight, when they too slept, ungracefully, in heaps and clumps by the road. But, except for the first night, he could not even remember Franz pulling his boots off.

His men had been excellent, admirable, indefatigable. That was, of course, due to the Leader and the State, but still, he would put it in his report. They had kept the stream moving, always. The attitude had been the newly prescribed one—not that of punishment, richly as that was deserved, but of complete aloofness, as if the Accursed People did not even exist. Naturally, now and then, the men had their fun. One could not blame them for that— some of the incidents had been extremely comic. There had been the old woman with the hen—a comedy character. Of course, she had not been permitted to keep the hen. They should have taken it away from her at the inspection point. But she had looked very funny, holding on to the squawking chicken by the tail feathers, with the tears running down her face.

Yes, the attitude of the men would certainly go in his report. He would devote a special paragraph to the musicians also—they had been indefatigable. They had played the prescribed tunes continually in spite of the dust and the heat. One would hope that those tunes would sink into the hearts of the Accursed People, to be forever a warning and a memory. Particularly if they happened to know the words. But one could never be sure about people like that.

Staff cars had come four times, the first morning, and once there had been a general. He had felt nervous, when they came, but there had been no complaint. After that, they had let him alone, except for an occasional visit— that must mean they thought him up to his work. Once, even, the road had been almost clear, for a few minutes—

he was moving them along faster than they did at the inspection point. The thought had gone to his head for an instant, but he kept cool—and, soon enough, the road had been crowded again.

As regarded casualties—he could not keep the exact figure in his head, but it was a minor one. A couple of heart attacks—one the man who had been a judge, or so the others said. Unpleasant but valuable to see the life drain out of a face like that. He had made himself watch it— one must harden oneself. They had wanted to remove the body—of course, that had not been allowed. The women taken in childbirth had been adequately dealt with—one could do nothing to assist. But he had insisted, for decency's sake, on a screen, and Franz had been very clever at rigging one up. Only two of those had died, the rest had gone on—they showed a remarkable tenacity. Then there were the five executions, including the man suddenly gone crazy, who had roared and foamed. A nasty moment, that—for a second the whole current had stopped flowing. But his men had jumped in at once—he himself had acted quickly. The others were merely incorrigible stragglers and of no account.

And now, it was almost over and soon the homeland would be free. Free as it never had been—for without the Accursed People, it would be unlike any other country on earth. They were gone, with their books and their music, their false, delusive science and their quick way of thinking. They were gone, all the people like Willi Schneider and his mother, who had spent so much time in talking and being friendly. They were gone, the willful people, who clung close together and yet so willfully supported the new and untried. The men who haggled over pennies, and the others who gave—the sweater, the mimic, the philosopher, the discoverer—all were gone. Yes, and with them went their slaves' religion, the religion of the weak and the humble, the religion that fought so bitterly and yet exalted the prophet above the armed man.

One could be a whole man, with them gone, without

their doubts and their mockery and their bitter, self-accusing laughter, their melancholy, deep as a well, and their endless aspiration for something that could not be touched with the hand. One could be solid and virile and untroubled, virile and huge as the old, thunderous gods. It was so that the Leader had spoken, so it must be true. And the countries who weakly received them would be themselves corrupted into warm unmanliness and mockery, into a desire for peace and a search for things not tangible. But the homeland would stand still and listen to the beat of its own heart—not even listen, but stand like a proud fierce animal, a perfect, living machine. To get children, to conquer others, to die gloriously in battle—that was the end of man. It had been a long time forgotten, but the Leader had remembered it. And, naturally, one could not do that completely with them in the land, for they had other ideas.

He thought of these things dutifully because it was right to think of them. They had been repeated and repeated in his ears till they had occupied his mind. But, meanwhile, he was very tired and the dust still rose. They were coming by clumps and groups, now—the last stragglers—they were no longer a solid, flowing current. The afternoon had turned hot—unseasonably hot. He didn't want any more brandy—the thought of it sickened his stomach. He wanted a glass of beer—iced beer, cold and dark, with foam on it—and a chance to unbutton his collar. He wanted to have the thing done and sit down and have Franz pull off his boots. If it were only a little cooler, a little quieter—if even these last would not wail so, now and then—if only the dust would not rise! He found himself humming, for comfort, a Christmas hymn —it brought a little frail coolness to his mind.

> "Silent night, holy night,
> All is calm, all is bright. . . ."

The old gods were virile and thunderous, but, down in the South, they would still deck the tree, in kindliness.

Call it a custom—call it anything you like—it still came out of the heart. And it was a custom of the homeland—it could not be wrong. Oh, the beautiful, crisp snow of Christmas Day, the greetings between friends, the bright, lighted tree! Well, there'd be a Christmas to come. Perhaps he'd be married, by then—he had thought of it, often. If he were, they would have a tree—young couples were sentimental, in the South. A tree and a small manger beneath it, with the animals and the child. They carved the figures out of wood, in his country, with loving care —the thought of them was very peaceful and cool. In the old days, he had always given Willi Schneider part of his almond cake—one knew it was not Willi's festival but one was friendly, for all that. And that must be forgotten. He had had no right to give Willi part of his almond cake—it was the tree that mattered, the tree and the tiny candles, the smell of the fresh pine and the clear, frosty sweetness of the day. They would keep that, he and his wife, keep it with rejoicing, and Willi would not look in through the window, with his old face or his new face. He would not look in at all, ever any more. For now the homeland was released, after many years.

Now the dust was beginning to settle—the current in the road had dwindled to a straggling trickle. He was able to think, for the first time, of the land to which that trickle was going—a hungry land, the papers said, in spite of its boastful ways. The road led blankly into it, beyond the rise of ground—hard to tell what it was like. But they would be dispersed, not only here, but over many lands. Of course, the situation was not comparable—all the same, it must be a queer feeling. A queer feeling, yes, to start out anew, with nothing but the clothes on your back and what you could push in a handcart, if you had a handcart. For an instant the thought came, unbidden, "It must be a great people that can bear such things." But they were the Accursed People—the thought should not have come.

He sighed and turned back to his duty. It was really wonderful—even on the third day there was such order, such precision. It was something to be proud of—something to remember long. The Leader would speak of it, undoubtedly. The ones who came now were the very last stragglers, the weakest, but they were being moved along as promptly as if they were strong. The dust actually no longer rose in a cloud—it was settling, slowly but surely.

He did not quite remember when he had last eaten. It did not matter, for the sun was sinking fast, in a red warm glow. In a moment, in an hour, it would be done—he could rest and undo his collar, have some beer. There was nobody on the road now—nobody at all. He stood rigidly at his post—the picture of an officer, though somewhat dusty—but he knew that his eyes were closing. Nobody on the road—nobody for a whole five minutes . . . for eight . . . for ten.

He was roused by Franz's voice in his ear—he must have gone to sleep, standing up. He had heard of that happening to soldiers on the march—he felt rather proud that, now, it had happened to him. But there seemed to be a little trouble on the road—he walked forward to it, stiffly, trying to clear his throat.

It was a commonplace grouping—he had seen dozens like it in the course of the three days—an older man, a young woman, and, of course, the child that she held. No doubt about them, either—the man's features were strongly marked, the woman had the liquid eyes. As for the child, that was merely a wrapped bundle. They should have started before—stupid people—the man looked strong enough. Their belongings were done up like all poor people's belongings.

He stood in front of them, now, erect and a soldier. "Well," he said. "Don't you know the orders? No livestock to be taken. Didn't they examine you, down the road?" ("And a pretty fool I'll look like, reporting one confiscated donkey to Headquarters," he thought, with irritation. "We've been able to manage, with the chickens, but this is really too much! What can they be thinking of at the inspection point? Oh, well, they're tired too, I suppose, but it's my responsibility.")

He put a rasp in his voice—he had to, they looked at him so stupidly. "Well?" he said. "Answer me! Don't you know an officer when you see one?"

"We have come a long way," said the man, in a low voice. "We heard there was danger to the child. So we are going. May we pass?" The voice was civil enough, but the eyes were dark and large, the face tired and worn. He was resting one hand on his staff, in a peasant gesture. The woman said nothing at all and one felt that she would say nothing. She sat on the back of the gray donkey and the child in her arms, too, was silent, though it moved.

The lieutenant tried to think rapidly. After all, these were the last. But the thoughts buzzed around his head and would not come out of his mouth. That was fatigue. It should be easy enough for a lieutenant to give an order.

He found himself saying, conversationally, "There are just the three of you?"

"That is all," said the man and looked at him with great simplicity. "But we heard there was danger to the child. So we could not stay any more. We could not stay at all."

"Indeed," said the lieutenant and then said again, "indeed."

"Yes," said the man. "But we shall do well enough—we have been in exile before." He spoke patiently and yet with a certain authority. When the lieutenant did not answer, he laid his other hand on the rein of the gray donkey. It moved forward a step and with it, also the child stirred and moved. The lieutenant, turning, saw the child's face now, and its hands, as it turned and moved its small hands to the glow of the sunset.

"If the lieutenant pleases—" said an eager voice, the voice of the Northern corporal.

"The lieutenant does not please," said the lieutenant. He nodded at the man. "You may proceed."

"But Lieutenant—" said the eager voice.

"Swine and dog," said the lieutenant, feeling something snap in his mind, "are we to hinder the Leader's plans because of one gray donkey? The order says—all out of the country by sunset. Let them go. You will report to me, Corporal, in the morning."

He turned on his heel and walked a straight line to the field hut, not looking back. When Franz, the orderly, came in a little later, he found him sitting in a chair.

"If the lieutenant would take some brandy—" he said, respectfully.

"The lieutenant has had enough brandy," said the lieutenant, in a hoarse, dusty voice. "Have my orders been obeyed?"

"Yes, Lieutenant."

"They are gone—the very last of them?"

"Yes, Lieutenant."

"They did not look back?"

"No, Lieutenant."

The lieutenant said nothing, for a while, and Franz busied himself with boots. After some time, he spoke.

"The lieutenant should try to sleep," he said. "We have carried out our orders. And now, they are gone."

"Yes," said the lieutenant, and, suddenly, he saw them again, the whole multitude, dispersed among every country—the ones who had walked his road, the ones at the points of embarkation. There were a great many of them, and that he had expected. But they were not dispersed as he had thought. They were not dispersed as he had thought, for, with each one went shame, like a visible burden. And the shame was not theirs, though they carried it—the shame belonged to the land that had driven them forth—his own land. He could see it growing and spreading like a black blot—the shame of his country spread over the whole earth.

"The lieutenant will have some brandy," he said. "Quickly, Franz."

When the brandy was brought, he stared at it for a moment, in the cup.

"Tell me, Franz," he said. "Did you know them well? Any of them? Before?"

"Oh yes, Lieutenant," said Franz, in his smooth, orderly's voice. "In the last war, I was billeted—well, the name of the town does not matter, but the woman was one of them. Of course that was before we knew about them," he said, respectfully. "That was more than twenty years ago. But she was very kind to me—I used to make toys for her children. I have often wondered what happened to her—she was very considerate and kind. Doubtless I was wrong, Lieutenant? But that was in another country."

"Yes, Franz," said the lieutenant. "There were children, you say?"

"Yes, Lieutenant."

"You saw the child today? The last one?"

"Yes, Lieutenant."

"Its hands had been hurt," said the lieutenant. "In the middle. Right through. I saw them. I wish I had not seen that. I wish I had not seen its hands."

# THE BLOOD OF THE MARTYRS

The man who expected to be shot lay with his eyes open, staring at the upper left-hand corner of his cell. He was fairly well over his last beating, and they might come for him any time now. There was a yellow stain in the cell corner near the ceiling; he had liked it at first, then disliked it; now he was coming back to liking it again.

He could see it more clearly with his glasses on, but he only put on his glasses for special occasions now—the first thing in the morning, and when they brought the food in, and for interviews with the General. The lenses of the glasses had been cracked in a beating some months before, and it strained his eyes to wear them too long. Fortunately, in his present life he had very few occasions demanding clear vision. But, nevertheless, the accident to his glasses worried him, as it worries all near-sighted people. You put your glasses on the first thing in the morning and the world leaps into proportion; if it does not do so, something is wrong with the world.

The man did not believe greatly in symbols, but his chief nightmare, nowadays, was an endless one in which, suddenly and without warning, a large piece of glass would drop out of one of the lenses and he would grope around the cell, trying to find it. He would grope very carefully and gingerly, for hours of darkness, but the end was always the same—the small, unmistakable crunch of irreplacable glass beneath his heel or his knee. Then he would wake up sweating, with his hands cold. This dream alternated with the one of being shot, but he found no great benefit in the change.

As he lay there, you could see that he had an intel-

lectual head—the head of a thinker or a scholar, old and
bald, with the big, domed brow. It was, as a matter of
fact, a well-known head; it had often appeared in the
columns of newspapers and journals, sometimes when
the surrounding text was in a language Professor Malzius
could not read. The body, though stooped and worn, was
still a strong peasant body and capable of surviving a
good deal of ill-treatment, as his captors had found out.
He had fewer teeth than when he came to prison, and
both the ribs and the knee had been badly set, but these
were minor matters. It also occurred to him that his blood
count was probably poor. However, if he could ever get
out and go to a first-class hospital, he was probably good
for at least ten years more of work. But, of course, he
would not get out. They would shoot him before that,
and it would be over.

Sometimes he wished passionately that it would be
over—tonight—this moment; at other times he was shaken
by the mere blind fear of death. The latter he tried to
treat as he would have treated an attack of malaria, knowing that it was an attack, but not always with success. He
should have been able to face it better than most—he
was Gregor Malzius, the scientist—but that did not always help. The fear of death persisted, even when one
had noted and classified it as a purely physical reac-
tion. When he was out of here, he would be able to write
a very instructive little paper on the fear of death. He
could even do it here, if he had writing materials, but
there was no use asking for those. Once they had been
given him and he had spent two days quite happily.
But they had torn up the work and spat upon it in front
of his face. It was a childish thing to do, but it discouraged
a man from working.

It seemed odd that he had never seen anybody shot, but
he never had. During the war, his reputation and his
bad eyesight had exempted him from active service. He
had been bombed a couple of times when his reserve bat-
talion was guarding the railway bridge, but that was

quite different. You were not tied to a stake, and the airplanes were not trying to kill you as an individual. He knew the place where it was done here, of course. But prisoners did not see the executions, they merely heard, if the wind was from the right quarter.

He had tried again and again to visualize how it would be, but it always kept mixing with an old steel engraving he had seen in boyhood—the execution of William Walker, the American filibuster, in Honduras. William Walker was a small man with a white semi-Napoleonic face. He was standing, very correctly dressed, in front of an open grave, and before him a ragged line of picturesque natives were raising their muskets. When he was shot he would instantly and tidily fall into the grave, like a man dropping through a trap door; as a boy, the extreme neatness of the arrangement had greatly impressed Gregor Malzius. Behind the wall there were palm trees, and, somewhere off to the right, blue and warm, the Caribbean Sea. It would not be like that at all, for his own execution; and yet, whenever he thought of it, he thought of it as being like that.

Well, it was his own fault. He could have accepted the new regime; some respectable people had done that. He could have fled the country; many honorable people had. A scientist should be concerned with the eternal, not with transient political phenomena; and a scientist should be able to live anywhere. But thirty years at the university were thirty years, and, after all, he was Malzius, one of the first biochemists in the world. To the last, he had not believed that they would touch him. Well, he had been wrong about that.

The truth, of course, was the truth. One taught it or one did not teach it. If one did not teach it, it hardly mattered what one did. But he had no quarrel with any established government; he was willing to run up a flag every Tuesday, as long as they let him alone. Most people were fools, and one government was as good as another for them—it had taken them twenty years to accept his theory of cell mutation. Now, if he'd been like his friend Bonnard—a fellow who signed protests, attended meetings for the cause of world peace, and generally played the fool in public—they'd have had some reason to complain. An excellent man in his field, Bonnard—none better—but outside of it, how deplorably like an actor, with his short gray beard, his pink cheeks and his impulsive enthusiasms! Any government could put a fellow like Bonnard in prison—though it would be an injury to science and, therefore, wrong. For that matter, he thought grimly, Bonnard would enjoy being a martyr. He'd walk gracefully to the execution post with a begged cigarette in his mouth, and some theatrical last quip. But Bonnard was safe in his own land—doubtless writing heated and generous articles on The Case of Professor Malzius—and he, Malzius, was the man who was going to be shot. He would like a cigarette, too, on his way to execution; he had not smoked in five months. But he certainly didn't intend to ask for one, and they wouldn't think of offering him any. That was the difference between him and Bonnard.

His mind went back with longing to the stuffy laboratory and stuffier lecture hall at the university; his feet yearned for the worn steps he had climbed ten thousand times, and his eyes for the long steady look through the truthful lens into worlds too tiny for the unaided eye. They had called him "The Bear" and "Old Prickly," but they had fought to work under him, the best of the young men. They said he would explain the Last Judgment in terms of cellular phenomena, but they had crowded to his lectures. It was Williams, the Englishman, who had made up the legend that he carried a chocolate éclair and a set of improper post cards in his battered brief case. Quite untrue, of course—chocolate always made him ill, and he had never looked at an improper post card in his life. And Williams would never know that he knew the legend, too: for Williams had been killed long ago in the war. For a moment, Professor Malzius felt blind hate at the thought of an excellent scientific machine like Williams being smashed in a war. But blind hate was an improper emotion for a scientist, and he put it aside.

He smiled grimly again; they hadn't been able to break up his classes—lucky he was The Bear! He'd seen one colleague hooted from his desk by a band of•determined young hoodlums—too bad, but if a man couldn't keep order in his own classroom, he'd better get out. They'd wrecked his own laboratory, but not while he was there.

It was so senseless, so silly. "In God's name," he said reasonably, to no one, "what sort of conspirator do you think I would make? A man of my age and habits! I am interested in cellular phenomena!" And yet they were beating him because he would not tell about the boys. As if he had even paid attention to half the nonsense! There were certain passwords and greetings—a bar of music you whistled, entering a restaurant; the address of a firm that specialized, ostensibly, in vacuum cleaners. But they were not his own property. They belonged to the young men who had trusted The Bear. He did not know what half of them meant, and the one time he had gone to a meeting, he had felt like a fool. For they were fools and childish—playing the childish games of conspiracy that people like Bonnard enjoyed. Could they even make a better world than the present? He doubted it extremely. And yet, he could not betray them; they had come to him, looking over their shoulders, with darkness in their eyes.

A horrible, an appalling thing—to be trusted. He had no wish to be a guide and counselor of young men. He wanted to do his work. Suppose they were poor and ragged and oppressed; he had been a peasant himself, he had eaten black bread. It was by his own efforts that he was Professor Malzius. He did not wish the confidences of boys like Gregopolous and the others—for, after all, what was Gregopolous? An excellent and untiring laboratory assistant—and a laboratory assistant he would remain to the end of his days. He had pattered about the laboratory like a fox terrier, with a fox terrier's quick bright eyes. Like a devoted dog, he had made a god of Professor Malzius. "I don't want your problems, man. I don't want to know what you are doing outside the laboratory." But Gregopolous had brought his problems and his terrible trust none the less, humbly and proudly, like a fox terrier with a bone. After that—well, what was a man to do?

He hoped they would get it over with, and quickly. The world should be like a chemical formula, full of reason and logic. Instead, there were all these young men, and their eyes. They conspired, hopelessly and childishly, for what they called freedom against the new regime. They wore no overcoats in winter and were often hunted and killed. Even if they did not conspire, they had miserable little love affairs and ate the wrong food—yes, even before, at the university, they had been the same. Why the devil would they not accept? Then they could do their work. Of course, a great many of them would not be allowed to accept—they had the wrong ideas or the wrong politics—but then they could run away. If Malzius, at twenty, had had to run from his country, he would still have been a scientist. To talk of a free world was a delusion; men were not free in the world. Those who wished got a space of time to get their work done. That was all. And yet, he had not accepted—he did not know why.

Now he heard the sound of steps along the corridor. His body began to quiver and the places where he had been beaten hurt him. He noted it as an interesting reflex. Sometimes they merely flashed the light in the cell and passed by. On the other hand, it might be death. It was a hard question to decide.

The lock creaked, the door opened. "Get up, Malzius!" said the hard, bright voice of the guard. Gregor Malzius got up, a little stiffly, but quickly.

"Put on your glasses, you old fool!" said the guard, with a laugh. "You are going to the General."

Professor Malzius found the stone floors of the corridor uneven, though he knew them well enough. Once or twice the guard struck him, lightly and without malice, as one strikes an old horse with a whip. The blows were familiar and did not register on Professor Malzius' consciousness; he merely felt proud of not stumbling. He was apt to stumble; once he had hurt his knee.

He noticed, it seemed to him, an unusual tenseness and officiousness about his guard. Once, even, in a brightly lighted corridor the guard moved to strike him, but refrained. However, that, too, happened occasionally, with one guard or another, and Professor Malzius merely noted the fact. It was a small fact, but an important one in the economy in which he lived.

But there could be no doubt that something unusual was going on in the castle. There were more guards than usual, many of them strangers. He tried to think, carefully, as he walked, if it could be one of the new national holidays. It was hard to keep track of them all. The General might be in a good humor. Then they would merely have a cat-and-mouse conversation for half an hour and nothing really bad would happen. Once, even, there had been a cigar. Professor Malzius, the scientist, licked his lips at the thought.

Now he was being turned over to a squad of other guards, with salutings. This was really unusual; Professor Malzius bit his mouth, inconspicuously. He had the poignant distrust of a monk or an old prisoner at any break in routine. Old prisoners are your true conservatives ;they only demand that the order around them remains exactly the same.

It alarmed him as well that the new guards did not laugh at him. New guards almost always laughed when they saw him for the first time. He was used to the laughter and missed it—his throat felt dry. He would have liked, just once, to eat at the university restaurant before he died. It was bad food, ill cooked and starchy, food good enough for poor students and professors, but he would have liked to be there, in the big smoky room that smelt of copper boilers and cabbage, with a small cup of bitter coffee before him and a cheap cigarette. He did not ask for his dog or his notebooks, the old photographs in his bedroom, his incomplete experiments or his freedom. Just to lunch once more at the university restaurant and have people point out The Bear. It seemed a small thing to ask, but of course it was quite impossible.

"Halt!" said a voice, and he halted. There were, for the third time, salutings. Then the door of the General's office opened and he was told to go in.

He stood, just inside the door, in the posture of attention, as he had been taught. The crack in the left lens of his glasses made a crack across the room, and his eyes were paining him already, but he paid no attention to that. There was the familiar figure of the General with his air of a well-fed and extremely healthy tomcat, and there was another man, seated at the General's desk. He could not see the other man very well—the crack made him bulge and waver—but he did not like his being there.

"Well, professor," said the General, in an easy, purring voice.

Malzius's entire body jerked. He had made a fearful, an unpardonable omission. He must remedy it at once. "Long live the state," he shouted in a loud thick voice, and saluted. He knew, bitterly, that his salute was ridiculous and that he looked ridiculous, making it. But perhaps the General would laugh—he had done so before. Then everything would be all right, for it was not quite as easy to beat a man after you had laughed at him.

The General did not laugh. He made a half turn instead, toward the man at the desk. The gesture said, "You see, he is well trained." It was the gesture of a man of the world, accustomed to deal with unruly peasants and animals—the gesture of a man fitted to be General.

The man at the desk paid no attention to the General's gesture. He lifted his head, and Malzius saw him more clearly and with complete unbelief. It was not a man but a picture come alive. Professor Malzius had seen the picture a hundred times; they had made him salute and take off his hat in front of it, when he had had a hat. Indeed, the picture had presided over his beatings. The man himself was a little smaller, but the picture was a good picture. There were many dictators in the world, and this was one type. The face was white, beaky and semi-Napoleonic; the lean, military body sat squarely in its chair. The eyes dominated the face, and the mouth was rigid. I remember also a hypnotist, and a woman Charcot showed me, at his clinic in Paris, thought Professor Malzius. But there is also, obviously, an endocrine unbalance. Then his thoughts stopped.

"Tell the man to come closer," said the man at the desk. "Can he hear me? Is he deaf?"

"No, Your Excellency," said the General, with enormous, purring respect. "But he is a little old, though perfectly healthy. . . . Are you not, Professor Malzius?"

"Yes, I am perfectly healthy. I am very well treated here," said Professor Malzius, in his loud thick voice. They were not going to catch him with traps like that, not even by dressing up somebody as the Dictator. He fixed his eyes on the big-old-fashioned inkwell on the General's desk—that, at least, was perfectly sane.

"Come closer," said the man at the desk to Professor Malzius, and the latter advanced till he could almost touch the inkwell with his fingers. Then he stopped with a jerk, hoping he had done right. The movement removed the man at the desk from the crack in his lenses, and Professor Malzius knew suddenly that it was true. This was, indeed, the Dictator, this man with the rigid mouth. He began to talk.

"I have been very well treated here and the General has acted with the greatest consideration," he said. "But I am Professor Gregor Malzius—professor of biochemistry. For thirty years I have lectured at the university; I am a fellow of the Royal Society, a corresponding member of the Academy of Sciences at Berlin, at Rome, at Boston, at Paris and Stockholm. I have received the Nottingham Medal, the Lamarck Medal, the Order of St. John of Portugal and the Nobel Prize. I think my blood count is low, but I have received a great many degrees and my experiments on the migratory cells are not finished. I do not wish to complain of my treatment, but I must continue my experiments."

He stopped, like a clock that has run down, surprised to hear the sound of his own voice. He noted, in one part of his mind, that the General had made a move to silence him, but had himself been silenced by the Dictator.

"Yes, Professor Malzius," said the man at the desk, in a harsh, toneless voice. "There has been a regrettable error." The rigid face stared at Professor Malzius. Professor Malzius stared back. He did not say anything.

"In these days," said the Dictator, his voice rising, "the nation demands the submission of every citizen. Encircled by jealous foes, our reborn land yet steps forward toward her magnificent destiny." The words continued for some time, the voice rose and fell. Professor Malzius listened respectfully; he had heard the words many times before and they had ceased to have meaning to him. He was thinking of certain cells of the body that rebel against the intricate processes of Nature and set up their own bellicose state. Doubtless they, too, have a destiny, he thought, but in medicine it is called cancer.

"Jealous and spiteful tongues in other countries have declared that it is our purpose to wipe out learning and science," concluded the Dictator. "That is not our purpose. After the cleansing, the rebirth. We mean to move forward to the greatest science in the world—our own science, based on the enduring principles of our nationhood." He ceased abruptly, his eyes fell into their dream. Very like the girl Charcot showed me in my young days, thought Professor Malzius; there was first the ebullition, then the calm.

"I was part of the cleansing? You did not mean to hurt me?" he asked timidly.

"Yes, Professor Malzius," said the General, smiling, "you were part of the cleansing. Now that is over. His Excellency has spoken."

"I do not understand," said Professor Malzius, gazing at the fixed face of the man behind the desk.

"It is very simple," said the General. He spoke in a slow careful voice, as one speaks to a deaf man or a child. "You are a distinguished man of science—you have received the Nobel Prize. That was a service to the state. You became, however, infected by the wrong political ideas. That was treachery to the state. You had, therefore, as decreed by His Excellency, to pass through a certain period for probation and rehabilitation. But that, we believe, is finished."

"You do not wish to know the names of the young men any more?" said Professor Malzius. "You do not want the addresses?"

"That is no longer of importance," said the General patiently. "There is no longer opposition. The leaders were caught and executed three weeks ago."

"There is no longer opposition," repeated Professor Malzius.

"At the trial, you were not even involved."

"I was not even involved," said Professor Malzius. "Yes."

"Now," said the General, with a look at the Dictator, "we come to the future. I will be frank—the new state is frank with its citizens."

"It is so," said the Dictator, his eyes still sunk in his dream.

"There has been—let us say—a certain agitation in foreign countries regarding Professor Malzius," said the General, his eyes still fixed on the Dictator. "That means nothing, of course. Nevertheless, your acquaintance, Professor Bonnard, and others have meddled in matters that do not concern them."

"They asked after me?" said Professor Malzius, with surprise. "It is true, my experiments were reaching a point that——"

"No foreign influence could turn us from our firm purpose," said the Dictator. "But it is our firm purpose to show our nation first in science and culture as we have already shown her first in manliness and statehood. For that reason, you are here, Professor Malzius." He smiled.

Professor Malzius stared. His cheeks began to tremble.

"I do not understand," said Professor Malzius. "You will give me my laboratory back?"

"Yes," said the Dictator, and the General nodded as one nods to a stupid child.

Professor Malzius passed a hand across his brow.

"My post at the university?" he said. "My experiments?"

"It is the purpose of our regime to offer the fullest encouragement to our loyal sons of science," said the Dictator.

"First of all," said Professor Malzius, "I must go to a hospital. My blood count is poor. But that will not take long." His voice had become impatient and his eyes glowed. "Then—my notebooks were burned, I suppose. That was silly, but we can start in again. I have a very good memory, an excellent memory. The theories are in my head, you know," and he tapped it. "I must have assistants, of course; little Gregopolous was my best one——"

"The man Gregopolous has been executed," said the General, in a stern voice. "You had best forget him."

"Oh," said Professor Malzius. "Well, then, I must have someone else. You see, these are important experiments. There must be some young men—clever ones—they cannot all be dead. I will know them." He laughed a little, nervously. "The Bear always got the pick of the crop," he said. "They used to call me The Bear, you know." He stopped and looked at them for a moment with ghastly eyes. "You are not fooling me?" he said. He burst into tears.

When he recovered he was alone in the room with the General. The General was looking at him as he himself had looked once at strange forms of life under the microscope, with neither disgust nor attraction, but with great interest.

"His Excellency forgives your unworthy suggestion," he said. "He knows you are overwrought."

"Yes," said Professor Malzius. He sobbed once and dried his glasses.

"Come, come," said the General, with a certain bluff heartiness. "We mustn't have our new president of the National Academy crying. It would look badly in the photographs."

"President of the Academy?" said Professor Malzius quickly. "Oh, no; I mustn't be that. They make speeches; they have administrative work. But I am a scientist, a teacher."

"I'm afraid you can't very well avoid it," said the General, still heartily, though he looked at Professor Malzius. "Your induction will be quite a ceremony. His Excellency himself will preside. And you will speak on the new glories of our science. It will be a magnificent answer to the petty and jealous criticisms of our neighbors. Oh, you needn't worry about the speech," he added quickly. "It will be prepared; you will only have to read it. His Excellency thinks of everything."

"Very well," said Professor Malzius; "and then may I go back to my work?"

"Oh, don't worry about that," said the General, smiling. "I'm only a simple soldier; I don't know about those things. But you'll have plenty of work."

"The more the better," said Malzius eagerly. "I still have ten good years."

He opened his mouth to smile, and a shade of dismay crossed the General's face.

"Yes," he said, as if to himself. "The teeth must be attended to. At once. And a rest, undoubtedly, before the photographs are taken. Milk. You are feeling sufficiently well, Professor Malzius?"

"I am very happy," said Professor Malzius. "I have been very well treated and I come of peasant stock."

"Good," said the General. He paused for a moment, and spoke in a more official voice.

"Of course, it is understood, Professor Malzius——" he said.

"Yes?" said Professor Malzius. "I beg your pardon. I was thinking of something else."

"It is understood, Professor Malzius," repeated the General, "that your—er—rehabilitation in the service of the state is a permanent matter. Naturally, you will be under observation, but, even so, there must be no mistake."

"I am a scientist," said Professor Malzius impatiently. "What have I to do with politics? If you wish me to take oaths of loyalty, I will take as many as you wish."

"I am glad you take that attitude," said the General. though he looked at Professor Malzius curiously. "I may say that I regret the unpleasant side of our interviews. I trust you bear no ill will."

"Why should I be angry?" said Professor Malzius. "You were told to do one thing. Now you are told to do another. That is all."

"It is not quite so simple as that," said the General rather stiffly. He looked at Professor Malzius for a third time. "And I'd have sworn you were one of the stiff-necked ones," he said. "Well, well, every man has his breaking point, I suppose. In a few moments you will receive the final commands of His Excellency. Tonight you will go to the capital and speak over the radio. You will have no difficulty there—the speech is written. But it will put a quietus on the activities of our friend Bonnard and the question that has been raised in the British Parliament. Then a few weeks of rest by the sea and the dental work, and then, my dear president of the National Academy, you will be ready to undertake your new duties. I congratulate you and hope we shall meet often under pleasant auspices." He bowed from the waist to Malzius, the bow of a man of the world, though there was still something feline in his mustaches. Then he stood to attention, and Malzius, too, for the Dictator had come into the room.

"It is settled?" said the Dictator. "Good. Gregor Malzius, I welcome you to the service of the new state. You have cast your errors aside and are part of our destiny."

"Yes," said Professor Malzius, "I will be able to do my work now."

The Dictator frowned a little.

"You will not only be able to continue your invaluable researches," he said, "but you will also be able—and it will be part of your duty—to further our national ideals. Our reborn nation must rule the world for the world's good. There is a fire within us that is not in other stocks. Our civilization must be extended everywhere. The future wills it. It will furnish the subject of your first discourse as president of the Academy."

"But," said Professor Malzius, in a low voice, "I am not a soldier. I am a biochemist. I have no experience in these matters you speak of."

The Dictator nodded. "You are a distinguished man of science," he said. "You will prove that our women must bear soldiers, our men abandon this nonsense of republics and democracies for trust in those born to rule them. You will prove by scientific law that certain races—our race in particular—are destined to rule the world. You will prove they are destined to rule by the virtues of war, and that was is part of our heritage."

"But," said Professor Malzius, "it is not like that. I mean," he said, "one looks and watches in the laboratory. One waits for a long time. It is a long process, very long. And then, if the theory is not proved, one discards the theory. That is the way it is done. I probably do not explain it well. But I am a biochemist; I do not know how to look for the virtues of one race against another, and I can prove nothing about war, except that it kills. If I said anything else, the whole world would laugh at me."

"Not one in this nation would laugh at you," said the Dictator.

"But if they do not laugh at me when I am wrong, there is no science," said Professor Malzius, knotting his brows.

He paused. "Do not misunderstand me," he said earnestly. "I have ten years of good work left; I want to get back to my laboratory. But, you see, there are the young men —if I am to teach the young men."

He paused again, seeing their faces before him. There were many. There was Williams, the Englishman, who had died in the war, and little Gregopolous with the fox-terrier eyes. There were all who had passed through his classrooms, from the stupidest to the best. They had shot little Gregopolous for treason, but that did not alter the case. From all over the world they had come—he remembered the Indian student and the Chinese. They wore cheap overcoats, they were hungry for knowledge, they ate the bad, starchy food of the poor restaurants, they had miserable little love affairs and played childish games, of politics, instead of doing their work. Nevertheless, a few were promising—all must be given the truth. It did not matter if they died, but they must be given the truth. Otherwise there could be no continuity and no science.

He looked at the Dictator before him—yes, it was a hysteric face. He would know how to deal with it in his classroom—but such faces should not rule countries or young men. One was willing to go through a great many meaningless ceremonies in order to do one's work—wear a uniform or salute or be president of the Academy. That did not matter; it was part of the due to Caesar. But not to tell lies to young men on one's own subject. After all, they had called him The Bear and said he carried improper post cards in his brief case. They had given him their terrible confidence—not for love or kindness, but because they had found him honest. It was too late to change.

The Dictator looked sharply at the General. "I thought this had been explained to Professor Malzius," he said.

"Why, yes," said Professor Malzius. "I will sign any papers. I assure you I am not interested in politics—a man like myself, imagine! One state is as good as another. And

I miss my tobacco—I have not smoked in five months. But, you see, one cannot be a scientist and tell lies."

He looked at the two men.

"What happens if I do not?" he said, in a low voice. But, looking at the Dictator, he had his answer. It was a fanatic face.

"Why, we shall resume our conversations, Professor Malzius," said the General, with a simper.

"Then I shall be beaten again," said Professor Malzius. He stated what he knew to be a fact.

"The process of rehabilitation is obviously not quite complete," said the General, "but perhaps, in time——"

"It will not be necessary," said Professor Malzius. "I cannot be beaten again." He stared wearily around the room. His shoulders straightened—it was so he had looked in the classroom when they had called him The Bear. "Call your other officers in," he said in a clear voice. "There are papers for me to sign. I should like them all to witness."

"Why——" said the General. "Why——" He looked doubtfully at the Dictator.

An expression of gratification appeared on the lean, semi-Napoleonic face. A white hand, curiously limp, touched the hand of Professor Malzius.

"You will feel so much better, Gregor," said the hoarse, tense voice. "I am so very glad you have given in."

"Why, of course, I give in," said Gregor Malzius. "Are you not the Dictator? And besides, if I do not, I shall be beaten again. And I cannot—you understand?—I cannot be beaten again."

He paused, breathing a little. But already the room was full of other faces. He knew them well, the hard faces of the new regime. But youthful some of them too.

The Dictator was saying something with regard to receiving the distinguished scientist, Professor Gregor Malzius, into the service of the state.

"Take the pen," said the General in an undertone.

"The inkwell is there, Professor Malzius. Now you may sign."

Professor Malzius stood, his fingers gripping the big, old-fashioned inkwell. It was full of ink—the servants of the Dictator were very efficient. They could shoot small people with the eyes of fox terriers for treason, but their trains arrived on time and their inkwells did not run dry.

"The state," he said, breathing. "Yes. But science does not know about states. And you are a little man—a little, unimportant man."

Then, before the General could stop him, he had picked up the inkwell and thrown it in the Dictator's face. The next moment the General's fist caught him on the side of the head and he fell behind the desk to the floor. But lying there, through his cracked glasses, he could still see the grotesque splashes of ink on the Dictator's face and uniform, and the small cut above his eye where the blood was gathering. They had not fired; he had thought he would be too close to the Dictator for them to fire in time.

"Take that man out and shoot him. At once," said the Dictator in a dry voice. He did not move to wipe the stains from his uniform—and for that Professor Malzius admired him. They rushed then, each anxious to be first. But Professor Malzius made no resistance.

As he was being hustled along the corridors, he fell now and then. On the second fall, his glasses were broken completely, but that did not matter to him. They were in a great hurry, he thought, but all the better—one did not have to think while one could not see.

Now and then he heard his voice make sounds of discomfort, but his voice was detached from himself. There was little Gregopolous—he could see him very plainly— and Williams, with his fresh English coloring—and all the men whom he had taught.

He had given them nothing but work and the truth; they had given him their terrible trust. If he had been beaten again, he might have betrayed them. But he had avoided that.

He felt a last weakness—a wish that someone might know. They would not, of course; he would have died of typhoid in the castle and there would be regretful notices in the newspapers. And then he would be forgotten, except for his work, and that was as it should be. He had never thought much of martyrs—hysterical people in the main. Though he'd like Bonnard to have known about the ink; it was in the coarse vein of humor that Bonnard could not appreciate. But then, he was a peasant; Bonnard had often told him so.

They were coming out into an open courtyard now; he felt the fresh air of outdoors. "Gently," he said. "A little gently. What's the haste?" But already they were tying him to the post. Someone struck him in the face and his eyes watered. "A schoolboy covered with ink," he muttered through his lost teeth. "A hysterical schoolboy too. But you cannot kill truth."

They were not good last words, and he knew that they were not. He must try to think of better ones—not shame Bonnard. But now they had a gag in his mouth; just as well; it saved him the trouble.

His body ached, bound against the post, but his sight and his mind were clearer. He could make out the evening sky, gray with fog, the sky that belonged to no country, but to all the world.

He could make out the gray high buttress of the castle. They had made it a jail, but it would not always be a jail. Perhaps in time it would not even exist. But if a little bit of truth were gathered, that would always exist, while there were men to remember and rediscover it. It was only the liars and the cruel who always failed.

Sixty years ago, he had been a little boy, eating black bread and thin cabbage soup in a poor house. It had been a bitter life, but he could not complain of it. He had had some good teachers and they had called him The Bear.

The gag hurt his mouth—they were getting ready now.

There had been a girl called Anna once; he had almost forgotten her. And his rooms had smelt a certain way and he had had a dog. It did not matter what they did with the medals. He raised his head and looked once more at the gray foggy sky. In a moment there would be no thought, but, while there was thought, one must remember and note. His pulse rate was lower than he would have expected and his breathing oddly even, but those were not the important things. The important thing was beyond, in the gray sky that had no country, in the stones of the earth and the feeble human spirit. The important thing was truth.

"Ready!" called the officer. "Aim! Fire!" But Professor Malzius did not hear the three commands of the officer. He was thinking about the young men.

# BLOSSOM AND FRUIT

When the spring was in its mid-term and the apple trees
entirely white they would walk down by the river, talking as they went, their voices hardly distinguishable from
the voices of birds or waters. Their love had begun with
the winter; they were both in their first youth. Those
who watched them made various prophecies—none of
which was fulfilled—laughed, criticized, or were sentimental according to the turn of their minds. But these two
were ignorant of the watching and, if they had heard
the prophecies, they would hardly have understood them.

Between them and the world was a wall of glass—between them and time was a wall of glass—they were not
conscious of being either young or old. The weather
passed over them as over a field or a stream—it was there
but they took no account of it. There was love and being
alive, there was the beating of the heart, apart or together. This had been, this would be, this was—it was
impossible to conceive of a world created otherwise. He
knew the shape of her face, in dreams and out of them;
she could shut her eyes, alone, and feel his hands on
her shoulders. So it went, so they spoke and answered,
so they walked by the river. Later on, once or twice, they
tried to remember what they had said—a great deal of
nonsense?—but the words were already gone. They could
hear the river running; he could remember a skein of
hair; she, a blue shirt open at the throat and an eager
face. Then, after a while, these two were not often remembered.

All this had been a number of years ago. But now
that the old man had returned at last to the place where

he had been born, he would often go down to the river-field. Sometimes a servant or a grandchild would carry the light camp chair and the old brown traveling-rug; more often he would go alone. He was still strong—he liked to do for himself; there was no use telling him he'd catch his death walking through the wet grass, it only set him in his ways.

When at last he had reached his goal—a certain ancient apple tree whose limbs were entirely crooked with bear-ing—he would set the chair under it, sit down, wrap his legs in the rug, and remain there till he was summoned to come in. He was alone but not lonely; if anyone passed by he would talk; if no one passed he was content to be silent. There was almost always a book in his lap, but he very seldom read it; his own life, after all, was the book that suited him best, it did not grow dull with rereading. There is little to add, he thought, little to add; but he was not sorry. The text remained; it was a long text, and many things that had seemed insignificant and obscure in the living took on sudden clarities and significances, now he remembered.

Yes, he thought, that is how most people live their ac-tual lives—skimming it through, in a hurry to get to the end and find out who got married and who got rich. Well, that's something that can't be helped. But when you know the end you can turn back and try to find out the story. Only most people don't want to, he thought, and smiled. Looks too queer to suit them—reading your own book backwards. But it's a great pleasure to me. He re-laxed, let his hands lie idle in his lap, let the pictures drift before his eyes.

The picture of the boy and girl by the river. He could stand off from it now and regard it, without sorrow or longing; no ghost cried in his flesh because of it, though it was a part of that flesh and with that flesh would die. And yet, for a moment, he had almost been in the old mood again, recovered the old ecstasy. Whatever love was, he had been in love at that time. But what was love?

They met by stealth because of reasons no longer important; it lasted through all of one long dry summer in the small town that later became a city. Outside, the street baked, the white dust blew up and down, but it was fresh and pleasant in the house.

She was a dark-haired woman, a widow, some years older than he—he was a young man in a tall collar, his face not yet lined or marked but his body set in the pattern which it would keep. Her name was Stella. She had a cool voice, sang sometimes; they talked a great deal. They made a number of plans which were not accomplished—they were hotly in love.

He remembered being with her one evening toward the end of summer, in the trivial room. On the table was a bowl of winesaps—he had been teasing her about them —she said she liked the unripened color best. They talked a little more, then she grew silent; her face, turned toward his, was white in the dusk.

That autumn an accident took him away from the town. When he came back, a year later, she had moved to another state. Later he heard that she had married again, and the name of the man. A great while later he read of her death.

The old man's rug had slipped from his knees; he gathered it up again and tucked it around him. He could not quite get back into the man who had loved and been loved by Stella, but he could not escape him, either. He saw that youth and the boy who had walked by the river. Each had a woman by his side, each stared at the other hostilely, each, pointing to his own companion, said, "This is love." He smiled a trifle dubiously at their frowning faces—both were so certain—and yet he included them both. Which was right, which wrong? He puzzled over the question but could come to no decision. And if neither were right—or both—why then, what was love?

You certainly strike some queer things when you read the book backwards, he thought. I guess I'd better call it a day and quit. But, even as he thought so, another picture arose.

They had been married for a little more than two years, their first child was eight months old. He was a man in his thirties, doing well, already a leader in the affairs of the growing town. She was five years younger, tall for a woman; she had high color in those days. They had known comparatively little of each other before their marriage—indeed, had not been very deeply in love; but living together had changed them.

He came back to the house on Pine Street, told the news of his day, heard about the neighbors, the errands, the child. After dinner they sat in the living room, he smoked and read the newspaper, she had sewing in her lap. They talked to each other in snatches; when their eyes met, something went, something came. At ten o'clock she went upstairs to feed the child; he followed some time later. The child was back in its crib again; they both looked at her a moment—sleep already lay upon her like a visible weight—how deeply, how swiftly she sank toward sleep! They went out, shut the door very softly, stood for a moment in the hallway, and embraced. Then the woman released herself.

"I'm going to bed now, Will," she said. "Be sure and turn out the lights when you come up."

"I won't be long," he said. "It's been a long day."

He stretched his arms, looking at her. She smiled deeply, turned away. The door of their room shut behind her.

When he had extinguished the lights and locked the doors he went up to the long garret that stretched the whole length of the house. They had had the house only two years, but the garret had already accumulated its collection of odds and ends; there were various discarded or crippled objects that would never be used again, that would stay here till the family moved, till someone died. But what he had come to see was a line of apples mellowing on a long shelf, in the dusty darkness. They had been sent in from the farm—you could smell their faint, unmistakable fragrance from the doorway. He took one up, turned it over in his hand, felt its weight and texture, firm and smooth and cool. You couldn't get a better eating apple than that, and this was the right place for them to mellow.

Mary's face came before him, looking at him in the hallway; the thought of it was like the deep stroke of a knife that left, as it struck, no pain. Yes, he thought, I'm alive—we're pretty fond of each other. Some impulse made him put down the apple and push up the little skylight of the garret to let the air blow in on his face. It was a clean cold—it was autumn; it made the blood run in him to feel it. He stood there for several minutes, drinking in cold autumn, thinking about his wife. Then at last he shut the skylight and went downstairs to their room.

A third couple had joined the others under the tree, a third image asserted itself, by every settled line in its body, the possessor not only of a woman but of a particular and unmistakable knowledge. The old man observed one and all, without envy but curiously. If they could only get to talking with one another, he thought, why then, maybe, we'd know something. But they could not do it—it was not in the cards. All each could do was to make an affirmation, "This is love."

The figures vanished, he was awake again. When you were old you slept lightly but more often, and these dreams came. Mary had been dead ten years; their children were men and women. He had always expected Mary to outlive him, but things had not happened so. She would have been a great comfort. Yet when he thought of her dead, though his grief was real, it came to him from a distance. He and she were nearer together than he and grief. And yet if he met her again it would be strange.

The flower came out on the branch, the fruit budded and grew. At last it fell or was picked, and the thing started over again. You could figure out every process of growth and decline, but that did not get you any nearer the secret. Only, he'd like to know.

He turned his eyes toward the house—somebody coming for him. His eyes were still better for far-away things than near, and he made out the figure quite plainly. It was the girl who had married his grandnephew, Robert. She called him "Father Hancock" or "Gramp" like the rest of them, but still, she was different from the rest.

For a moment her name escaped him. Then he had it. Jenny. A dark-haired girl, pleasant spoken, with a good free walk to her—girls stepped out freer, on the whole, than they had in his day. As for cutting their hair and the rest of it—well, why shouldn't they? It was only the kind of people who wrote to newspapers who made a fuss about such things. And they always had to make a fuss about something. He chuckled deeply, wondering what a newspaper would make of it if a highly respected old citizen wrote and asked them what was love. "Crazy old fool—ought to be in an asylum." Well, maybe at that, they'd be right.

He watched the girl coming on as he would have watched a rabbit run through the grass or a cloud march along the sky. There was something in her walk that matched both rabbit and cloud—something light and free and unbroken. But there was something else in her walk as well.

"Lunch, Father Hancock!" she called while she was still some yards away. "Snapper beans and black-cherry pie!"

"Well, I'm hungry," said the old man. "You know me, Jenny—never lost appetite yet. But you can have my slice of pie; you've got younger teeth than mine."

"Stop playing you're a centenarian, Father Hancock," said the girl. "I've seen you with Aunt Maria's pies before."

"I might take a smidgin', at that," said the old man reflectively, "just to taste. But you can have all I don't eat, Jenny—and that's a fair offer."

"It's too fair," said the girl. "I'd eat you out of house and home to-day." She stretched her arms toward the sky. "Gee, I feel hungry!" she said.

"It's right you should," said the old man, placidly. "And don't be ashamed of your dinner either. Eat solid and keep your strength up."

"Do I look as if I needed to keep my strength up?" she said with a laugh.

"No. But it's early to tell," said the old man, gradually disentangling himself from his coverings. He stood up, declining her offered hand. "Thank you, my dear," he said. "I never expected to see my own great-grandnephew. But don't be thinking of that. It'll be your baby, boy or girl, and that's what's important."

The girl's hand went slowly to her throat while color rose in her face. Then she laughed.

"Father Hancock!" she said. "You—you darned old wizard! Why, Robert doesn't know about it yet and——"

"He wouldn't," said the old man briefly. "Kind of inexperienced at that age. But you can't fool me, my dear. I've seen too much and too many."

She looked at him with trouble in her eyes.

"Well, as long as you know . . ." she said. "But you won't let on to the rest of them . . . of course I'll tell Robert soon, but—"

"I know," said the old man. "They carry on. Never could see so much sense in all that carrying on, but relations do. And being the first great-grandchild. No, I won't tell 'em. And I'll be as surprised as Punch when they finally tell me."

"You're a good egg," said the girl gratefully. "Thanks ever so much. I don't mind your knowing."

They stood for a moment in silence, his hand on her shoulder. The girl shivered suddenly.

"Tell me, Father Hancock," she said suddenly, in a muffled voice, not looking at him, "is it going to be pretty bad?"

"No, child, it won't be so bad." She said nothing, but he could feel the tenseness in her body relax.

"It'll be for around November, I expect?" he said, and went on without waiting for her reply. "Well, that's a good time, Jenny. You take our old cat, Marcella— she generally has her second lot of kittens around in October or November. And those kittens, they do right well."

"Father Hancock! You're a positive disgrace!" So she said, but he knew from the tone of her voice that she was not angry with him and once more, as they went together toward the house, he felt the stroke of youth upon him, watching her walk so well.

About the middle of summer, when the green of the fields had turned to yellow and brown, Will Hancock's old friend John Sturgis drove over one day to visit him.

A son and a granddaughter accompanied John Sturgis, as well as two other vaguer female relatives whom the young people called indiscriminately "Cousin" and "Aunt"; and for a while the big porch of the Hancock house knew the bustle of tribal ceremony. Everyone was a little anxious, everyone was a little voluble; this was neither a funeral nor a wedding but, as an occasion, it ranked with those occasions, and in the heart of every Hancock and Sturgis present was a small individual grain of gratitude and pride at being there to witness the actual meeting of two such perishable old men.

The relatives possessed the old men and displayed them. The old men sat quietly, their tanned hands resting on their knees. They knew they were being possessed, but they too felt pride and pleasure. It was, after all, remarkable that they should be here. The young people didn't know how remarkable it was.

Finally, however, Will Hancock rose.

"Come along down-cellar, John," he said gruffly. "Got something to show you."

It was the familiar opening of an immemorial gambit. And it brought the expected reply.

"Now, father," said Will Hancock's eldest daughter, "if you'll only wait a minute, Maria will be out with the lemonade, and I had her bake some brownies."

"Lemonade!" said Will Hancock and sniffed. "Hold your tongue, Mary," he said gently. "I'm going to give John Sturgis something good for what ails him."

As he led the way down-cellar he smiled to himself. They would be still protesting, back on the porch. They would be saying that cellars were damp and old men delicate, that cider turned into acid, and that at their age you'd think they'd have more sense. But there would be no real heart in the protestations. And if the ceremonial visit to the cellar had been omitted there would have been disappointment. Because then their old men would not have been quite so remarkable, after all.

They passed through the dairy-cellar, with its big tin milk-pans, and into the cider-cellar. It was cool there but with a sweet-smelling coolness; there was no scent of damp or mold. Three barrels stood in a row against the wall; on the floor was a yellow patch of light. Will Hancock took a tin cup from a shelf and silently tapped the farthest barrel. The liquid ran in the cup. It was old cider, yellow as wheat-straw, 'and when he raised it toward his nostrils the soul of the bruised apple came to him.

"Take a seat, John," he said, passing over the full cup. His friend thanked him and sank into the one disreputable armchair. Will Hancock filled another cup and sat down upon the middle barrel.

"Well, here's to crime, John!" he said. It was the time-honored phrase.

"Mud in your eye!" said John Sturgis fiercely. He sipped the cider.

"Ah!" he said, "tastes better every year, Will."

"She ought to, John. She's goin' along with us."

They both sat silent for a time, sipping appreciatively, their worn eyes staring at each other, taking each other in. Each time they met again now was a mutual triumph for both; they looked forward to each time and back upon it, but they had known each other so long that speech had become only a minor necessity between them.

"Well," said John Sturgis at last, when the cups had been refilled, "I hear you got some more expectations in your family, Will. That's fine."

"That's what they tell me," said Will Hancock. "She's a nice girl, Jenny."

"Yes, she's a nice girl," said John Sturgis indifferently. "It'll be some news for Molly when I get home. She'll be right interested. She was hopin' we might beat you to it, with young Jack and his wife. But no signs yet."

He shook his head and a shadow passed over his face.

"Well, I don't know that you set so much store by it," said Will Hancock consolingly, "though it's interesting."

"Oh, they'll have a piece in the paper," said John Sturgis with a trace of bitterness. "Four generations. Even if it isn't a great-grandchild, so to speak. I know 'em." He took a larger sip of cider.

"That won't do me a speck of good when I get home," he confided. "And Molly, she'll think I was crazy. But what's the use of livin' if you've got to live so tetchy all the time?"

"I never saw you looking better, John," said Will Hancock, heartily. "Never did."

"I'm spry enough most days," admitted John Sturgis. "And as for you, you look like a four-year-old. But it's the winter——"

He left the sentence uncompleted, and both fell silent for a moment, thinking of the coming winter. Winter, the foe of old men.

At last John Sturgis leaned forward. His cheeks had a ghost of color in them now, his eyes an unexpected brightness.

"Tell me, Will," he said, eagerly, "you and me—we've seen a good deal in our time. Well, tell me this—just how do you figure it all out?"

Will Hancock could not pretend to misunderstand the question. Nor could he deny his friend the courtesy of a reply.

"I haven't a notion," he said at last, slowly and gravely. "I've thought about it, Lord knows—but I haven't a notion, John."

The other sank back into his chair, disappointedly.

"Well now, that's too bad," he grumbled, "for I've been thinkin' about it. Seems to me as if I didn't do much else *but* think most of the time. But you're the educated one; and if you haven't a notion—well——"

His eyes stared into space, without fear or anger, but soberly. Will Hancock tried to think of some way to help his friend.

He saw again before him those three figures under the apple tree, each a part of himself, each with a woman beside it, each saying, "This is love." Now, as he fell into reverie, a fourth couple joined them—an old man, still erect, and a girl who still walked with a light step though her body was heavy now.

He stared at these last visitors, incredulously at first, and then with a little smile. Nearly every day of the summer Jenny had come to call him when he sat under his tree. He could see her looking across the gulf that separated them—and finding things not so bad as she had thought they might be. Why, I might have been an old tree myself, he thought. Or an old rock you went out to when you wanted to be alone.

There had been her relatives and his. There had been all the women. But it was to him that she had come. To the others he was and would be "Father Hancock" and their own remarkable old man. But Jenny was not really

one of his own; and because of that she had from him a
certain calming wisdom that he did not know he possessed.

He heard an insect cry in the deep grass and smelled
the smell of the hay, the smell of summer days. Love? It
was not love, of course, nor could be, by any stretch of
language. To her it had been summer and an old tree;
and to him, he knew what it had been. He was fond of
her, naturally, but that was not the answer. It was not she
who had moved him. But for an instant, on the cords
of the defeated flesh, he had heard a note struck clearly,
the vibration of a single and silver wire. As he thought of
this, the wire vibrated anew, the imperishable accent rang.
Then it was mute—it would not be struck again.

"I tried to figure it out the other day," he said to John
Sturgis, "what love was, first. But——"

Then he stopped. It was useless. John Sturgis was his
old friend, but there was no way to tell John Sturgis the
thoughts in his mind.

"It's funny your sayin' that," said John Sturgis reflectively. "You know I came back to the house the other
day, and there was Molly asleep in the chair. I was
scared for a minute but then I saw she was sleeping. Only
she didn't wake up right away—I guess I came in light.
Well, I stood there looking at her. You came to our
golden wedding, Will; but her cheeks were pink and she
looked so pretty in her sleep. I just went over and kissed
her, like an old fool. Now what makes a man act like
that?"

He paused for a moment.

"It's so blame' hard to figure out," he said. "When
you're young you've got the strength but you haven't got
the time. And when you're old you've got time enough,
but I'm always goin' to sleep."

He drained the last drop in his cup and rose.

"Well, Sam'll be lookin' for me," he said. "It was good
cider."

As they passed through the dairy a black, whiskered

face appeared at the small barred window and vanished guiltily at the sound of Will Hancock's voice.

"That old cat's always trying to get in to the milk," he said. "She ought to take shame on her, all the kittens she's had. But I guess this'll be her last litter, this fall. She's getting on."

The tribal ceremonies of departure were drawing toward a close. Will Hancock shook John Sturgis' hand.

"Come over again, John, and bring along Molly next time," he said. "There's always a drop in the barrel."

"And it's a prize drop," said John Sturgis. "Thank you, Will. But I don't figure on gettin' over again this summer. Next spring, maybe."

"Sure," said Will. But between them both, as they knew, lay the shadow of the cold months, the shadow to be lived through. Will Hancock watched his friend being helped into the car, watched the car drive away. "John's beginning to go," he thought with acceptance. "And that's probably just what John's telling Sam about me."

He turned back toward his family. He was tired, but he could not give in. The family clustered about him, talking and questioning. John's visit had made him, for the moment, an even more remarkable old man than ever; and he must play his role for the rest of them, worthily, now John had gone. So he played it, and they saw no difference. But he kept wondering what day the winter would set in.

The first gales of autumn had come and passed; when Will Hancock got up in the morning he saw white rime on the ground. It had melted away by eleven, but next morning it was back again. At last, when he walked down to his apple tree he walked under bare boughs.

That night he went early to his room, but before he got in bed he stood for a while at the window, looking at the sky. It was a winter sky, the stars were hard in it. Yet the day had been mild enough. Jenny wanted her child

born in the Indian Summer. Perhaps she would still have
her wish.

He slept more lightly than ever these nights—the first
thing roused him. So when the noises began in the house
he was awake at once. But he lay there for some time,
dreamily, not even looking at his watch. The footsteps
went up and down stairs, and he listened to them; a
voice said something sharply and was hushed; somebody
was trying to telephone. He knew them all, those sounds
of whispering haste that wake up a house at night.

Yes, he thought, all the same it's hard on the women.
Or the men too, for that matter. But sooner or later, the
doctor would come and take from his small black bag
the miraculous doll wrapped up in the single cabbage
leaf. He himself had once been such a doll, though he
couldn't remember it. Now they would not want him
out there, but he would go all the same.

He rose, put on his dressing-gown, and tiptoed down
the long corridor. He heard a shrill whisper in his ear,
*"Father!* Are you *crazy?* Go back to *bed!"* But he shook
his head at the whisper and went on. At the head of the
stairs he met his grandnephew, Robert. There was sweat
on the boy's face and he breathed as if he had been running. They looked at each other a moment, with sym-
pathy but without understanding.

"How is she?" said Will Hancock.

"All right, thanks, Gramp," said the boy in a grateful
voice as he kept fumbling in his dressing-gown pocket for
a cigarette that was not there. "The doctor's coming over
but we—we don't think it's the real thing yet."

Someone called to the boy, and he disappeared again.
The corridor abruptly seemed very full of Will Hancock's family. They were clustering around him, buzzing
reassuringly, but he paid little attention.

Suddenly, from behind a closed door, he heard Jenny's
voice, clear and amused. "Why, how perfectly sweet of
Father Hancock, Bob! But I'm sorry they woke him—
and all for a false alarm."

The reassuring buzzes around him recommenced. He shook them off impatiently and walked back toward his room. But when he was hidden from the others he gave a single guilty look behind him and made for the back stairs. They won't follow me, he thought; got too much to talk about.

He switched on the light in the cider-cellar, drawing his dressing-gown closer about him. It was cold in the cellar now and it would be colder still. But cider was always cider, and he felt thirsty.

He drank the yellow liquid reflectively, swinging his heels against the side of the barrel. Upstairs they would still be whispering and consulting. And maybe the doctor would come with his black bag after all, and to-morrow there would be a piece in the paper to make John Sturgis jealous. But there wasn't anything he could do about it.

No, even for Jenny, there was nothing more he could do. She had taken his wisdom, such as it was, and used it. And he was glad of that. But now he knew from the light tone of her voice that she was beyond such wisdom as he had. The wire had ceased its vibration, the leaves of the tree were shed, like dry wisdom on the ground. Well, she was a nice girl and Robert a decent boy. They would have other children doubtless, and those children children in their turn.

He heard a low sound from the other corner of the cellar and went over to see what had made it. Then he whistled. "Well, old lady," he said, "you certainly don't waste your time." It was the old black house-cat who had stared through the dairy window at himself and John Sturgis. Already she was licking the third of her new kittens while the two first-born nuzzled at her, squeaking from time to time.

He bent over and stroked her head. She looked at him troubledly. "It's all right," he said reassuringly. "They've forgotten about us both—and no wonder. But I'll stick around."

He refilled his cup and sat down upon the barrel, swinging his heels. There was nothing here that he could do, either—cats were wiser than humans in such matters. But, nevertheless, he would stay.

As the cider sank in the cup and he grew colder he fell into a waking dream. Now and then he went over to stroke the cat, but he did it automatically. He was here, in a bare old cellar, drinking cider which would doubtless disagree with him, and in all probability catching his death of cold. And upstairs, perhaps, were life and death and the doctor—new life fighting to come into the world and death waiting a chance to seize it as it came, as death always did. Moreover, these lives and deaths were his lives and deaths, after a fashion, for he was part of their chain. But, for the moment, he was disconnected from them. He was beyond life and death.

He saw again, in front of him, the three couples of his first dream—and himself and Jenny—himself giving Jenny, unconsciously, the wisdom he did not know. "This is love—this is love—this is love—" and so it was, each phase of it, for each man there spoke the truth of his own heart. Then he looked at the apple tree and saw that it was in flower, but fruit hung on it as well, green fruit and ripe, and even as he looked a wind was blowing the last leaves from the bare bough.

He shivered a little, he was very cold. He put his cup back on the shelf and went over for a last look at the old cat. The travail was over—she lay on her side, beset by the new-born. There was green, inexplicable light in her eyes as he stooped over her, and when he patted her head she stretched one paw out over her kittens like an arm.

He rose stiffly and left her, turning out the light. As he went up the stairs, "Adorable life," he thought, "I know you. I know you were given only to be given away."

The house was silent again, as he tiptoed back to his room. His vigil had been unsuspected, his watch quite useless; and yet he had kept a vigil and a watch. To-morrow might have been too late for it—even now he trembled with cold. Yet, when he stood before the window, he looked long at the winter sky. The stars were still hard points of light, and he would not see them soft again, but earth would continue to turn round, in spite of all these things.

# EVERYBODY WAS VERY NICE

Yes, I guess I have put on weight since you last saw me—not that you're any piker yourself, Spike. But I suppose you medicos have to keep in shape—probably do better than we downtown. I try to play golf in the week-ends, and I do a bit of sailing. But four innings of the baseball game at reunion was enough for me. I dropped out, after that, and let Art Corliss pitch.

You really should have been up there. After all, the Twentieth is quite a milestone—and the class is pretty proud of its famous man. What was it that magazine article said: "most brilliant young psychiatrist in the country"? I may not know psychiatry from marbles, but I showed it to Lisa, remarking that it was old Spike Garrett, and for once she was impressed. She thinks brokers are pretty dumb eggs. I wish you could stay for dinner—I'd like to show you the apartment and the twins. No, they're Lisa's and mine. Boys, if you'll believe it. Yes, the others are with Sally—young Barbara's pretty grown up, now.

Well, I can't complain. I may not be famous like you, Spike, but I manage to get along, in spite of the brain trusters, and having to keep up the place on Long Island. I wish you got East oftener—there's a pretty view from the guest house, right across the Sound—and if you wanted to write a book or anything, we'd know enough to leave you alone. Well, they started calling me a partner two years ago, so I guess that's what I am. Still fooling them, you know. But, seriously, we've got a pretty fine organization. We run a conservative business, but we're not all stuffed shirts, in spite of what the radicals say. As a matter of fact, you ought to see what the boys

131

ran about us in the last Bawl Street Journal. Remind me to show it to you.

But it's your work I want to hear about—remember those bull-sessions we used to have in Old Main? Old Spike Garrett, the Medical Marvel! Why, I've even read a couple of your books, you old horse thief, believe it or not! You got me pretty tangled up on all that business about the id and the ego, too. But what I say is, there must be something in it if a fellow like Spike Garrett believes it. And there is, isn't there? Oh, I know you couldn't give me an answer in five minutes. But as long as there's a system—and the medicos know what they're doing.

I'm not asking for myself, of course—remember how you used to call me the 99 per-cent normal man? Well, I guess I haven't changed. It's just that I've gotten to thinking recently, and Lisa says I go around like a bear with a sore head. Well, it isn't that. I'm just thinking. A man has to think once in a while. And then, going back to reunion brought it all up again.

What I mean is this—the thing seemed pretty clear when we were in college. Of course, that was back in '15, but I can remember the way most of us thought. You fell in love with a girl and married her and settled down and had children and that was that. I'm not being simple-minded about it—you knew people get divorced, just as you knew people died, but it didn't seem something that was likely to happen to you. Especially if you came from a small Western city, as I did. Great Scott, I can remember when I was just a kid and the Prentisses got divorced. They were pretty prominent people and it shook the whole town.

That's why I want to figure things out for my own satisfaction. Because I never expected to be any Lothario—I'm not the type. And yet Sally and I got divorced and we're both remarried, and even so, to tell you the truth, things aren't going too well. I'm not saying a word against Lisa. But that's the way things are. And it isn't as if I were the only one. You can look around anywhere and see it, and it starts you wondering.

I'm not going to bore you about myself and Sally. Good Lord, you ushered at the wedding, and she always liked you. Remember when you used to come out to the house? Well, she hasn't changed—she's still got that little smile—though, of course, we're all older. Her husband's a doctor, too—that's funny, isn't it?—and they live out in Montclair. They've got a nice place there and he's very well thought of. We used to live in Meadowfield, remember?

I remember the first time I saw her after she married McConaghey—oh, we're perfectly friendly, you know. She had on red nail polish and her hair was different, a different bob. And she had one of those handbags with her new initials on it. It's funny, the first time, seeing your wife in clothes you don't know. Though Lisa and I have been married eight years, for that matter, and Sally and I were divorced in '28.

Of course, we have the children for part of the summer. We'll have Barbara this summer—Bud'll be in camp. It's a little difficult sometimes, but we all co-operate. You have to. And there's plenty to do on Long Island in the summer, that's one thing. But they and Lisa get along very well—Sally's brought them up nicely that way. For that matter, Doctor McConaghey's very nice when I see him. He gave me a darn good prescription for a cold and I get it filled every winter. And Jim Blake—he's Lisa's first husband—is really pretty interesting, now we've got to seeing him again. In fact, we're all awfully nice—just as nice and polite as we can be. And sometimes I get to wondering if it mightn't be a good idea if somebody started throwing fits and shooting rockets, instead. Of course I don't really mean that.

You were out for a week end with us in Meadowfield—maybe you don't remember it—but Bud was about six months old then and Barbara was just running around. It wasn't a bad house, if you remember the house. Dutch Colonial, and the faucet in the pantry leaked. The landlord was always fixing it, but he never quite fixed it right. And you had to cut hard to the left to back into the garage. But Sally liked the Japanese cherry tree and it wasn't a bad house. We were going to build on Rose Hill Road eventually. We had the lot picked out, if we didn't have the money, and we made plans about it. Sally never could remember to put in the doors in the plan, and we laughed about that.

It wasn't anything extraordinary, just an evening. After supper, we sat around the lawn in deck chairs and drank Sally's beer—it was long before Repeal. We'd repainted the deck chairs ourselves the Sunday before and we felt pretty proud of them. The light stayed late, but there was a breeze after dark, and once Bud started yipping and Sally went up to him. She had on a white dress, I think —she used to wear white a lot in the summers—it went with her blue eyes and her yellow hair. Well, it wasn't anything extraordinary—we didn't even stay up late. But we were all there. And if you'd told me that within three years we'd both be married to other people, I'd have thought you were raving.

Then you went West, remember, and we saw you off on the train. So you didn't see what happened, and as a matter of fact, it's hard to remember when we first started meeting the Blakes. They'd moved to Meadow-field then, but we hadn't met them.

Jim Blake was one of those pleasant, ugly-faced people with steel glasses who get right ahead in the law and never look young or old. And Lisa was Lisa. She's dark, you know, and she takes a beautiful burn. She was the first girl there to wear real beach things or drink a special kind of tomato juice when everybody else was drinking cocktails. She was very pretty and very good fun to be with— she's got lots of ideas. They entertained a good deal be-cause Lisa likes that—she had her own income, of course. And she and Jim used to bicker a good deal in public in an amusing way—it was sort of an act or seemed like it. They had one little girl, Sylvia, that Jim was crazy about.

I mean it sounds normal, doesn't it, even to their having the kind of Airedale you had then? Well, it all seemed normal enough to us, and they soon got to be part of the crowd. You know, the young married crowd in every suburb.

Of course, that was '28 and the boom was booming and everybody was feeling pretty high. I suppose that was part of it—the money—and the feeling you had that everything was going faster and faster and wouldn't stop. Why, it was Sally herself who said that we owed ourselves a whirl and mustn't get stodgy and settled while we were still young. Well, we had stuck pretty close to the grindstone for the past few years, with the children and everything. And it was fun to feel young and sprightly again and buy a new car and take in the club gala without having to worry about how you'd pay your house account. But I don't see any harm in that.

And then, of course, we talked and kidded a lot about freedom and what have you. Oh, you know the kind of talk—everybody was talking it then. About not being Victorians and living your own life. And there was the older generation and the younger generation. I've forgotten a lot of it now, but I remember there was one piece about love not being just a form of words mumbled by a minister, but something pretty special. As a matter of fact, the minister who married us was old Doctor Snell and he had the kind of voice you could hear in the next county. But I used to talk about that mumbling minister myself. I mean, we were enlightened, for a suburb, if you get my point. Yes, and pretty proud of it, too. When they banned a book in Boston, the lending library ordered six extra copies. And I still remember the big discussion we had about perfect freedom in marriage when even the straight Republicans voted the radical ticket. All except Chick Bewleigh, and he was a queer sort of bird, who didn't even believe that stocks had reached a permanently high plateau.

But, meanwhile, most of us were getting the 8:15 and

our wives were going down to the chain store and asking
if that was a really nice head of lettuce. At least that's the
way we seemed. And, if the crowd started kidding me
about Mary Sennett, or Mac Church kissed Sally on the
ear at a club revel, why, we were young, we were modern,
and we could handle that. I wasn't going to take a shot-
gun to Mac, and Sally wasn't going to put on the jealous
act. Oh, we had it all down to a science. We certainly did.

Good Lord, we had the Blakes to dinner, and they had
us. They'd drop over for drinks or we'd drop over there.
It was all perfectly normal and part of the crowd. For
that matter, Sally played with Jim Blake in the mixed
handicap and they got to the semi-finals. No, I didn't
play with Lisa—she doesn't like golf. I mean that's the
way it was.

And I can remember the minute it started, and it wasn't
anything, just a party at the Bewleighs'. They've got a
big, rambling house and people drift around. Lisa and I
had wandered out to the kitchen to get some drinks for
the people on the porch. She had on a black dress, that
night, with a big sort of orange flower on it. It wouldn't
have suited everybody, but it suited her.

We were talking along like anybody and suddenly we
stopped talking and looked at each other. And I felt, for
a minute, well, just the way I felt when I was first in love
with Sally. Only this time, it wasn't Sally. It happened
so suddenly that all I could think of was, "Watch your
step!" Just as if you'd gone into a room in the dark and
hit your elbow. I guess that makes it genuine, doesn't it?

We picked it up right away and went back to the party.
All she said was, "Did anybody ever tell you that you're
really quite a menace, Dan?" and she said that in the way
we all said those things. But, all the same, it had happened. I could hear her voice all the way back in the car.
And yet, I was as fond of Sally as ever. I don't suppose
you'll believe that, but it's true.

And next morning, I tried to kid myself that it didn't
have any importance. Because Sally wasn't jealous, and

we were all modern and advanced and knew about life. But the next time I saw Lisa, I knew it had.

I want to say this. If you think it was all romance and rosebuds, you're wrong. A lot of it was merry hell. And yet, everybody whooped us on. That's what I don't un-derstand. They didn't really want the Painters and the Blakes to get divorced, and yet they were pretty inter-ested. Now, why do people do that? Some of them would carefully put Lisa and me next to each other at table and some of them would just as carefully not. But it all added up to the same thing in the end—a circus was going on and we were part of the circus. It's interesting to watch the people on the high wires at the circus and you hope they don't fall. But, if they did, that would be interesting too. Of course, there were a couple of people who tried, as they say, to warn us. But they were older people and just made us mad.

Everybody was so nice and considerate and understand-ing. Everybody was so nice and intelligent and fine. Don't misunderstand me. It was wonderful, being with Lisa. It was new and exciting. And it seemed to be wonderful for her, and she'd been unhappy with Jim. So, anyway, that made me feel less of a heel, though I felt enough of a heel, from time to time. And then, when we were together, it would seem so fine.

A couple of times we really tried to break it, too—at least twice. But we all belonged to the same crowd, and what could you do but run away? And, somehow, that meant more than running away—it meant giving in to the Victorians and that mumbling preacher and all the things we'd said we didn't believe in. Or I suppose Sally might have done like old Mrs. Pierce, back home. She horsewhipped the dressmaker on the station platform and then threw herself crying into Major Pierce's arms and he took her to Atlantic City instead. It's one of the town's great stories and I always wondered what they talked about on the train. Of course, they moved to Des Moines after that—I remember reading about their

golden wedding anniversary when I was in college. Only
nobody could do that nowadays, and, besides, Lisa wasn't
a dressmaker.

So, finally, one day, I came home, and there was Sally,
perfectly cold, and, we talked pretty nearly all night.
We'd been awfully polite to each other for quite a while
before—the way you are. And we kept polite, we kept a
good grip on ourselves. After all, we'd said to each other
before we were married that if either of us ever—and there
it was. And it was Sally who brought that up, not me. I
think we'd have felt better if we'd fought. But we didn't
fight.

Of course, she was bound to say some things about
Lisa, and I was bound to answer. But that didn't last
long and we got our grip right back again. It was funny,
being strangers and talking so politely, but we did it. I
think it gave us a queer kind of pride to do it. I think it
gave us a queer kind of pride for her to ask me politely
for a drink at the end, as if she were in somebody else's
house, and for me to mix it for her, as if she were a guest.

Everything was talked out by then and the house felt
very dry and empty, as if nobody lived in it at all. We'd
never been up quite so late in the house, except after a
New Year's party or when Buddy was sick, that time. I
mixed her drink very carefully, the way she liked it, with
plain water, and she took it and said "Thanks." Then
she sat for a while without saying anything. It was so
quiet you could hear the little drip of the leaky faucet in
the pantry, in spite of the door being closed. She heard it
and said, "It's dripping again. You better call up Mr.
Vye in the morning—I forgot. And I think Barbara's getting a cold—I meant to tell you." Then her face twisted
and I thought she was going to cry, but she didn't.

She put the glass down—she'd only drunk half her
drink—and said, quite quietly, "Oh, damn you, and
damn Lisa Blake, and damn everything in the world!"
Then she ran upstairs before I could stop her and she
still wasn't crying.

I could have run upstairs after her, but I didn't. I stood looking at the glass on the table and I couldn't think. Then, after a while, I heard a key turn in a lock. So I picked up my hat and went out for a walk—I hadn't been out walking that early in a long time. Finally, I found an all-night diner and got some coffee. Then I came back and read a book till the maid got down—it wasn't a very interesting book. When she came down, I pretended I'd gotten up early and had to go into town by the first train, but I guess she knew.

I'm not going to talk about the details. If you've been through them, you've been through them; and if you haven't, you don't know. My family was fond of Sally, and Sally's had always liked me. Well, that made it tough. And the children. They don't say the things you expect them to. I'm not going to talk about that.

Oh, we put on a good act, we put on a great show! There weren't any fists flying or accusations. Everybody said how well we did it, everybody in town. And Lisa and Sally saw each other, and Jim Blake and I talked to each other perfectly calmly. We said all the usual things. He talked just as if it were a case. I admired him for it. Lisa did her best to make it emotional, but we wouldn't let her. And I finally made her see that, court or no court, he'd simply have to have Sylvia. He was crazy about her, and while Lisa's a very good mother, there wasn't any question as to which of them the kid liked best. It happens that way, sometimes.

For that matter, I saw Sally off on the train to Reno. She wanted it that way. Lisa was going to get a Mexican divorce—they'd just come in, you know. And nobody could have told, from the way we talked in the station. It's funny, you get a queer bond, through a time like that. After I'd seen her off—and she looked small in the train—the first person I wanted to see wasn't Lisa, but Jim Blake. You see, other people are fine, but unless you've been through things yourself, you don't quite understand them. But Jim Blake was still in Meadowfield, so I went back to the club.

I hadn't ever really lived in the club before, except for three days one summer. They treat you very well, but, of course, being a college club, it's more for the youngsters and the few old boys who hang around the bar. I got awfully tired of the summer chintz in the dining room and the Greek waiter I had who breathed on my neck. And you can't work all the time, though I used to stay late at the office. I guess it was then I first thought of getting out of Spencer Wilde and making a new connection. You think about a lot of things at a time like that.

Of course, there were lots of people I could have seen, but I didn't much want to—somehow, you don't. Though I did strike up quite a friendship with one of the old boys. He was about fifty-five and he'd been divorced four times and was living permanently at the club. We used to sit up in his little room—he'd had his own furniture moved in and the walls were covered with pictures—drinking Tom Collinses and talking about life. He had lots of ideas about life, and about matrimony, too, and I got quite interested, listening to him. But then he'd go into the dinners he used to give at Delmonico's, and while that was interesting, too, it wasn't much help, except to take your mind off the summer chintz.

He had some sort of small job, downtown, but I guess he had an income from his family too. He must have. But when I'd ask him what he did, he'd always say, "I'm retired, my boy, very much retired, and how about a touch more beverage to keep out the sun?" He always called it beverage, but they knew what he meant at the bar. He turned up at the wedding, when Lisa and I were married, all dressed up in a cutaway, and insisted on making us a little speech—very nice it was too. Then we had him to dinner a couple of times, after we'd got back, and somehow or other, I haven't seen him since. I suppose he's still at the club—I've got out of the habit of going there, since I joined the other ones, though I still keep my membership.

Of course, all that time, I was crazy about Lisa and writing her letters and waiting till we could be married. Of course I was. But, now and then, even that would get shoved into the background. Because there was so much to do and arrangements to make and people like lawyers to see. I don't like lawyers very much, even yet, though the people we had were very good. But there was all the telephoning and the conferences. Somehow, it was like a machine—a big machine—and you had to learn a sort of new etiquette for everything you did. Till, finally, it got so that about all you wanted was to have the fuss over and not talk about it any more.

I remember running into Chick Bewleigh in the club, three days before Sally got her decree. You'd like Chick— he's the intellectual type, but a darn good fellow too. And Nan, his wife, is a peach—one of those big, rangy girls with a crazy sense of humor. It was nice to talk to him because he was natural and didn't make any cracks about grass-bachelors or get that look in his eye. You know the look they get. We talked about Meadowfield—just the usual news—the Bakers were splitting up and Don Sikes had a new job and the Wilsons were having a baby. But it seemed good to hear it.

"For that matter," he said, drawing on his pipe, "we're adding to the population again ourselves. In the fall. How we'll ever manage four of them! I keep telling Nan she's cockeyed, but she says they're more fun than a swimming pool and cost less to keep up, so what can you do!"

He shook his head and I remembered that Sally always used to say she wanted six. Only now it would be Lisa, so I mustn't think about that.

"So that's your recipe for a happy marriage," I said. "Well, I always wondered."

I was kidding, of course, but he looked quite serious.

"*Kinder, Küche und Kirche?*" he said. "Nope, that

doesn't work any more, what with pre-schools, automats and the movies. Four children or no four children, Nan could still raise hell if she felt like raising hell. And so could I, for that matter. Add blessings of civilization," and his eyes twinkled.

"Well then," I said, "what is it?" I really wanted to know.

"Oh, just bull luck, I suppose. And happening to like what you've got," he answered, in a sort of embarrassed way.

"You can do that," I said. "And yet——"

He looked away from me.

"Oh, it was a lot simpler in the old days," he said. "Everything was for marriage—church, laws, society. And when people got married, they expected to stay that way. And it made a lot of people as unhappy as hell. Now the expectation's rather the other way, at least in this great and beautiful nation and among people like us. If you get a divorce, it's rather like going to the dentist—unpleasant sometimes, but lots of people have been there before. Well, that's a handsome system, too, but it's got its own casualty list. So there you are. You takes your money and you makes your choice. And some of us like freedom better than the institution and some of us like the institution better, but what most of us would like is to be Don Juan on Thursdays and Benedick, the married man, on Fridays, Saturdays and the rest of the week. Only that's a bit hard to work out, somehow," and he grinned.

"All the same," I said, "you and Nan——"

"Well," he said. "I suppose we're exceptions. You see, my parents weren't married till I was seven. So I'm a conservative. It might have worked out the other way."

"Oh," I said.

"Yes," he said. "My mother was English, and you may have heard of English divorce laws. She ran away with my father and she was perfectly right—her husband was a very extensive brute. All the same, I was brought up on the other side of the fence, and I know something about what it's like. And Nan was a minister's daughter who thought she ought to be free. Well, we argued about things a good deal. And, finally, I told her that I'd be very highly complimented to live with her on any terms at all, but if she wanted to get married, she'd have to expect a marriage, not a trip to Coney Island. And I made my point rather clear by blacking her eye, in a taxi, when she told me she was thinking seriously of spending a week end with my deadly rival, just to see which one of us she really loved. You can't spend a romantic week end with somebody when you've got a black eye. But you can get married with one and we did. She had raw beefsteak on it till two hours before the wedding, and it was the prettiest sight I ever saw. Well, that's our simple story."

"Not all of it," I said.

"No," he said, "not all of it. But at least we didn't start in with any of this bunk about if you meet a handsomer fellow it's all off. We knew we were getting into something. Bewleigh's Easy Guide to Marriage in three installments—you are now listening to the Voice of Experience, and who cares? Of course, if we hadn't—ahem—liked each other, I could have blacked her eye till doomsday and got nothing out of it but a suit for assault and battery. But nothing's much good unless it's worth fighting for. And she doesn't look exactly like a downtrodden wife."

"Nope," I said, "but all the same——"

He stared at me very hard—almost the way he used to when people were explaining that stocks had reached a permanently high plateau.

"Exactly," he said. "And there comes a time, no matter what the intention, when a new face heaves into view and a spark lights. I'm no Adonis, God knows, but it's happened to me once or twice. And I know what I do then. I run. I run like a rabbit. It isn't courageous or adventurous or fine. It isn't even particularly moral, as I think about morals. But I run. Because, when all's said and done, it takes two people to make a love affair and you can't have it when one of them's not there. And, dammit, Nan knows it, that's the trouble. She'd ask Helen of Troy to dinner just to see me run. Well, goodbye, old man, and our best to Lisa, of course——"

After he was gone, I went and had dinner in the grill. I did a lot of thinking at dinner, but it didn't get me anywhere. When I was back in the room, I took the receiver off the telephone. I was going to call long distance. But your voice sounds different on the phone, and, anyway, the decree would be granted in three days. So when the girl answered, I told her it was a mistake.

Next week Lisa came back and she and I were married. We went to Bermuda on our wedding trip. It's a very pretty place. Do you know, they won't allow an automobile on the island?

The queer thing was that at first I didn't feel married to Lisa at all. I mean, on the boat, and even at the hotel. She said, "But how exciting, darling!" and I suppose it was.

Now, of course, we've been married eight years, and that's always different. The twins will be seven in May—two years older than Sally's Jerry. I had an idea for a while that Sally might marry Jim Blake—he always admired her. But I'm glad she didn't—it would have made things a little too complicated. And I like McConaghey—I like him fine. We gave them an old Chinese jar for a wedding present. Lisa picked it out. She has very good taste and Sally wrote us a fine letter.

I'd like to have you meet Lisa sometime—she's interested in intelligent people. They're always coming to the apartment—artists and writers and people like that.

Of course, they don't always turn out the way she expects. But she's quite a hostess and she knows how to handle things. There was one youngster that used to rather get in my hair. He'd call me the Man of Wall Street and ask me what I thought about Picabia or one of those birds, in a way that sort of said, "Now watch this guy stumble!" But as soon as Lisa noticed it, she got rid of him. That shows she's considerate.

Of course, it's different, being married to a person. And I'm pretty busy these days and so is she. Sometimes, if I get home and there's going to be a party, I'll just say good night to the twins and fade out after dinner. But Lisa understands about that, and I've got my own quarters. She had one of her decorator friends do the private study and it really looks very nice.

I had Jim Blake in there one night. Well, I had to take him somewhere. He was getting pretty noisy and Lisa gave me the high sign. He's doing very well, but he looks pretty hard these days and I'm afraid he's drinking a good deal, though he doesn't often show it. I don't think he ever quite got over Sylvia's dying. Four years ago. They had scarlet fever at the school. It was a great shock to Lisa, too, of course, but she had the twins and Jim never married again. But he comes to see us, every once in a while. Once, when he was tight, he said it was to convince himself about remaining a bachelor, but I don't think he meant that.

Now, when I brought him into the study, he looked around and said, "Shades of Buck Rogers! What one of Lisa's little dears produced this imitation Wellsian nightmare?"

"Oh, I don't remember," I said. "I think his name was Slivovitz."

"It looks as if it had been designed by a man named Slivovitz," he said. "All dental steel and black glass. I recognize the Lisa touch. You're lucky she didn't put murals of cogwheels on the walls."

"Well, there was a question of that," I said.

"I bet there was," he said. "Well, here's how, old man! Here's to two great big wonderful institutions, marriage and divorce!"

I didn't like that very much and told him so. But he just wagged his head at me.

"I like you, Painter," he said. "I always did. Sometimes I think you're goofy, but I like you. You can't insult me— I won't let you. And it isn't your fault."

"What isn't my fault?" I said.

"The setup," he said. "Because, in your simple little heart, you're an honest monogamous man, Painter—monogamous as most. And if you'd stayed married to Sally, you'd have led an honest monogamous life. But they loaded the dice against you, out at Meadowfield, and now Lord knows where you'll end up. After all, I was married to Lisa myself for six years or so. Tell me, isn't it hell?"

"You're drunk," I said.

*"In vino veritas,"* said he. "No, it isn't hell—I take that back. Lisa's got her damn-fool side, but she's an attractive and interesting woman—or could be, if she'd work at it. But she was brought up on the idea of Romance with a big R, and she's too bone-lazy and bone-selfish to work at it very long. There's always something else, just over the horizon. Well, I got tired of fighting that, after a while. And so will you. She doesn't want husbands—she wants clients and followers. Or maybe you're tired already."

"I think you'd better go home, Jim," I said. "I don't want to have to ask you."

"Sorry," he said. *"In vino veritas.* But it's a funny setup, isn't it? What Lisa wanted was a romantic escapade—and she got twins. And what you wanted was marriage—and you got Lisa. As for me," and for a minute his face didn't look drunk any more, "what I principally wanted was Sylvia and I've lost that. I could have married again, but I didn't think that'd be good for her. Now, I'll probably marry some client I've helped with her decree—we don't touch divorce, as a rule, just a very, very special line of business for a few important patrons. I know those—I've had them in the office. And won't that be fun for us all! What a setup it is!" and he slumped down in his chair and went to sleep. I let him sleep for a while and then had Briggs take him down in the other elevator. He called up next day and apologized—said he knew he must have been noisy, though he couldn't remember anything he said.

The other time I had somebody in the study was when Sally came back there once, two years ago. We'd met to talk about college for Barbara and I'd forgotten some papers I wanted to show her. We generally meet downtown. But she didn't mind coming back—Lisa was out, as it happened. It made me feel queer, taking her up in the elevator and letting her in at the door. She wasn't like Jim—she thought the study was nice.

Well, we talked over our business and I kept looking at her. You can see she's older, but her eyes are still that very bright blue, and she bites her thumb when she's interested. It's a queer feeling. Of course, I was used to seeing her, but we usually met downtown. You know, I wouldn't have been a bit surprised if she'd pushed the bell and said, "Tea, Briggs. I'm home." She didn't, naturally.

I asked her, once, if she wouldn't take off her hat and she looked at me in a queer way and said, "So you can show me your etchings? Dan, Dan, you're a dangerous man!" and for a moment we both laughed like fools.

"Oh, dear," she said, drying her eyes, "that's very funny. And now I must be going home."

"Look here, Sally," I said, "I've always told you—but, honestly, if you need anything—if there's anything——"

"Of course, Dan," she said. "And we're awfully good friends, aren't we?" But she was still smiling.

I didn't care. "Friends!" I said. "You know how I think about you. I always have. And I don't want you to think——"

She patted my shoulder—I'd forgotten the way she used to do that.

"There," she said. "Mother knows all about it. And we really are friends, Dan. So——"

"I was a fool."

She looked at me very steadily out of those eyes.

"We were all fools," she said. "Even Lisa. I used to hate her for a while. I used to hope things would happen to her. Oh, not very bad things. Just her finding out that you never see a crooked picture without straightening it, and hearing you say: 'A bird can't fly on one wing,' for the dozenth time. The little things everybody has to find out and put up with. But I don't even do that any more."

"If you'd ever learned to put a cork back in a bottle," I said. "I mean the right cork in the right bottle. But——"

"I do so! No, I suppose I never will." And she laughed. She took my hands. "Funny, funny, funny," she said. "And funny to have it all gone and be friends."

"Is it all gone?" I said.

"Why, no, of course not," she said. "I don't suppose it ever is, quite. Like the boys who took you to dances. And there's the children, and you can't help remembering. But it's gone. We had it and lost it. I should have fought for it more, I suppose, but I didn't. And then I was terribly hurt and terribly mad. But I got over that. And now I'm married to Jerry. And I wouldn't give him up, or Jerry Junior, for anything in the world. The only thing that worries me is sometimes when I think it isn't quite a fair deal for him. After all, he could have married—well, somebody else. And yet he knows I love him."

"He ought to," I said rather stiffly. "He's a darn lucky guy, if you ask me."

"No, Dan. I'm the lucky girl. I'm hoping this minute that Mrs. Potter's X-rays turn out all right. He did a beautiful job on her. But he always worries."

I dropped her hands.

"Well, give him my best," I said.

"I will, Dan. He likes you, you know. Really he does. By the way, have you had any more of that bursitis? There's a new treatment—he wanted me to ask you——"

"Thanks," I said, "but that all cleared up."

"I'm glad. And now I must fly. There's always shopping when you come in from the suburbs. Give my best to

Lisa and tell her I was sorry not to see her. She's out. I suppose."

"Yes," I said. "She'll be sorry to miss you—you wouldn't stay for a cocktail? She's usually in around then."

"It sounds very dashing, but I mustn't. Jerry Junior lost one of his turtles and I've got to get him another. Do you know a good pet shop? Well, Bloomingdale's, I suppose—after all, I've got other things to get."

"There's a good one two blocks down on Lexington," I said. "But if you're going to Bloomingdale's—— Well, goodbye, Sally, and good luck."

"Goodbye, Dan. And good luck to you. And no regrets."

"No regrets," I said, and we shook hands.

There wasn't any point in going down to the street with her, and besides I had to phone the office. But before I did, I looked out, and she was just getting into a cab. A person looks different, somehow, when they don't know you're seeing them. I could see the way she looked to other people—not young any more, not the Sally I'd married, not even the Sally I'd talked with, all night in that cold house. She was a nice married woman who lived in Montclair and whose husband was a doctor; a nice woman, in shopping for the day, with a new spring hat and a fifty-trip ticket in her handbag. She'd had trouble in her life, but she'd worked it out. And, before she got on the train, she'd have a black-and-white soda, sitting on a stool at the station, or maybe she didn't do that any more. There'd be lots of things in her handbag, but I wouldn't know about any of them nor what locks the keys fitted. And, if she were dying, they'd send for me, because that would be etiquette. And the same if I were dying. But we'd had something and lost it—the way she said—and that was all that was left.

Now she was that nice Mrs. McConaghey. But she'd never be quite that to me. And yet, there was no way to go back. You couldn't even go back to the house in Meadowfield—they'd torn it down and put up an apartment instead.

So that's why I wanted to talk to you. I'm not complaining and I'm not the kind of fellow that gets nerves. But I just want to know—I just want to figure it out. And sometimes it keeps going round and round in your head. You'd like to be able to tell your children something, especially when they're growing up. Well, I know what we'll tell them. But I wonder if it's enough.

Not that we don't get along well when Bud and Barbara come to see us. Especially Barbara—she's very tactful and she's crazy about the twins. And now they're growing up, it's easier. Only, once in a while, something happens that makes you think. I took Barbara out sailing last summer. She's sixteen and a very sweet kid, if I say it myself. A lot of kids that age seem pretty hard, but she isn't.

Well, we were just talking along, and naturally, you like to know what your children's plans are. Bud thinks he wants to be a doctor like McConaghey and I've no objection. I asked Barbara if she wanted a career, but she said she didn't think so.

"Oh, I'd like to go to college," she said, "and maybe work for a while, afterwards, the way mother did, you know. But I haven't any particular talents, dad. I could kid myself, but I haven't. I guess it's just woman's function and home and babies for me."

"Well, that sounds all right to me," I said, feeling very paternal.

"Yes," she said, "I like babies. In fact, I think I'll get married pretty young, just for the experience. The first time probably won't work, but it ought to teach you some things. And then, eventually, you might find somebody to tie to."

"So that's the way it is with the modern young woman?" I said.

"Why, of course," she said. "That's what practically all the girls say—we've talked it all over at school. Of course, sometimes it takes you quite a while. Like Helen Hastings' mother. She just got married for the fourth time last year, but he really is a sweet! He took us all to the matinee when I was visiting Helen and we nearly died. He's a count, of course, and he's got the darlingest accent. I don't know whether I'd like a count, though it must be fun to have little crowns on your handkerchiefs like Helen's mother. What's the matter, daddy? Are you shocked?"

"Don't flatter yourself, young lady—I've been shocked by experts," I said. "No, I was just thinking. Suppose we —well, suppose your mother and I had stayed together? How would you have felt about it then?"

"But you didn't, did you?" she said, and her voice wasn't hurt or anything, just natural. "I mean, almost nobody does any more. Don't worry, daddy. Bud and I understand all about it—good gracious, we're grown up! Of course, if you and mother had," she said, rather dutifully, "I suppose it would have been very nice. But then we'd have missed Mac, and he really is a sweet, and you'd have missed Lisa and the twins. Anyhow, it's all worked out now. Oh, of course, I'd rather hope it would turn out all right the first time, if it wasn't too stodgy or sinister. But you've got to face facts, you know."

"Face facts!" I said. "Dammit, Barbara!"

Then I stopped, because what did I have to say?

Well, that's the works, and if you've got any dope on it, I wish you'd tell me. There are so few people you can talk to—that's the trouble. I mean everybody's very nice, but that's not the same thing. And, if you start thinking too much, the highballs catch up on you. And you can't afford that—I've never been much of a drinking man.

The only thing is, where does it stop, if it does? That's the thing I'm really afraid of.

It may sound silly to you. But I've seen other people —well, take this Mrs. Hastings, Barbara talked about. Or my old friend at the club. I wonder if he started in, want-

:ng to get married four times. I know I didn't—I'm not the type and you know it.

And yet, suppose, well, you do meet somebody who treats you like a human being. I mean somebody who doesn't think you're a little goofy because you know more about American Can than who painted what. Supposing, even, they're quite a lot younger. That shouldn't make all the difference. After all, I'm no Lothario. And Lisa and I aren't thinking of divorce or anything like that. But, naturally, we lead our own lives, and you ought to be able to talk to somebody. Of course, if it could have been Sally. That was my fault. But it isn't as if Maureen were just in the floor show. She's got her own specialty number. And, really, when you get to know her, she's a darned intelligent kid.

# JOHNNY PYE AND THE FOOL-KILLER

You don't hear so much about the Fool-Killer these days, but when Johnny Pye was a boy there was a good deal of talk about him. Some said he was one kind of person, and some said another, but most people agreed that he came around fairly regular. Or, it seemed so to Johnny Pye. But then, Johnny was an adopted child, which is, maybe, why he took it so hard.

The miller and his wife had offered to raise him, after his own folks died, and that was a good deed on their part. But, as soon as he lost his baby teeth and started acting the way most boys act, they began to come down on him like thunder, which wasn't so good. They were good people, according to their lights, but their lights were terribly strict ones, and they believed that the harder you were on a youngster, the better and brighter he got. Well, that may work with some children, but it didn't with Johnny Pye.

He was sharp enough and willing enough—as sharp and willing as most boys in Martinsville. But, somehow or other, he never seemed to be able to do the right things or say the right words—at least when he was home. Treat a boy like a fool and he'll act like a fool, I say, but there's some folks need convincing. The miller and his wife thought the way to smarten Johnny was to treat him like a fool, and finally they got so he pretty much believed it himself.

And that was hard on him, for he had a boy's imagination, and maybe a little more than most. He could stand the beatings and he did. But what he couldn't stand was the way things went at the mill. I don't suppose the miller intended to do it. But, as long as Johnny Pye could remember, whenever he heard of the death of somebody he didn't like, he'd say, "Well, the Fool-Killer's come for so-and-so," and sort of smack his lips. It was, as you might say, a family joke, but the miller was a big man with a big red face, and it made a strong impression on Johnny Pye. Till, finally, he got a picture of the Fool-Killer, himself. He was a big man, too, in a checked shirt and corduroy trousers, and he went walking the ways of the world, with a hickory club that had a lump of lead in the end of it. I don't know how Johnny Pye got that picture so clear, but, to him, it was just as plain as the face of any human being in Martinsville. And, now and then, just to test it, he'd ask a grown-up person, kind of timidly, if that was the way the Fool-Killer looked. And, of course, they'd generally laugh and tell him it was. Then Johnny would wake up at night, in his room over the mill, and listen for the Fool-Killer's step on the road and wonder when he was coming. But he was brave enough not to tell anybody that.

Finally, though, things got a little more than he could bear. He'd done some boy's trick or other—let the stones grind a little fine, maybe, when the miller wanted the meal ground coarse—just carelessness, you know. But he'd gotten two whippings for it, one from the miller and one from his wife, and, at the end of it, the miller had said, "Well, Johnny Pye, the Fool-Killer ought to be along for you most any day now. For I never did see a boy that was such a fool." Johnny looked to the miller's wife to see if she believed it, too, but she just shook her head and looked serious. So he went to bed that night, but he couldn't sleep, for every time a bough rustled or the mill wheel creaked, it seemed to him it must be the Fool-Killer. And, early next morning, before anybody was up, he packed such duds as he had in a bandanna handkerchief and ran away.

He didn't really expect to get away from the Fool-Killer very long—as far as he knew, the Fool-Killer got you wherever you went. But he thought he'd give him a run for his money, at least. And when he got on the road, it was a bright spring morning, and the first peace and quiet he'd had in some time. So his spirits rose, and he chunked a stone at a bullfrog as he went along, just to show he was Johnny Pye and still doing business.

He hadn't gone more than three or four miles out of Martinsville, when he heard a buggy coming up the road behind him. He knew the Fool-Killer didn't need a buggy to catch you, so he wasn't afraid of it, but he stepped to the side of the road to let it pass. But it stopped, instead, and a black-whiskered man with a stovepipe hat looked out of it.

"Hello, bub," he said. "Is this the road for East Liberty?"

"My name's John Pye and I'm eleven years old," said Johnny, polite but firm, "and you take the next left fork for East Liberty. They say it's a pretty town—I've never been there myself." And he sighed a little, because he thought he'd like to see the world before the Fool-Killer caught up with him.

"H'm," said the man. "Stranger here, too, eh? And what brings a smart boy like you on the road so early in the morning?"

"Oh," said Johnny Pye, quite honestly, "I'm running away from the Fool-Killer. For the miller says I'm a fool and his wife says I'm a fool and almost everybody in Martinsville says I'm a fool except little Susie Marsh. And the miller says the Fool-Killer's after me—so I thought I'd run away before he came."

The black-whiskered man sat in his buggy and wheezed for a while. When he got his breath back, "Well, jump in, bub," he said. "The miller may say you're a fool, but I think you're a right smart boy to be running away from the Fool-Killer all by yourself. And I don't hold with small-town prejudices and I need a right smart boy, so I'll give you a lift on the road."

"But, will I be safe from the Fool-Killer, if I'm with you?" said Johnny. "For, otherwise, it don't signify."

"Safe?" said the black-whiskered man, and wheezed again. "Oh, you'll be safe as houses. You see, I'm a herb doctor—and some folks think, a little in the Fool-Killer's line of business, myself. And I'll teach you a trade worth two of milling. So jump in, bub."

"Sounds all right the way you say it," said Johnny, "but my name's John Pye," and he jumped into the buggy. And they went rattling along toward East Liberty with the herb doctor talking and cutting jokes till Johnny thought he'd never met a pleasanter man. About half a mile from East Liberty, the doctor stopped at a spring.

"What are we stopping here for?" said Johnny Pye.

"Wait and see," said the doctor, and gave him a wink. Then he got a haircloth trunk full of empty bottles out of the back of the buggy and made Johnny fill them with spring water and label them. Then he added a pinch of pink powder to each bottle and shook them up and corked them and stowed them away.

"What's that?" said Johnny, very interested.

"That's Old Doctor Waldo's Unparalleled Universal Remedy," said the doctor, reading from the label.

"Made from the purest snake oil and secret Indian herbs, it cures rheumatism, blind staggers, headache, malaria, five kinds of fits, and spots in front of the eyes. It will also remove oil or grease stains, clean knives and silver, polish brass, and is strongly recommended as a general tonic and blood purifier. Small size, one dollar—family bottle, two dollars and a half."

"But I don't see any snake oil in it," said Johnny, puzzled, "or any secret Indian herbs."

"That's because you're not a fool," said the doctor, with another wink. "The Fool-Killer wouldn't, either. But most folks will."

And, that very same night, Johnny saw. For the doctor made his pitch in East Liberty and he did it handsome. He took a couple of flaring oil torches and stuck them on the sides of the buggy; he put on a diamond stickpin and did card tricks and told funny stories till he had the crowd goggle-eyed. As for Johnny, he let him play on the tambourine. Then he started talking about Doctor Waldo's Universal Remedy, and, with Johnny to help him, the bottles went like hot cakes. Johnny helped the doctor count the money afterward, and it was a pile.

"Well," said Johnny, "I never saw money made easier. You've got a fine trade, Doctor."

"It's cleverness does it," said the doctor, and slapped him on the back.

"Now a fool's content to stay in one place and do one thing, but the Fool-Killer never caught up with a good pitchman yet."

"Well, it's certainly lucky I met up with you," said Johnny, "and, if it's cleverness does it, I'll learn the trade or bust."

So he stayed with the doctor quite a while—in fact, till he could make up the remedy and do the card tricks almost as good as the doctor. And the doctor liked Johnny, for Johnny was a biddable boy. But one night they came into a town where things didn't go as they usually did. The crowd gathered as usual, and the doctor did his tricks. But, all the time, Johnny could see a sharp-faced little fellow going through the crowd and whispering to one man and another. Till, at last, right in the middle of the doctor's spiel, the sharp-faced fellow gave a shout of "That's him all right! I'd know them whiskers anywhere!" and, with that, the crowd growled once and began to tear slats out of the nearest fence. Well, the next thing Johnny knew, he and the doctor were being ridden out of town on a rail, with the doctor's long coattails flying at every jounce.

They didn't hurt Johnny particular—him only being a boy. But they warned 'em both never to show their faces in that town again, and then they heaved the doctor into a thistle patch and went their ways.

"Owoo!" said the doctor, "ouch!" as Johnny was helping him out of the thistle patch. "Go easy with those thistles! And why didn't you give me the office, you blame little fool?"

"Office?" said Johnny. "What office?"

"When that sharp-nosed man started snooping around," said the doctor. "I thought that infernal main street looked familiar—I was through there two years ago, selling solid gold watches for a dollar apiece."

"But the works to a solid gold watch would be worth more than that," said Johnny.

"There weren't any works," said the doctor, with a groan, "but there was a nice lively beetle inside each case and it made the prettiest tick you ever heard."

"Well, that certainly was a clever idea," said Johnny. "I'd never have thought of that."

"Clever?" said the doctor. "Ouch—it was ruination! But who'd have thought the fools would bear a grudge for two years? And now we've lost the horse and buggy, too —not to speak of the bottles and the money. Well, there's lots more tricks to be played and we'll start again."

But, though he liked the doctor, Johnny began to feel dubious. For it occurred to him that, if all the doctor's cleverness got him was being ridden out of town on a rail, he couldn't be so far away from the Fool-Killer as he thought. And, sure enough, as he was going to sleep that night, he seemed to hear the Fool-Killer's footsteps coming after him—step, step, step. He pulled his jacket up over his ears, but he couldn't shut it out. So, when the doctor had got in the way of starting business over again, he and Johnny parted company. The doctor didn't bear any grudge; he shook hands with Johnny and told him to remember that cleverness was power. And Johnny went on with his running away.

He got to a town, and there was a store with a sign in the window, BOY WANTED, so he went in. There, sure enough, was the merchant, sitting at his desk, and a fine, important man he looked, in his black broadcloth suit.

Johnny tried to tell him about the Fool-Killer, but

the merchant wasn't interested in that. He just looked Johnny over and saw that he looked biddable and strong for his age. "But, remember, no fooling around, boy!" said the merchant sternly, after he'd hired him.

"No fooling around?" said Johnny, with the light of hope in his eyes.

"No," said the merchant, meaningly. "We've no room for fools in this business, I can tell you! You work hard, and you'll rise. But, if you've got any foolish notions, just knock them on the head and forget them."

Well, Johnny was glad enough to promise that, and he stayed with the merchant a year and a half. He swept out the store, and he put the shutters up and took them down; he ran errands and wrapped up packages and learned to keep busy twelve hours a day. And, being a biddable boy and an honest one, he rose, just like the merchant had said. The merchant raised his wages and let him begin to wait on customers and learn accounts. And then, one night, Johnny woke up in the middle of the night. And it seemed to him he heard, far away but getting nearer, the steps of the Fool-Killer after him—tramping, tramping.

He went to the merchant next day and said, "Sir, I'm sorry to tell you this, but I'll have to be moving on."

"Well, I'm sorry to hear that, Johnny," said the merchant, "for you've been a good boy. And, if it's a question of salary—"

"It isn't that," said Johnny, "but tell me one thing, sir, if you don't mind my asking. Supposing I did stay with you—where would I end?"

The merchant smiled. "That's a hard question to answer," he said, "and I'm not much given to compliments. But I started, myself, as a boy, sweeping out the store. And you're a bright youngster with lots of go-ahead. I don't see why, if you stuck to it, you shouldn't make the same kind of success that I have."

"And what's that?" said Johnny.

The merchant began to look irritated, but he kept his smile.

"Well," he said, "I'm not a boastful man, but I'll tell you this. Ten years ago I was the richest man in town. Five years ago, I was the richest man in the county. And five years from now—well, I aim to be the richest man in the state."

His eyes kind of glittered as he said it, but Johnny was looking at his face. It was sallow-skinned and pouchy, with the jaw as hard as a rock. And it came upon Johnny that moment that, though he'd known the merchant a year and a half, he'd never really seen him enjoy himself except when he was driving a bargain.

"Sorry, sir," he said, "but, if it's like that, I'll certainly have to go. Because, you see, I'm running away from the Fool-Killer, and if I stayed here and got to be like you, he'd certainly catch up with me in no—"

"Why, you impertinent young cub!" roared the merchant, with his face gone red all of a sudden. "Get your money from the cashier!" and Johnny was on the road again before you could say "Jack Robinson." But, this time, he was used to it, and walked off whistling.

Well, after that, he hired out to quite a few different people, but I won't go into all of his adventures. He worked for an inventor for a while, and they split up because Johnny happened to ask him what would be the good of his patent, self-winding, perpetual-motion machine, once he did get it invented. And, while the inventor talked big about improving the human race and the beauties of science, it was plain he didn't know. So that night, Johnny heard the steps of the Fool-Killer, far off but coming closer, and, next morning, he went away. Then he stayed with a minister for a while, and he certainly hated to leave him, for the minister was a good man. But they got talking one evening and, as it chanced, Johnny asked him what happened to people who didn't believe in his particular religion. Well, the minister was broad-minded, but there's only one answer to that. He

admitted they might be good folks—he even admitted
they mightn't exactly go to hell—but he couldn't let them
into heaven, no, not the best and the wisest of them, for
there were the specifications laid down by creed and
church, and, if you didn't fulfill them, you didn't.

So Johnny had to leave him, and, after that, he went
with an old drunken fiddler for a while. He wasn't a
good man, I guess, but he could play till the tears ran
down your cheeks. And, when he was playing his best, it
seemed to Johnny that the Fool-Killer was very far away.
For, in spite of his faults and his weaknesses, while he
played, there was might in the man. But he died drunk
in a ditch, one night, with Johnny to hold his head, and,
while he left Johnny his fiddle, it didn't do Johnny much
good. For, while Johnny could play a tune, he couldn't
play like the fiddler—it wasn't in his fingers.

Then it chanced that Johnny took up with a company
of soldiers. He was still too young to enlist, but they
made a kind of pet of him, and everything went swim-
mingly for a while. For the captain was the bravest man
Johnny had ever seen, and he had an answer for everything, out of regulations and the Articles of War. But
then they went West to fight Indians and the same old
trouble cropped up again. For one night the captain said
to him, "Johnny, we're going to fight the enemy tomorrow, but you'll stay in camp."

"Oh, I don't want to do that," said Johnny; "I want
to be in on the fighting."

"It's an order," said the captain, grimly. Then he gave
Johnny certain instructions and a letter to take to his
wife.

"For the colonel's a copper-plated fool," he said, "and
we're walking straight into an ambush."

"Why don't you tell him that?" said Johnny.

"I have," said the captain, "but he's the colonel."

"Colonel or no colonel," said Johnny, "if he's a fool,
somebody ought to stop him."

"You can't do that, in an army," said the captain.

"Orders are orders." But it turned out the captain was wrong about it, for, next day, before they could get moving, the Indians attacked and got badly licked. When it was all over, "Well, it was a good fight," said the captain, professionally. "All the same, if they'd waited and laid an ambush, they'd have had our hair. But, as it was, they didn't stand a chance."

"But why didn't they lay an ambush?" said Johnny.

"Well," said the captain, "I guess they had their orders too. And now, how would you like to be a soldier?"

"Well, it's a nice outdoors life, but I'd like to think it over," said Johnny. For he knew the captain was brave and he knew the Indians had been brave—you couldn't find two braver sets of people. But, all the same, when he thought the whole thing over, he seemed to hear steps in the sky. So he soldiered to the end of the campaign and then he left the army, though the captain told him he was making a mistake.

By now, of course, he wasn't a boy any longer; he was getting to be a young man with a young man's thoughts and feelings. And, half the time, nowadays, he'd forget about the Fool-Killer except as a dream he'd had when he was a boy. He could even laugh at it now and then, and think what a fool he'd been to believe there was such a man.

But, all the same, the desire in him wasn't satisfied, and something kept driving him on. He'd have called it ambitiousness, now, but it came to the same thing. And with every new trade he tried, sooner or later would come the dream—the dream of the big man in the checked shirt and corduroy pants, walking the ways of the world with his hickory stick in one hand. It made him angry to have that dream, now, but it had a singular power over him. Till, finally, when he was turned twenty or so, he got scared.

"Fool-Killer or no Fool-Killer," he said to himself. "I've got to ravel this matter out. For there must be some one thing a man could tie to, and be sure he wasn't a fool.

I've tried cleverness and money and half a dozen other things, and they don't seem to be the answer. So now I'll try book learning and see what comes of that."

So he read all the books he could find, and whenever he'd seem to hear the steps of the Fool-Killer coming for the authors—and that was frequent—he'd try and shut his ears. But some books said one thing was best and some another, and he couldn't rightly decide.

"Well," he said to himself, when he'd read and read till his head felt as stuffed with book learning as a sausage with meat, "it's interesting, but it isn't exactly contemporaneous. So I think I'll go down to Washington and ask the wise men there. For it must take a lot of wisdom to run a country like the United States, and if there's people who can answer my questions, it's there they ought to be found."

So he packed his bag and off to Washington he went. He was modest for a youngster, and he didn't intend to try and see the President right away. He thought probably a congressman was about his size. So he saw a congressman, and the congressman told him the thing to be was an upstanding young American and vote the Republican ticket—which sounded all right to Johnny Pye, but not exactly what he was after.

Then he went to a senator, and the senator told him to be an upstanding young American and vote the Democratic ticket—which sounded all right, too, but not what he was after, either. And, somehow, though both men had been impressive and affable, right in the middle of their speeches he'd seemed to hear steps—you know.

But a man has to eat, whatever else he does, and Johnny found he'd better buckle down and get himself a job. It happened to be with the first congressman he struck, for that one came from Martinsville, which is why Johnny went to him in the first place. And, in a little while, he forgot his search entirely and the Fool-Killer, too, for the congressman's niece came East to visit him, and she was the Susie Marsh that Johnny had sat next in school. She'd been pretty then, but she was prettier now, and as soon as Johnny Pye saw her, his heart gave a jump and a thump.

"And don't think we don't remember you in Martinsville, Johnny Pye," she said, when her uncle had explained who his new clerk was. "Why, the whole town'll be excited when I write home. We've heard all about your killing Indians and inventing perpetual motion and traveling around the country with a famous doctor and making a fortune in dry goods and—oh, it's a wonderful story!"

"Well," said Johnny, and coughed, "some of that's just a little bit exaggerated. But it's nice of you to be interested. So they don't think I'm a fool any more, in Martinsville?"

"I never thought you were a fool," said Susie with a little smile, and Johnny felt his heart give another bump.

"And I always knew you were pretty, but never how pretty till now," said Johnny, and coughed again. "But, speaking of old times, how's the miller and his wife? For I did leave them right sudden, and while there were faults on both sides, I must have been a trial to them too."

"They've gone the way of all flesh," said Susie Marsh, "and there's a new miller now. But he isn't very well-liked, to tell the truth, and he's letting the mill run down."

"That's a pity," said Johnny, "for it was a likely mill." Then he began to ask her more questions and she began to remember things too. Well, you know how the time can go when two youngsters get talking like that.

Johnny Pye never worked so hard in his life as he did that winter. And it wasn't the Fool-Killer he thought about—it was Susie Marsh. First he thought she loved him and then he was sure she didn't, and then he was betwixt and between, and all perplexed and confused. But, finally, it turned out all right and he had her promise, and Johnny Pye knew he was the happiest man in the world. And that night, he waked up in the night and heard the Fool-Killer coming after him—step, step, step.

He didn't sleep much after that, and he came down to breakfast hollow-eyed. But his uncle-to-be didn't notice that—he was rubbing his hands and smiling.

"Put on your best necktie, Johnny!" he said, very cheerful, "for I've got an appointment with the President today, and, just to show I approve of my niece's fiancé, I'm taking you along."

"The President!" said Johnny, all dumb founded.

"Yes," said Congressman Marsh, "you see, there's a little bill—well, we needn't go into that. But slick down your back hair, Johnny—we'll make Martinsville proud of us this day!"

Then a weight seemed to go from Johnny's shoulders and a load from his heart. He wrung Mr. Marsh's hand.

"Thank you, Uncle Eben!" he said. "I can't thank you enough." For, at last, he knew he was going to look upon a man that was bound to be safe from the Fool-Killer— and it seemed to him if he could just once do that, all his troubles and searchings would be ended.

Well, it doesn't signify which President it was—you can take it from me that he was President and a fine-looking man. He'd just been elected, too, so he was lively as a trout, and the saddle galls he'd get from Congress hadn't even begun to show. Anyhow, there he was, and Johnny feasted his eyes on him. For if there was anybody in the country the Fool-Killer couldn't bother, it must be a man like this.

The President and the congressman talked politics for a while, and then it was Johnny's turn.

"Well, young man," said the President, affably, "and what can I do for you—for you look to me like a fine, upstanding young American."

The congressman cut in quick before Johnny could open his mouth.

"Just a word of advice, Mr. President," he said. "Just a word in season. For my young friend's led an adventurous life, but now he's going to marry my niece and settle down. And what he needs most of all is a word of ripe wisdom from you."

"Well," said the President, looking at Johnny rather keenly, "if that's all he needs, a short horse is soon curried. I wish most of my callers wanted as little."

But, all the same, he drew Johnny out, as such men can, and before Johnny knew it, he was telling his life story.

"Well," said the President, at the end, "you certainly have been a rolling stone, young man. But there's nothing wrong in that. And, for one of your varied experience there's one obvious career. Politics!" he said, and slapped his fist in his hand.

"Well," said Johnny, scratching his head, "of course, since I've been in Washington, I've thought of that. But I don't know that I'm rightly fitted."

"You can write a speech," said Congressman Marsh, quite thoughtful, "for you've helped me with mine. You're a likeable fellow too. And you were born poor and worked up—and you've even got a war record—why, hell! Excuse me, Mr. President!—he's worth five hundred votes just as he stands!"

"I—I'm more than honored by you two gentlemen," said Johnny, abashed and flattered, "but supposing I did go into politics—where would I end up?"

The President looked sort of modest.

"The Presidency of the United States," said he, "is within the legitimate ambition of every American citizen. Provided he can get elected, of course."

"Oh," said Johnny, feeling dazzled, "I never thought of that. Well, that's a great thing. But it must be a great responsibility too."

"It is," said the President, looking just like his pictures on the campaign buttons.

"Why, it must be an awful responsibility!" said Johnny.

"I can't hardly see how a mortal man can bear it. Tell me, Mr. President," he said, "may I ask you a question?"

"Certainly," said the President, looking prouder and more responsible and more and more like his picture on the campaign buttons every minute.

"Well," said Johnny, "it sounds like a fool question, but it's this: This is a great big country of ours, Mr. President, and it's got the most amazing lot of different people in it. How can any President satisfy all those people at one time? Can you yourself, Mr. President?"

The President looked a bit taken aback for a minute. But then he gave Johnny Pye a statesman's glance.

"With the help of God," he said, solemnly, "and in accordance with the principles of our great party, I intend . . ."

But Johnny didn't even hear the end of the sentence. For, even as the President was speaking, he heard a step outside in the corridor and he knew, somehow, it wasn't the step of a secretary or a guard. He was glad the President had said "with the help of God" for that sort of softened the step. And when the President finished, Johnny bowed.

"Thank you, Mr. President," he said; "that's what I wanted to know. And now I'll go back to Martinsville, I guess."

"Go back to Martinsville?" said the President, surprised.

"Yes, sir," said Johnny. "For I don't think I'm cut out for politics."

"And is that all you have to say to the President of the United States?" said his uncle-to-be, in a fume.

But the President had been thinking, meanwhile, and he was a bigger man than the congressman.

"Wait a minute, Congressman," he said. "This young man's honest, at least, and I like his looks. Moreover, of all the people who've come to see me in the last six

months, he's the only one who hasn't wanted something
—except the White House cat, and I guess she wanted
something, too, because she meowed. You don't want to
be President, young man—and, confidentially, I don't
blame you. But how would you like to be postmaster at
Martinsville?"    ·

"Postmaster at Martinsville?" said Johnny. "But—"

"Oh, it's only a tenth-class post office," said the President, "but, for once in my life, I'll do something because
I want to, and let Congress yell its head off. Come—is it
yes or no?"

Johnny thought of all the places he'd been and all
the trades he'd worked at. He thought, queerly enough,
of the old drunk fiddler dead in the ditch, but he knew
he couldn't be that. Mostly, though, he thought of Martinsville and Susie Marsh. And, though he'd just heard
the Fool-Killer's step, he defied the Fool-Killer.

"Why, it's yes, of course, Mr. President," he said, "for
then I can marry Susie."

"That's as good a reason as you'll find," said the President. "And now, I'll just write a note."

Well, he was as good as his word, and Johnny and his
Susie were married and went back to live in Martinsville.
And, as soon as Johnny learned the ways of postmaster-
ing, he found it as good a trade as most. There wasn't
much mail in Martinsville, but, in between whiles, he
ran the mill, and that was a good trade too. And all the
time, he knew, at the back of his mind, that he hadn't
quite settled accounts with the Fool-Killer. But he didn't
much care about that, for he and Susie were happy. And
after a while they had a child, and that was the most remarkable experience that had ever happened to any
young couple, though the doctor said it was a perfectly
normal baby.

One evening, when his son was about a year old,
Johnny Pye took the river road, going home. It was a

mite longer than the hill road, but it was the cool of the evening, and there's times when a man likes to walk by himself, fond as he may be of his wife and family.

He was thinking of the way things had turned out for him, and they seemed to him pretty astonishing and singular, as they do to most folks, when you think them over. In fact, he was thinking so hard that, before he knew it, he'd almost stumbled over an old scissors grinder who'd set up his grindstone and tools by the side of the road. The scissors grinder had his cart with him, but he'd turned the horse out to graze—and a lank, old, white horse it was, with every rib showing. And he was very busy, putting an edge on a scythe.

"Oh, sorry," said Johnny Pye. "I didn't know anybody was camping here. But you might come around to my house tomorrow—my wife's got some knives that need sharpening."

Then he stopped, for the old man gave him a long, keen look.

"Why, it's you, Johnny Pye," said the old man. "And how do you do, Johnny Pye! You've been a long time coming—in fact, now and then, I thought I'd have to fetch you. But you're here at last."

Johnny Pye was a grown man now, but he began to tremble.

"But it isn't you!" he said, wildly. "I mean you're not him! Why, I've known how he looks all my life! He's a big man, with a checked shirt, and he carries a hickory stick with a lump of lead in one end."

"Oh, no," said the scissors grinder, quite quiet. "You may have thought of me that way, but that's not the way I am." And Johnny Pye heard the scythe go whet-whet-whet on the stone. The old man ran some water on it and looked at the edge. Then he shook his head as if the edge didn't quite satisfy him. "Well, Johnny, are you ready?" he said, after a while.

"Ready?" said Johnny, in a hoarse voice. "Of course I'm not ready."

"That's what they all say," said the old man, nodding his head, and the scythe went whet-whet on the stone.

Johnny wiped his brow and started to argue it out.

"You see, if you'd found me earlier," he said, "or later. I don't want to be unreasonable, but I've got a wife and a child."

"Most has wives and many has children," said the old man, grimly, and the scythe went whet-whet on the stone as he pushed the treadle. And a shower of sparks flew, very clear and bright, for the night had begun to fall.

"Oh, stop that damn racket and let a man think for a minute!" said Johnny, desperate. "I can't go, I tell you. I won't. It isn't time. It's—"

The old man stopped the grindstone and pointed with the scythe at Johnny Pye.

"Tell me one good reason," he said. "There's men would be missed in the world, but are you one of them? A clever man might be missed, but are you a clever man?"

"No," said Johnny, thinking of the herb doctor. "I had a chance to be clever, but I gave it up."

"One," said the old man, ticking off on his fingers. "Well, a rich man might be missed—by some. But you aren't rich, I take it."

"No," said Johnny, thinking of the merchant, "nor wanted to be."

"Two," said the old man. "Cleverness—riches—they're done. But there's still martial bravery and being a hero. There might be an argument to make, if you were one of those."

Johnny Pye shuddered a little, remembering the way that battlefield had looked, out West, when the Indians were dead and the fight over.

"No," he said, "I've fought, but I'm not a hero."

"Well, then, there's religion," said the old man, sort

of patient, "and science, and—but what's the use? We know what you did with those. I might feel a trifle of compunction if I had to deal with a President of the United States. But—"

"Oh, you know well enough I ain't President," said Johnny, with a groan. "Can't you get it over with and be done?"

"You're not putting up a very good case," said the old man, shaking his head. "I'm surprised at you, Johnny. Here you spend your youth running away from being a fool. And yet, what's the first thing you do, when you're man grown? Why, you marry a girl, settle down in your home town, and start raising children when you don't know how they'll turn out. You might have known I'd catch up with you, then—you just put yourself in my way."

"Fool I may be," said Johnny Pye in his agony, "and if you take it like that, I guess we're all fools. But Susie's my wife, and my child's my child. And, as for work in the world—well, somebody has to be postmaster, or folks wouldn't get the mail."

"Would it matter much if they didn't?" said the old man, pointing his scythe.

"Well, no, I don't suppose it would, considering what's on the post cards," said Johnny Pye. "But while it's my business to sort it, I'll sort it as well as I can."

The old man whetted his scythe so hard that a long shower of sparks flew out on the grass.

"Well," he said, "I've got my job, too, and I do it likewise. But I'll tell you what I'll do. You're coming my way, no doubt of it, but, looking you over, you don't look quite ripe yet. So I'll let you off for a while. For that matter," said he, "if you'll answer one question of mine— how a man can be a human being and not be a fool— I'll let you off permanent. It'll be the first time in history," he said, "but you've got to do something on your own hook, once in a while. And now you can walk along, Johnny Pye."

With that he grounded the scythe till the sparks flew out like the tail of a comet and Johnny Pye walked along. The air of the meadow had never seemed so sweet to him before.

All the same, even with his relief, he didn't quite forget, and sometimes Susie had to tell the children not to disturb father because he was thinking. But time went ahead, as it does, and pretty soon Johnny Pye found he was forty. He'd never expected to be forty, when he was young, and it kind of surprised him. But there it was, though he couldn't say he felt much different, except now and then when he stooped over. And he was a solid citizen of the town, well-liked and well-respected, with a growing family and a stake in the community, and when he thought those things over, they kind of surprised him too. But, pretty soon, it was as if things had always been that way.

It was after his eldest son had been drowned out fishing that Johnny Pye met the scissors grinder again. But this time he was bitter and distracted, and, if he could have got to the old man, he'd have done him a mortal harm. But, somehow or other, when he tried to come to grips with him, it was like reaching for air and mist. He could see the sparks fly from the ground scythe, but he couldn't even touch the wheel.

"You coward!" said Johnny Pye. "Stand up and fight like a man!" But the old man just nodded his head and the wheel kept grinding and grinding.

"Why couldn't you have taken me?" said Johnny Pye, as if those words had never been said before. "What's the sense in all this? Why can't you take me now?"

Then he tried to wrench the scythe from the old man's hands, but he couldn't touch it. And then he fell down and lay on the grass for a while.

"Time passes," said the old man, nodding his head. "Time passes."

"It will never cure the grief I have for my son," said Johnny Pye.

"It will not," said the old man, nodding his head. "But time passes. Would you leave your wife a widow and your other children fatherless for the sake of your grief?"

"No, God help me!" said Johnny Pye. "That wouldn't be right for a man."

"Then go home to your house, Johnny Pye," said the old man. And Johnny Pye went, but there were lines in his face that hadn't been there before.

And time passed, like the flow of the river, and Johnny Pye's children married and had houses and children of their own. And Susie's hair grew white, and her back grew bent, and when Johnny Pye and his children followed her to her grave, folks said she'd died in the fullness of years, but that was hard for Johnny Pye to believe. Only folks didn't talk as plain as they used to, and the sun didn't heat as much, and sometimes, before dinner, he'd go to sleep in his chair.

And once, after Susie had died, the President of those days came through Martinsville and Johnny Pye shook hands with him and there was a piece in the paper about his shaking hands with two Presidents, fifty years apart. Johnny Pye cut out the clipping and kept it in his pocketbook. He liked this President all right, but, as he told people, he wasn't a patch on the other one fifty years ago. Well, you couldn't expect it—you didn't have Presidents these days, not to call them Presidents. All the same, he took a lot of satisfaction in the clipping.

He didn't get down to the river road much any more —it wasn't too long a walk, of course, but he just didn't often feel like it. But, one day, he slipped away from the granddaughter that was taking care of him, and went.

It was kind of a steep road, really—he didn't remember
its being so steep.

"Well," said the scissors grinder, "and good afternoon
to you, Johnny Pye."

"You'll have to talk a little louder," said Johnny Pye.
"My hearing's perfect, but folks don't speak as plain as
they used to. Stranger in town?"

"Oh, so that's the way it is," said the scissors grinder.

"Yes, that's the way it is," said Johnny Pye. He knew
he ought to be afraid of this fellow, now he'd put on his
spectacles and got a good look at him, but for the life
of him, he couldn't remember why.

"I know just who you are," he said, a little fretfully.
"Never forgot a face in my life, and your name's right
on the tip of my tongue—"

"Oh, don't bother about names," said the scissors grinder. "We're old acquaintances. And I asked you a question, years ago—do you remember that?"

"Yes," said Johnny Pye, "I remember." Then he began
to laugh—a high, old man's laugh. "And of all the fool
questions I ever was asked," he said, "that certainly took
the cake."

"Oh?" said the scissors grinder.

"Uh-huh," said Johnny Pye. "For you asked me how
a man could be a human being and yet not be a fool.
And the answer is—when he's dead and gone and buried.
Any fool would know that."

"That so?" said the scissors grinder.

"Of course," said Johnny Pye. "I ought to know. I'll be
ninety-two next November, and I've shook hands with
two Presidents. The first President I shook—"

"I'll be interested to hear about that," said the scissors
grinder, "but we've got a little business, first. For, if all
human beings are fools, how does the world get ahead?"

"Oh, there's lots of other things," said Johnny Pye,
kind of impatient. "There's the brave and the wise and

the clever—and they're apt to roll it ahead as much as an inch. But it's all mixed in together. For, Lord, it's only some fool kind of creature that would have crawled out of the sea to dry land in the first place—or got dropped from the Garden of Eden, if you like it better that way. You can't depend on the kind of folks people think they are—you've got to go by what they do. And I wouldn't give much for a man that some folks hadn't thought was a fool, in his time."

"Well," said the scissors grinder, "you've answered my question—at least as well as you could, which is all you can expect of a man. So I'll keep my part of the bargain."

"And what was that?" said Johnny. "For, while it's all straight in my head, I don't quite recollect the details."

"Why," said the scissors grinder, rather testy, "I'm to let you go, you old fool! You'll never see me again till the Last Judgment. There'll be trouble in the office about it," said he, "but you've got to do what you like, once in a while."

"Phew!" said Johnny Pye. "That needs thinking over!" And he scratched his head.

"Why?" said the scissors grinder, a bit affronted. "It ain't often I offer a man eternal life."

"Well," said Johnny Pye, "I take it very kind, but, you see, it's this way." He thought for a moment. "No," he said, "you wouldn't understand. You can't have touched seventy yet, by your looks, and no young man would."

"Try me," said the scissors grinder.

"Well," said Johnny Pye, "it's this way," and he scratched his head again. "I'm not saying—if you'd made the offer forty years ago, or even twenty. But, well, now, let's just take one detail. Let's say 'teeth.'"

"Well, of course," said the scissors grinder, "naturally —I mean you could hardly expect me to do anything about that."

"I thought so," said Johnny Pye. "Well, you see, these are good, bought teeth, but I'm sort of tired of hearing them click. And spectacles, I suppose, the same?"

"I'm afraid so," said the scissors grinder. "I can't interfere with time, you know—that's not my department. And, frankly, you couldn't expect, at a hundred and eighty, let's say, to be quite the man you was at ninety. But still, you'd be a wonder!"

"Maybe so," said Johnny Pye, "but, you see—well, the truth is, I'm an old man now. You wouldn't think it to look at me, but it's so. And my friends—well, they're gone —and Susie and the boy—and somehow you don't get as close to the younger people, except the children. And to keep on just going and going till Judgment Day, with nobody around to talk to that had real horse sense—well, no, sir, it's a handsome offer but I just don't feel up to accepting it. It may not be patriotic of me, and I feel sorry for Martinsville. It'd do wonders for the climate and the chamber of commerce to have a leading citizen live till Judgment Day. But a man's got to do as he likes, at least once in his life." He stopped and looked at the scissors grinder. "I'll admit, I'd kind of like to beat out Ike Leavis," he said. "To hear him talk, you'd think nobody had ever pushed ninety before. But I suppose—"

"I'm afraid we can't issue a limited policy," said the scissors grinder.

"Well," said Johnny Pye, "I just thought of it. And Ike's all right." He waited a moment. "Tell me," he said in a low voice. "Well, you know what I mean. Afterwards. I mean, if you're likely to see"—he coughed— "your friends again. I mean, if it's so—like some folks believe."

"I can't tell you that," said the scissors grinder. "I only go so far."

"Well, there's no harm in asking," said Johnny Pye, rather humbly. He peered into the darkness; a last shower of sparks flew from the scythe, then the whir of the wheel stopped.

"H'm," said Johnny Pye, testing the edge. "That's a well-ground scythe. But they used to grind 'em better in the old days." He listened and looked, for a moment, anxiously. "Oh, Lordy!" he said, "there's Helen coming to look for me. She'll take me back to the house."

"Not this time," said the scissors grinder. "Yes, there isn't bad steel in that scythe. Well, let's go, Johnny Pye."

# A LIFE AT ANGELO'S

I don't know why everybody keeps on going to Angelo's.
The drinks aren't any better—in fact, they're a little
worse, if anything—and the dinner never was much. I'm
getting so I can hardly look a sardine in the eye any
more.

Of course it's a quiet place, and they don't let in many
college boys. It's generally just the old crowd from five
o'clock on. Oh, people come and go naturally—the way
they do in New York. If they didn't, I don't suppose
Angelo could keep on running. But what I mean is, you
can drop in almost any time after curfew and find somebody you know to have a quick one or a couple of quick
ones with. And then, if that's your weakness, you can
stay and get dinner; though I wish they'd try another
brand of sardines.

Suppose everyone stopped coming, all at once? Or
suppose the place closed? I don't like to think about that.
I suppose it's bound to happen, sooner or later, when
Angelo's made his pile—they always go back to Italy.
Then there'll be all the trouble and bother of finding
another place; and the crowd won't be the same. You
can't keep a crowd together, once you move the place, in
New York. It seems pretty safe, though, at the moment,
I'm glad to say. There's never been any real trouble, you
see; no one ever gets shot at Angelo's, and when the visiting firemen get too noisy, Rocco just eases them out.
Rocco's the little one with the grin, and he doesn't look
strong, but how he can ease a fellow out when it's necessary! He did it to me only once, and I've never held it

against him. That was just after Evie and I had broken
up.

No, I don't think there's any need to worry for a while
yet. And when there is, I'm sure Angelo will tell me about
it far enough ahead so I can make my arrangements.
After all, I'm one of his oldest customers. I don't go back
to the Twelfth Street place, the way Mr. Forman does,
but seven years is a long time in this man's town. They're
easing Mr. Forman out at 11:30 these days. It used to be
all hours when I first knew him, but a man can't expect
to drink like that at his age and not show it in the whites
of the eyes. That's another thing I have against all this
changing around. You get started going from one place
to another and buying taxis and going in for general
snake dancing; and before you know where you are you're
on a party, and the whole next day is bad. Well, now, if
you work at all, you can't afford to have the week days
go bad on you. I'm not talking of Saturday night—there's
a law about that. And of course those impromptu harvest
homes are a lot of fun when you're young and new to the
town. But when you've had a little sense knocked into
you you're a fool if you don't run on schedule. Isn't that
so?

Now, at Angelo's, you always know where you are. A
couple of quick ones or so before dinner, and the red at
dinner—or the white, if you're dining with a girl. Then
a little touch after the coffee and a couple of long ones
and a nightcap, and home at twelve by the old college
clock. And all the time you're talking with somebody
you know—about their wives, or their husbands, or religion, or the market, or what's new in the crowd—just ra-
tional conversation and maybe a little quiet singing, like
"Work is the Curse of the Drinking Classes." Sometimes
Mr. Forman sits down and tells one of his long stories,
but generally he'd rather stand at the bar. And sometimes the whole crowd clicks, and sometimes it doesn't,
and sometimes that Page girl gets started on her imita-
tions.

But anyway, it's something you're used to, and you're doing it again, and it's warm, and you know the people, and you don't have to go home. And Angelo's there, getting a little fatter and sleeker every year, and with a little bigger white edge around his waistcoat. Now and then he'll set up some *strega* for you, if he's feeling right. I don't like *strega* myself, but it would hurt his feelings to refuse. And then, in summer, there's the little back garden, and the fat cat that always has kittens, and the pink shades on the lamps. Rocco will be telling you the fish is ver' fine—and you know it isn't, but who cares?—and you can sit and watch the lights in the skyscrapers and hear the roar of the town, going by outside. You don't have to think at all. It's restful that way.

I can remember when I used to think a lot. And wonder about the people who came to places like Angelo's, and who they were, and why they came, and what they did with the rest of their time. I used to make up stories about them, going back to the apartment with Evie, and we'd both get excited over them; and forget to turn off at our own corner, we were talking so hard. That was when everybody we met was brand-new and bound to be interesting, and it was fun going to shows together in the gallery and having pancakes afterward at Childs'. I was always going to write some of those stories down, and she helped me make notes of them. I found the start of the one about Mr. Forman the other day. Well, what was the percentage in keeping it? I've seen a good deal of this writing racket since; and I ought to know what will sell and what won't. And anyhow, I'd just made him an old soak, and he's really a pretty interesting man.

Besides, that's something you get over. Wondering, I mean. Once you're on a normal schedule, you don't have time. I used to think it was funny—meeting people the way you do and having them tell you all sorts of inside things, the way it happens, and yet not really knowing them or tying them up with anything outside. But that's

stopped bothering me. You just have to let them come
and go, or it breaks the charm.

Going home to dinner with Jim Hewitt was what
cured me, finally. I never met a fellow I liked better at
Angelo's, and we told our real names. So, when he suggested breaking the family bread one evening, I took him
up. Good Lord, he lived at Scarsdale and they had three
children! The baby was sounding off like a police siren
as we came in, and we had one round of weak orange
blossoms before the fodder. Mrs. Hewitt liked orange
blossoms. Then, afterward, we sat around and played
three-handed bridge and Mrs. Hewitt and Jim discussed
the squeak in the car. I couldn't have stayed all night;
I'd have had the mimies. Jim was sort of ritzy for a while
after that, but he got all right again, finally. I guess they
must have hitched up the sled dogs and moved north to
White Plains or something, for I haven't seem him in I
don't know how long.

Of course, now and then something comes along that
you have to take notice of. People get married or divorced,
and Angelo will always open a bottle of champagne, no
matter which it is, if they're really old customers. I remember the party the crowd of us gave to cheer up Helen
Ashland when she heard about Jake's remarriage. She
certainly took it like a sport—we were thinking up funny
telegrams to send the bridal couple all evening. I don't
believe she really had hysterics either. That was just Bing
Otis' idea. And she couldn't have meant it when she said
she hated us—she'd always been the life of the crowd. Anyhow, I think she got married again last year—somebody
was broadcasting about it. If she ever comes back to
Angelo's, I'll have to get the low-down.

That's another thing about the crowd—the way they
stick together when anything happens. I'll never forget
the night Ted Harrison went out. Of course, he'd been
going into reverse for quite a while, and whenever he
got particularly sunk, he'd talk about doing a one-way
jump through a window; but we knew Ted and just kid-

ded him along. So when he did do it, after all, it was mean. Anyhow, he had the sense not to stage his act at Angelo's.

We went to the service afterward—those of us that could. That's what I mean by all of us sticking together. It was one of those gray winter days, and cold. There was a little boy, and he was crying. I don't see why they brought him there. I didn't know Ted had a boy. I know the rest of Ted's family sort of upstaged us. But we felt we ought to be there; though it was funny how little you could remember about Ted except parties. Well, there isn't much to those services, the way I look at it. But then we went back to Angelo's and he was fine.

Evie never took to Angelo's somehow, even at first. She felt she had to like the dinner, because it was cheap, but the atmosphere of the place never really appealed to her. She liked going to places where there was music or where somebody famous might be sitting at the next table. Of course, it was generally an out-of-town buyer or a cloak model, really, but she got just as big a kick out of pretending. We used to have dinner home a lot, too, that first year. It's wonderful how much food you can get for the money, living like that. Though, of course, it's really cheaper for me to eat at Angelo's, now I'm alone.

I've thought sometimes of getting a regular maid or one of those Japs who just come in and get dinner and clear away. There'd be money enough, for Evie never would take alimony, and now she's married again she doesn't need it anyway. But then, what would you do after dinner? You can't go to the movies every night in the week, and a man who works all day needs some relaxation.

When Evie and I were married, we used to go to all sorts of places—we even went to museums on Sundays and to those concerts they have way uptown. But there's not much point in doing that sort of thing by yourself. And if you start trotting a girl around, why, anybody knows how that finishes. You may not mean to get hooked up together at all, but some little thing happens and you're in for it, one way or the other. And if it's one way, you're bound to feel like a bum sooner or later, while if it's the other—well, I've been married to Evie, and once is enough. I'm not going to repeat at my age. This child is too wise.

Now, you can see as much of a girl as you like at Angelo's, and that's all right because you're both part of the crowd. You've got protection, if you see what I mean. And even if you should stop playing for matches, it wouldn't mean much to either of you. We're all pretty modern in the crowd and we understand about things like that. Of course, we've had some fairly wild birds at one time or another, and I don't say I agree with all the talk I hear. But there's no use being Victorian, like people were in 1910. You just have to be wise.

It's queer, though—you certainly couldn't call Evie Victorian. And yet she never genuinely fitted in with the crowd. She wasn't a gloom either, or a bluenose; she was really awfully pretty and the kind of girl that everybody likes right off. Why, Mr. Forman took a great shine to her and used to come over and sit at our table and tell her how he wished he had a daughter her age. But she just couldn't stand him. She said it was the look of his hands. Now, when anybody's been drinking for thirty semesters or so, like Mr. Forman, I think they're lucky if they have any hands at all. And if they do remind you of an alligator-skin bag, you ought to overlook it and be broad-minded. But Evie simply couldn't see it that way.

She was always wanting us to make friends with other young married people, even when they lived up by Grant's Tomb, where the climate's different. Well, that's all right, but once you go in for that sort of thing, you might as well stay in Waynesburg. That's what I kept telling her: "This is New York," I said, "this is New York." Let the Weather Bureau worry about the wide-open spaces. But all the same, after she was gone, I found a whole envelope full of real-estate ads—you know those mortgage manors with the built-in kiddie coops that all the Westchester cowboys come home to on the 5:49. Now, can you can imagine that in a sensible girl?

So there it was, you see, and we didn't make a go of it. Well, it's no use crying over spilt giggle water, as they say, and a man has to take things like that in his stride. If he doesn't, he's lost in the shuffle in this man's hamlet. I can see it wasn't anybody's fault; I'm modern. Maybe if Evie had really liked the crowd—but there, I won't blame her. She's happy the way she is, I guess; and you can see the way I am. The only thing that ever hurts this little head is to think of Angelo's closing down, sardines or no sardines. But I'm sure he'll give me the eye, long enough ahead, if it does. He's always shot square with me.

Of course, occasionally you get sort of philosophic about this time in the evening, and wonder how things would have turned out if they'd been different. But I've almost quit doing that. There's no percentage in it.

I remember Mr. Forman, one of the first times Evie and I were here. She hadn't noticed his hands then, and when he got talking to us, we both thought he was a pretty quaint old character. I guess he took to us so because we both of us must have looked young and green. Anyhow, he started philosophizing. "Youth," he says. "Youth against the city; coming in every day—" Oh, he ought to have had it syndicated! "I've watched 'em come," says he, "and I've seen 'em go. And some it makes, and some it breaks, and some just dry up gradually till the whitewing sweeps 'em away. Go back to your cornfields, young people," says he—as if Waynesburg didn't have car tracks!—"Go back and raise a family of nice little mortgages, because I'm a bad old man and you're breaking my heart"—and pretty soon he's crying into his glass.

We didn't pay any attention to him. We knew we were going to lick the world. But all the same, there's something in what he said. This town is a tough spot till you get wise to it—and it's too bad to see a fine man like Mr. Forman going to pieces the way he has these last two years. But then he's got what I call too much system in his drinking. You have to have just enough so it doesn't worry you.

Take me. If I'm stepping out a little more than usual tonight, it's just because of seeing Evie again. Of course it was bound to happen sometime, the way people come to New York; but a thing like that is apt to make you a little nervous just the same. It's easier, being modern the way we are. All the same, when I stepped out of the elevator and saw her waiting where she generally used to wait . . .

She hadn't come upstairs to the office, and that was decent of her. That girl at the front desk never could see me, and it's a laugh, your ex-wife ringing you up to pass the time of day or waiting out in the reception room. Though it wouldn't have been exactly a laugh to me.

I'd thought of all sorts of things to say to her when we did meet, but I didn't say any of them. I even forgot to take off my hat. I just said, "Hello, Evie. I didn't know you were in town," and she said, "Hello, Dick. I'm just here between trains"—and then we stared at each other.

I knew her right away, and yet I didn't know her, if you can get that. She was just as pretty as ever, but we weren't married any more. And then, her face was different. It didn't have that sort of quiet look on it when we were married. Of course, she'd let her hair grow too. She always had pretty hair. It had been five years. Well, there we were.

I must have looked like something, for, when we were out on the street she touched me on the arm.

"Don't worry, Dick," she said. "Everything's all right. I just thought, as long as I was in New York, it was silly not to see each other. Do you mind?"

"Not a bit," I said. . . . Well, you have to be polite, haven't you?

"How's Mr. Barris?" I said. . . . That's Evie's husband. It's a funny name.

"Oh, he's fine . . ." she said, "just fine."

"And the children?" I said. . . . I couldn't imagine them. "I suppose they're fine too?"

"Oh, they're fine," she said.

"Well, I'm glad to hear that, Evie," I said.

I don't know why it was so hard to talk; we ought to have been used to talking to each other.

She looked at me and laughed, quite the way she used to. "We can't stand here and gape at each other, Dick," she said.

"That's right," I said, so I flagged a taxi and told him Angelo's. Then I remembered she didn't like Angelo's. But she was decent and said that it was all right.

I'll hand it to Rocco. He knew who she was, all right, but he didn't even bat an eye—just took the order. We were the only people in the little room. She said she wanted some sherry; so that was that, with a double old-fashioned for me.

When he was gone, "Was that Rocco?" she said. "He didn't remember me."

"Well," said I, "you've been away a long time."

Then we looked at each other and knew we had nothing to say. She made rings with the bottom of the sherry glass.

"Oh, Dick," she said, "it's all so different from the way I thought it would be. Tell me about yourself."

"Oh, I'm still at the old stand," I said. "Same desk, as a matter of fact. Same salary, just about."

"How about the novel?"

"Oh," I said, "I'm working at it."

But she saw through me. "It's been five years," she said.

"A good idea's worth putting time on," said I, so she gave that up. Well, I wasn't going to cry on her.

"How about yourself?" said I. "Still living in Des Moines?"

"You know Mr. Barris lives in Cleveland," she said.

"I never can keep those two towns straight," I said. I felt better now, with that old-fashioned inside me, especially as Rocco was bringing another.

"Who came from Waynesburg?" she said, trying to kid me out of it.

"Me," I said. "But you'll have to admit I've come a long way."

I don't know why that made her look as if she wanted to cry. She hardly ever did cry—that was one thing about her.

"Oh, show me the snapshots!" I said. "I know you've got them." So she did. There was the house and the children and everything, including Mr. Barris in golf pants, and the family sedan. The little girl looks like Evie. That's a break for her. I don't know what our kids would have looked like. Terrible, I suppose.

I passed the pictures back. "They're nice," I said. "It's quite a house. I suppose you've even got a garbage incinerator."

"Of course," she said. "Why?"

"It looks like a house that would have a garbage incinerator," I said. "But you'd think Barris could afford a better car now he's a family man."

"Don't talk about George," she said.

"I'm through," I said. "So you're happy, Evie?"

She looked straight at me. "I am happy," she said—and that's the hell of it; I could see she was.

"Well," I said, "skoal!"—and that was the end of that old-fashioned. I was certainly coming back to normal in grand style. I could feel it creeping all over me. Then I heard her sort of talking to herself.

"It was a mistake," she was saying. "I ought to have known, but I couldn't help it. I thought—"

"Why say that?" I said. "It's always nice to revive

old times. . . . Rocco! . . . . Ah, there you are, sir. And
in a minute some of the crowd may blow in."

She started putting on her gloves. "I suppose they're
the same too," she said.

"Who?"

"Oh, the Parsons, and that man you called the Poached
Egg, and—what was her name?—Ruth something . . . .
and—"

"Wait a minute," I said. "You're moving too fast
for me. The Parsons broke up, and they say she's up
at Saranac for her lungs. I don't know whatever did
happen to the Poached Egg. As for that Ruth girl—well,
after Ted Harrison popped himself—"

"Ted Harrison?" she said. "Who was Ted Harrison?"

Well, there we were. We just didn't have any point
of contact at all. Of course, it wasn't her fault; she'd
been away, and you do get quick action in this town.
But she didn't even know who Ted Harrison had been.

"Oh, well," I said, "it doesn't signify. Just wait around
a little. Some people I want you to meet will be coming
in pretty soon. You'll like them; they're really awfully
nice people."

"I don't think I can wait, Dick," she said. "I've got
to get back to the hotel. I'm taking the night train."

"Back to Cleveland?" I said.

"Back to Cleveland," she said.

"Well," I said, "if you must, you must. And I won't
tell Barris on you." I felt pretty cheery by now. She
looked at me. "I'm sorry," I said.

"Oh, Dick, Dick!" she said. "Whatever are you going
to do with your life? You had such a lot. I can't stand it."

"If you mean my hair," I said, "it's the barber's fault,
not mine."

But she didn't pay any attention. "I didn't come back
to show off," she said. "Really I didn't. I hoped—I really
did—I'd come back and find you—"

"Clean and sober?" said I. "Well, I'm all of that."

"I—oh, what's the use?—I even thought you might be married."

"To some nice girl?" I said. "No, thanks. I've been."

"I held on as long as I could," she said.

"I'm not denying it," said I. "Let's leave it at that. No hard feelings."

She looked as if she wanted to say a whole lot more. Then she looked around the room and at Rocco coming in with the fresh supply. I don't know what she saw to make her look like that.

"No, it wouldn't have been," she said, sort of low to herself. "It couldn't have been. Good-by, Dick, and thank you."

"The pleasure is all mine," said I. "Only sorry you won't have another. Just a second and I'll get you a taxi."

But when I'd settled the bill and got my hat and coat, she was gone.

I went back to the little room and sat down again. I didn't feel like thinking, but I couldn't help it. For one thing, Evie's asking about all those people who had been in the crowd—why, they'd just disappeared. And I hadn't even realized it. Come to think of it, the only two left of that particular crowd who still came to Angelo's were Mr. Forman and myself. And what was that novel about that I'd been going to write?

"Rocco!" I called.

"Right with you, mister."

"You have the right idea," I said, but when he came in, I made him stay.

"Rocco," I said, "tell me something. How do I look today?"

"Oh, mister look ver' fine; seem ver' well."

That's the trouble with Rocco. He's always so darn pleasant.

"Don't two-time me, Rocco," I said. "Do you remember when I first started coming here?"

"Oh, yes: remember ver' well. Mister ver' good customer; ver' steady customer. Wish we had all like mister."

"Leave that outside," I said. "Just tell me one thing: Do I look a lot different?"

He spread out his hands. "Sure, mister look little different. Why not? Time pass. Rocco look different too."

"You're a liar," I said. "You haven't changed that Dago grin in twenty years. . . . All right, I look different, but how old do I look?"

He spread out his hands again. "Rocco don't know. Mister maybe forty, forty-one—mister in his prime."

"You low snake," I said. "I'm thirty-two." This was serious.

"Thirty-two? That's right. That's what Rocco mean" —and he grinned. But I didn't feel so funny.

"Tell me, Rocco," I said. "You've always been a friend of mine. Now be a friend. Tell me honestly. Do you think I drink too much?"

Gosh, you couldn't get anywhere with him! He just kept on grinning.

"Mister ver' good customer," he said; "ver' old, ver' steady customer. Mister carry what he drink ver' well."

"I know that!" I said. I was getting mad by now. "But is it too much? Be sensible, Rocco. I don't put away half what Mr. Forman does."

"Nobody drink so much as Mr. Forman. Some day Mr. Forman go pop. Rocco ver' sorry then, for Mr. Forman old customer."

"Well, that's a swell way of encouraging me. How about yourself, Rocco? How's your health?"

"Fine; thanks, mister. We have new bambino only other day."

"Well, I'm certainly glad to hear that. But look here, Rocco; you take a snifter—"

"Sure. Rocco drink wine—strega—ver' good. But Rocco have to work. Can't drink all time."

"I get that. But I work too."

"Sure, mister work. But Rocco work alla time. Rocco

have wife, tree bambini; have to work. Work to go back to Italy, buy *trattoria,* buy farm, have more bambini, be big man in town. That work for a man. Mister have another old-fashioned?"

He wouldn't talk any more. And the next one didn't go so well, because I'd started looking at myself in the mirror.

Oh, it just shows what a state I was in. And it shows you never ought to go back on your tracks. You know, for a while there I didn't like my face a bit.

That's why I say, modern or not, things like seeing Evie again don't do you any good. Because, when Mr. Forman came in and touched me on the shoulder, I jumped a mile. And just before I jumped I caught his face in the glass right over mine. I've apologized to him since, and I guess he's forgotten it. But they all must have thought I was crazy, running out like that and leaving the money on the table. And all that week I just got crazier and crazier, getting up and taking a cold shower in the mornings, and eating at tearooms and coming right back after dinner and hunting around to see if I could find whatever became of that novel. One good thing, I did get the room pretty well cleaned up. That woman who comes in never really cleans.

But what's the use of all that when you keep getting the fidgets? And getting the fidgets makes you think too much. Anyway, one evening it was nice and warm, and I thought, "I'll just take a walk. I can't sit here any more."

Well, I didn't have any particular direction in mind, but after a while, sure enough, there I was in front of Angelo's. Man, you should have seen the welcome they gave me. Angelo set up the drinks himself, and Rocco was grinning all over.

"Angelo think we lose our mos' steady customer," he said, "but mister come back. I know he come back."

And Mr. Forman never said a word about how I'd acted.

He wasn't a bit standoffish; in fact, Rocco had to ease him out at eleven that night.

Now, the only worry I've got is Angelo's retiring, as I say. But even if he does, maybe Rocco will keep the place on. Of course, even that would be a change, but I'd hardly mind. We've known each other a long while, and he knows I'm a good customer.

# THE CURFEW TOLLS

"It is not enough to be the possessor of genius—the time and the man must conjoin. An Alexander the Great, born into an age of profound peace, might scarce have troubled the world—a Newton, grown up in a thieves' den, might have devised little but a new and ingenious picklock. . . ."

*Diversions of Historical Thought by*
*John Cleveland Cotton.*

(The following extracts have been made from the letters of General Sir Charles William Geoffrey Estcourt, C.B., to his sister Harriet, Countess of Stokely, by permission of the Stokely family. Omissions are indicated by triple dots, thus . . .)

St. Philippe-des-Bains, September 3d, 1788.
My Dear Sister: . . . I could wish that my excellent Paris physician had selected some other spot for my convalescence. But he swears by the waters of St. Philip and I swear by him, so I must resign myself to a couple of yawning months ere my constitution mends. Nevertheless, you will get long letters from me, though I fear they may be dull ones. I cannot bring you the gossip of Baden or Aix—except for its baths. St. Philip is but one of a dozen small white towns on this agreeable coast. It has its good inn and its bad inn, its dusty, little square with its dusty, fleabitten beggar, its posting-station and its promenade of scrubby lindens and palms. From the heights one may see Corsica on a clear day, and the Mediterranean is of an unexampled blue. To tell the truth, it is all agreeable enough, and an old Indian campaigner, like myself, should not complain. I am well treated at the Cheval Blanc—am I not an English milord? —and my excellent Gaston looks after me devotedly.

But there is a blue-bottle drowsiness about small watering places out of season, and our gallant enemies, the French, know how to bore themselves more exquisitely in their provinces than any nation on earth. Would you think that the daily arrival of the diligence from Toulon would be an excitement? Yet it is to me, I assure you, and to all St. Philip. I walk, I take the waters, I read Ossian, I play piquet with Gaston, and yet I seem to myself but half-alive. . . .

. . . You will smile and say to me, "Dear brother, you have always plumed yourself on being a student of human nature. Is there no society, no character for you to study, even in St. Philippe-des-Bains?" My dear sister, I bend myself earnestly to that end, yet so far with little result. I have talked to my doctor—a good man but unpolished; I have talked to the curé—a good man but dull. I have even attempted the society of the baths, beginning with Monsieur le Marquis de la Percedragon, who has ninety-six quarterings, soiled wristbands, and a gloomy interest in my liver, and ending with Mrs. Macgregor Jenkins, a worthy and red-faced lady whose conversation positively cannonades with dukes and duchesses. But, frankly, I prefer my chair in the garden and my Ossian to any of them, even at the risk of being considered a bear. A witty scoundrel would be the veriest godsend to me, but do such exist in St. Philip? I trow not. As it is, in my weakened condition, I am positively agog when Gaston comes in every morning with his budget of village scandal. A pretty pass to come to, you will say, for a man who has served with Eyre Coote and but for the mutabilities of fortune, not to speak of a most damnable cabal . . . (A long passage dealing with General Estcourt's East Indian services and his personal and unfavorable opinion of Warren Hastings is here omitted from the manuscript.) . . . But, at fifty, a man is either a fool or a philosopher. Nevertheless, unless Gaston provides me with a character to try my wits on,

shortly, I shall begin to believe that they too have de-
teriorated with Indian suns. . . .

September 21st, 1788.
My Dear Sister: . . . Believe me, there is little sound-
ness in the views of your friend, Lord Martindale. The
French monarchy is not to be compared with our own,
but King Louis is an excellent and well-beloved prince,
and the proposed summoning of the States-General cannot but have the most salutary effect. . . . (Three pages
upon French politics and the possibility of cultivating
sugar-cane in Southern France are here omitted.) . . .
As for news of myself, I continue my yawning course,
and feel a decided improvement from the waters. . . .
So I shall continue them though the process is slow. . . .

You ask me, I fear a trifle mockingly, how my studies
in human nature proceed?

No so ill, my dear sister—I have, at least, scraped
acquaintance with one odd fish, and that, in St. Philip,
is a triumph. For some time, from my chair in the promenade, I have observed a pursy little fellow, of my age or
thereabouts, stalking up and down between the lindens.
His company seems avoided by such notables of the place
as Mrs. Macgregor Jenkins and at first I put him down as
a retired actor, for there is something a little theatrical
in his dress and walk. He wears a wide-brimmed hat of
straw, loose nankeen trousers and a quasi-military coat,
and takes his waters with as much ceremony as Monsieur ·
le Marquis, though not quite with the same *ton*. I should
put him down as a Meridional, for he has the quick, dark
eye, the sallow skin, the corpulence and the rodomontish
airs that mark your true son of the Midi, once he has
passed his lean and hungry youth.

And yet, there is some sort of unsuccessful oddity about
him, which sets him off from your successful bourgeois.
I cannot put my finger on it yet, but it interests me.

At any rate, I was sitting in my accustomed chair, reading Ossian, this morning, as he made his solitary rounds

of the promenade. Doubtless I was more than usually absorbed in my author, for I must have pronounced some lines aloud as he passed. He gave me a quick glance at the time, but nothing more. But on his next round, as he was about to pass me, he hesitated for a moment, stopped, and then, removing his straw hat, saluted me very civilly.

"Monsieur will pardon me," he said, with a dumpy hauteur, "but surely monsieur is English? And surely the lines that monsieur just repeated are from the great poet, Ossian?"

I admitted both charges, with a smile, and he bowed again.

"Monsieur will excuse the interruption," he said, "but I myself have long admired the poetry of Ossian"—and with that he continued my quotation to the end of the passage, in very fair English, too, though with a strong accent. I complimented him, of course, effusively—after all, it is not every day that one runs across a fellow-admirer of Ossian on the promenade of a small French watering place—and after that, he sat down in the chair beside me and we fell into talk. He seems, astonishingly for a Frenchman, to have an excellent acquaintance with our English poets—perhaps he has been a tutor in some English family. I did not press him with questions on this first encounter, though I noted that he spoke French with a slight accent also, which seems odd.

There is something a little rascally about him, to tell you the truth, though his conversation with me was both forceful and elevated. An ill man, too, and a disappointed one, or I miss my mark, yet his eyes, when he talks, are strangely animating. I fancy I would not care to meet him in a *guet-apens,* and yet, he may be the most harmless of broken pedagogues. We took a glass of waters together, to the great disgust of Mrs. Macgregor Jenkins, who ostentatiously drew her skirts aside. She let me know, afterward, in so many words, that my acquaintance was a noted bandit, though, when pressed, she could give no better reason than that he lives a little removed from the town, that "nobody knows where he comes from" and that his wife is "no better than she should be," whatever that portentous phrase entails. Well, one would hardly call him a gentleman, even by Mrs. Macgregor's somewhat easy standards, but he has given me better conversation than I have had in a month—and if he is, a bandit, we might discuss thuggee together. But I hope for nothing so stimulating, though I must question Gaston about him. . . .

October 11th.

. . . But Gaston could tell me little, except that my acquaintance comes from Sardinia or some such island originally, has served in the French army and is popularly supposed to possess the evil eye. About Madame he hinted that he could tell me a great deal, but I did not labor the point. After all, if my friend has been c-ck-ld-d—do not blush, my dear sister!—that, too, is the portion of a philosopher, and I find his wide range of conversation much more palatable than Mrs. Macgregor Jenkins' rewarmed London gossip. Nor has he tried to borrow money from me yet, something which, I am frank to say, I expected and was prepared to refuse. . . .

November 20th.

. . . Triumph! My character is found—and a character of the first water, I assure you! I have dined with him in his house, and a very bad dinner it was. Madame is not a good housekeeper, whatever else she may be. And what she has been, one can see at a glance—she has all the little faded coquetries of the garrison coquette. Good-tempered, of course, as such women often are, and must have been pretty in her best days, though with shocking bad teeth. I suspect her of a touch of the tarbrush, though there I may be wrong. No doubt she caught my friend young—I have seen the same thing happen in India often enough—the experienced woman and the youngster fresh from England. Well, 'tis an old story—an old one with him, too—and no doubt Madame has her charms, though she is obviously one reason why he has not risen.

After dinner, Madame departed, not very willingly, and he took me into his study for a chat. He had even procured a bottle of port, saying he knew the Englishman's taste for it, and while it was hardly the right Cockburn, I felt touched by the attention. The man is desperately lonely—one reads that in his big eyes. He is also desperately proud, with the quick, touchy sensitiveness of the failure, and I quite exerted myself to draw him out.

And indeed, the effort repaid me. His own story is simple enough. He is neither bandit nor pedagogue, but, like myself, a broken soldier—a major of the French Royal Artillery, retired on half pay for some years. I think it creditable of him to have reached so respectable a rank, for he is of foreign birth—Sardinian, I think I told you— and the French service is by no means as partial to foreigners as they were in the days of the first Irish Brigade. Moreover, one simply does not rise in that service, unless one is a gentleman of quarterings, and that he could hardly claim. But the passion of his life has been India, and that is what interests me. And, 'pon my honor, he was rather astonishing about it.

As soon as, by a lucky chance, I hit upon the subject, his eyes lit up and his sickness dropped away. Pretty soon he began to take maps from a cabinet in the wall and ply me with questions about my own small experiences. And very soon indeed, I am abashed to state, I found myself stumbling in my answers. It was all book knowledge on his part, of course, but where the devil he could have got some of it, I do not know. Indeed, he would even correct me, now and then, as cool as you please. "Eight twelve pounders, I think, on the north wall of the old fortifications of Madras——" and the deuce of it is, he would be right. Finally, I could contain myself no longer.

"But, major, this is incredible," I said. "I have served

twenty years with John Company and thought that I
had some knowledge. But one would say you had fought
over every inch of Bengal!"

He gave me a quick look, almost of anger, and began
to roll up his maps.

"So I have, in my mind," he said, shortly, "but, as my
superiors have often informed me, my hobby is a tedious
one."

"It is not tedious to me," I said boldly. "Indeed, I
have often marveled at your government's neglect of their
opportunities in India. True, the issue is settled now——"

"It is by no means settled," he said, interrupting me
rudely. I stared at him.

"It was settled, I believe, by Baron Clive, at a spot
named Plassey," I said frigidly. "And afterward, by my
own old general, Eyre Coote, at another spot named Wan-
dewash."

"Oh, yes—yes—yes," he said impatiently, "I grant you
Clive—Clive was a genius and met the fate of geniuses.
He steals an empire for you, and your virtuous English
Parliament holds up its hands in horror because he steals
a few lakhs of rupees for himself as well. So he blows out
his brains in disgrace—you inexplicable English!—and you
lose your genius. A great pity. I would not have treated
Clive so. But then, if I had been Milord Clive, I would
not have blown out my brains."

"And what would you have done, had you been Clive?"
I said, for the man's calm, staring conceit amused me.

His eyes were dangerous for a moment and I saw why
the worthy Mrs. Macgregor Jenkins had called him a
bandit.

"Oh," he said coolly, "I would have sent a file of grena-
diers to your English Parliament and told it to hold its
tongue. As Cromwell did. Now there was a man. But your
Clive—faugh!—he had the ball at his feet and he refused
to kick it. I withdraw the word genius. He was a nincom-
poop. At the least, he might have made himself a rajah."

This was a little too much, as you may imagine. "Gen-

eral Clive had his faults," I said icily, "but he was a true
Briton and a patriot."

"He was a fool," said my puffy little major, flatly, his
lower lip stuck out. "As big a fool as Dupleix, and that is
saying much. Oh, some military skill, some talent for
organization, yes. But a genius would have brushed him
into the sea! It was possible to hold Arcot, it was possible
to win Plassey—look!" and, with that, he ripped another
map from his cabinet and began to expound to me eagerly exactly what he would have done in command of the
French forces in India, in 1757, when he must have been
but a lad in his twenties. He thumped the paper, he
strewed corks along the table for his troops—corks taken
from a supply in a tin box, so it must be an old game
with him. And, as I listened, my irritation faded, for
the man's monomania was obvious. Nor was it, to tell
the truth, an ill-designed plan of campaign, for corks on
a map. Of course these things are different, in the field.

I could say, with honesty, that his plan had features
of novelty, and he gulped the words down hungrily—he
has a great appetite for flattery.

"Yes, yes," he said. "That is how it should be done—
the thickest skull can see it. And, ill as I am, with a fleet
and ten thousand picked men—- " He dreamed, obviously, the sweat of his exertions on his waxy face—it was ab-
surd and yet touching to see him dream.

"You would find a certain amount of opposition," I
said, in an amused voice.

"Oh, yes, yes," he said quickly, "I do not underrate
the English. Excellent horse, solid foot. But no true
knowledge of cannon, and I am a gunner——"

I hated to bring him down to earth and yet I felt that
I must.

"Of course, major," I said, "you have had great experience in the field."

He looked at me for a moment, his arrogance quite un-
shaken.

"I have had very little," he said, quietly, "but one

knows how the thing should be done or one does not know. And that is enough."

He stared at me for an instant with his big eyes. A little mad, of course. And yet I found myself saying, "But surely, major—what happened?"

"Why," he said, still quietly, "what happens to folk who have naught but their brains to sell? I staked my all on India when I was young—I thought that my star shone over it. I ate dirty puddings—*corpo di Baccho!*— to get there—I was no De Rohan or Soubise to win the king's favor! And I reached there indeed, in my youth, just in time to be included in the surrender of Pondicherry." He laughed, rather terribly, and sipped at his glass.

"You English were very courteous captors," he said. "But I was not released till the Seven Years War had ended—that was in '63. Who asks for the special exchange of an unknown artillery lieutenant? And then ten years odd of garrison duty at Mauritius. It was there that I met Madame—she is a Creole. A pleasant spot, Mauritius. We used to fire the cannon at the sea birds when we had enough ammunition for target practice," and he chuckled drearily. "By then I was thirty-seven. They had to make me a captain—they even brought me back to France. To garrison duty. I have been on garrison duty, at Toulon, at Brest, at——" He ticked off the names on his fingers but I did not like his voice.

"But surely," I said, "the American war, though a small affair—there were opportunities——"

"And who did they send?" he said quickly. "Lafayette —Rochambeau—De Grasse—the sprigs of the nobility. Oh, at Lafayette's age, I would have volunteered like Lafayette. But one should be successful in youth—after that, the spring is broken. And when one is over forty, one has responsibilities. I have a large family, you see, though not of my own begetting," and he chuckled as if at a secret joke. "Oh, I wrote the Continental Congress," he said reflectively, "but they preferred a dolt like Von Steuben.

A good dolt, an honest dolt, but there you have it. I also wrote your British War Office," he said in an even voice. "I must show you that plan of campaign—sometime—they could have crushed General Washington with it in three weeks."

I stared at him, a little appalled.

"For an officer who has taken his king's shilling to send to an enemy nation a plan for crushing his own country's ally," I said, stiffly—"well, in England, we would call that treason."

"And what is treason?" he said lightly. "If we call it unsuccessful ambition we shall be nearer the truth." He looked at me, keenly. "You are shocked, General Estcourt, he said. "I am sorry for that. But have you never known the curse"—and his voice vibrated—"the curse of not being employed when you should be employed? The curse of being a hammer with no nail to drive? The curse —the curse of sitting in a dusty garrison town with dreams that would split the brain of a Caesar, and no room on earth for those dreams?"

"Yes," I said, unwillingly, for there was something in him that demanded the truth, "I have known that."

"Then you know hells undreamed of by the Christian," he said, with a sigh, "and if I committed treason—well, I have been punished for it. I might have been a brigadier, otherwise—I had Choiseul's ear for a few weeks, after great labor. As it is, I am here on half pay, and there will not be another war in my time. Moreover, M. de Ségur has proclaimed that all officers now must show sixteen quarterings. Well, I wish them joy of those officers, in the next conflict. Meanwhile, I have my corks, my maps and my family ailment." He smiled and tapped his side. "It killed my father at thirty-nine—it has not treated me quite so ill, but it will come for me soon enough."

And indeed, when I looked at him, I could well believe it, for the light had gone from his eyes and his cheeks were flabby. We chatted a little on indifferent subjects after that, then I left him, wondering whether to pursue the acquaintance. He is indubitably a character, but some of his speeches leave a taste in my mouth. Yet he can be greatly attractive—even now, with his mountainous failure like a cloak upon him. And yet why should I call it mountainous? His conceit is mountainous enough, but what else could he have expected of his career? Yet I wish I could forget his eyes. . . . To tell the truth, he puzzles me and I mean to get to the bottom of him. . . .

February 12th, 1789.

. . . I have another sidelight on the character of my friend, the major. As I told you, I was half of a mind to break off the acquaintance entirely, but he came up to me so civilly, the following day, that I could find no excuse. And since then, he has made me no embarrassingly treasonable confidences, though whenever we discuss the art of war, his arrogance is unbelievable. He even informed me, the other day, that while Frederick of Prussia was a fair general, his tactics might have been improved upon. I merely laughed and turned the question. Now and then I play a war game with him, with his corks and maps, and when I let him win, he is as pleased as a child. . . . His illness increases visibly, despite the waters, and he shows an eagerness for my company which I cannot but find touching. . . . After all, he is a man of intelligence, and the company he has had to keep must have galled him at times. . . .

Now and then I amuse myself by speculating what might have happened to him, had he chosen some other profession than that of arms. He has, as I have told you, certain gifts of the actor, yet his stature and figure must have debarred him from tragic parts, while he certainly does not possess the humors of the comedian. Perhaps his best choice would have been the Romish church, for there, the veriest fisherman may hope, at least, to succeed to the keys of St. Peter. . . . And yet, Heaven knows, he would have made a very bad priest! . . .

But, to my tale. I had missed him from our accustomed

walks for some days and went to his house—St. Helen's
it is called; we live in a pother of saints' names hereabouts
—one evening to inquire. I did not hear the quarreling
voices till the tousle-haired servant had admitted me and
then it was too late to retreat. Then my friend bounced
down the corridor, his sallow face bored and angry.

"Ah, General Estcourt!" he said, with a complete
change of expression as soon as he saw me. "What fortune! I was hoping you would pay us a call—I wish to in-
troduce you to my family!"

He had told me previously of his pair of stepchildren
by Madame's first marriage, and I must confess I felt
curious to see them. But it was not of them he spoke, as I
soon gathered.

"Yes," he said. "My brothers and sisters, or most of
them, are here for a family council. You come in the nick
of time!" He pinched my arm and his face glowed with
the malicious naïveté of a child. "They do not believe that
I really know an English general—it will be a great blow
to them!" he whispered as we passed down the corridor.
"Ah, if you had only worn your uniform and your Garters! But one cannot have everything in life!"

Well, my dear sister, what a group, when we entered
the salon! It is a small room, tawdrily furnished in the
worst French taste, with a jumble of Madame's feminin-
ities and souvenirs from the Island of Mauritius, and they
were all sitting about in the French after-dinner fashion, drinking tisane and quarreling. And, indeed, had the
room been as long as the nave of St. Peter's, it would yet
have seemed too small for such a crew! An old mother,
straight as a ramrod and as forbidding, with the burning
eyes and the bitter dignity one sees on the faces of certain
Italian peasants—you could see that they were all a little
afraid of her except my friend, and he, I must say, treated
her with a filial courtesy that was greatly to his credit.
Two sisters, one fattish, swarthy and spiteful, the other
with the wreck of great beauty and the evident marks of a
certain profession on her shabby-fine *toilette* and her

pinkened cheeks. An innkeeper brother-in-law called
Buras or Durat, with a jowlish, heavily handsome face
and the manners of a cavalry sergeant—he is married to
the spiteful sister. And two brothers, one sheep-like, one
fox-like, yet both bearing a certain resemblance to my
friend.

The sheep-like brother is at least respectable, I gathered—a provincial lawyer in a small way of business whose
great pride is that he has actually appeared before the
Court of Appeals at Marseilles. The other, the fox-like
one, makes his living more dubiously—he seems the sort
of fellow who orates windily in taprooms about the
Rights of Man, and other nonsense of M. Rousseau's. I
would certainly not trust him with my watch, though he
is trying to get himself elected to the States-General. And
as regards family concord, it was obvious at first glance
that not one of them trusted the others. And yet, that is
not all of the tribe. There are, if you will believe me, two
other brothers living, and this family council was called to
deal with the affairs of the next-to-youngest, who seems
even in this mélange, to be a black sheep.

I can assure you, my head swam, and when my friend
introduced me, proudly, as a Knight of the Garters, I did
not even bother to contradict him. For they admitted me
to their intimate circle at once—there was no doubt about
that. Only the old lady remained aloof, saying little and
sipping her camomile tea as if it were the blood of her
enemies. But, one by one, the others related to me, with
an unasked-for frankness, the most intimate and scandal-
ous details of their brothers' and sisters' lives. They
seemed united only on two points, jealousy of my friend
the major, because he is his mother's favorite, and dislike
of Madame Josephine because she gives herself airs. Except for the haggard beauty—I must say, that, while her
remarks anent her sister-in-law were not such as I would
care to repeat, she seemed genuinely fond of her brother
the major, and expounded his virtues to me through an
overpowering cloud of scent.

It was like being in a nest of Italian smugglers, or a den of quarrelsome foxes, for they all talked, or rather barked at once, even the brother-in-law, and only Madame Mère could bring silence among them. And yet, my friend enjoyed it. It was obvious he showed them off before me as he might have displayed the tricks of a set of performing animals. And yet with a certain fondness, too —that is the inexplicable part of it. I do not know which sentiment was upmost in my mind—respect for this family feeling or pity for his being burdened with such a clan.

For though not the eldest, he is the strongest among them, and they know it. They rebel, but he rules their family conclaves like a petty despot. I could have laughed at the farce of it, and yet, it was nearer tears. For here, at least, my friend was a personage.

I got away as soon as I could, despite some pressing looks from the haggard beauty. My friend accompanied me to the door.

"Well, well," he said, chuckling and rubbing his hands, "I am infinitely obliged to you, general. They will not forget this in a hurry. Before you entered, Joseph"—Joseph is the sheep-like one—"was boasting about his acquaintance with a *sous-intendant,* but an English general, bah! Joseph will have green eyes for a fortnight!" And he rubbed his hands again in a perfect paroxysm of delight.

It was too childlike to make me angry. "I am glad, of course, to have been of any service," I said.

"Oh, you have been a great service," he said. "They will not plague my poor Josie for at least half an hour. Ah, this is a bad business of Louis'—a bad business!"—Louis is the black sheep—"but we will patch it up somehow. Hortense is worth three of him—he must go back to Hortense!"

"You have a numerous family, major," I said, for want of something better to say.

"Oh, yes," he said, cheerfully. "Pretty numerous—I am sorry you could not meet the others. Though Louis is a

fool—I pampered him in his youth. Well! He was a baby
—and Jerome a mule. Still, we haven't done so badly for
ourselves; not badly. Joseph makes a go of his law practice
—there are fools enough in the world to be impressed by
Joseph—and if Lucien gets to the States-General, you may
trust Lucien to feather his nest! And there are the grandchildren, and a little money—not much," he said, quickly. "They mustn't expect that from me. But it's a step up
from where we started—if papa had lived, he wouldn't
have been so ill-pleased. Poor Elisa's gone, but the rest of
us have stuck together, and, while we may seem a little
rough, to strangers, our hearts are in the right place.
When I was a boy," and he chuckled again, "I had other
ambitions for them. I thought, with luck on my side, I
could make them all kings and queens. Funny, isn't it, to
think of a numskull like Joseph as a king! Well, that was
the boy of it. But, even so, they'd all be eating chestnuts
back on the island without me, and that's something."

He said it rather defiantly, and I did not know which
to marvel at most—his preposterous pride in the group or
his cool contempt of them. So I said nothing but shook
his hand instead. I could not help doing the latter. For
surely, if anyone started in life with a millstone about
his neck . . . and yet they are none of them ordinary
people. . . .

March 13th, 1789.
. . . My friend's complaint has taken a turn for the
worse and it is I who pay him visits now. It is the act of
a Christian to do so and, to tell the truth, I have become
oddly attached to him, though I can give no just reason
for the attachment. He makes a bad patient, by the way,
and is often abominably rude to both myself and Madame, who nurses him devotedly though unskillfully. I
told him yesterday that I could have no more of it and he
looked at me with his strangely luminous eyes. "So," he
said, "even the English desert the dying." . . . Well, I
stayed; after that, what else might a gentleman do? . . .

Yet I cannot feel that he bears me any real affection—he exerts himself to charm, on occasion, but one feels he is playing a game . . . yes, even upon his deathbed, he plays a game . . . a complex character. . . .

April 28th, 1789.
. . . My friend the major's malady approaches its term —the last few days find him fearfully enfeebled. He knows that the end draws nigh; indeed he speaks of it often, with remarkable calmness. I had thought it might turn his mind toward religion, but while he has accepted the ministrations of his Church, I fear it is without the sincere repentance of a Christian. When the priest had left him, yesterday, he summoned me, remarking, "Well, all that is over with," rather more in the tone of a man who has just reserved a place in a coach than one who will shortly stand before his Maker.

"It does no harm," he said, reflectively. "And, after all, it might be true. Why not?" and he chuckled in a way that repelled me. Then he asked me to read to him— not the Bible, as I had expected, but some verses of the poet Gray. He listened attentively, and when I came to the passage, "Hands, that the rod of empire might have swayed," and its successor, "Some mute inglorious Milton here may rest," he asked me to repeat them. When I had done so, he said, "Yes, yes. That is true, very true. I did not think so in boyhood—I thought genius must force its own way. But your poet is right about it."

I found this painful, for I had hoped that his illness had brought him to a juster, if less arrogant, estimate of his own abilities.

"Come, major," I said, soothingly, "we cannot all be great men, you know. And you have no need to repine. After all, as you say, you have risen in the world——"

"Risen?" he said, and his eyes flashed. "Risen? Oh, God, that I should die alone with my one companion an Englishman with a soul of suet! Fool, if I had had Alexander's chance, I would have bettered Alexander! And it will

come, too, that is the worst of it. Already Europe is shaking with a new birth. If I had been born under the Sun-
King, I would be a Marshal of France; if I had been
born twenty years ago, I would mold a new Europe with
my fists in the next half-dozen years. Why did they put
my soul in my body at this infernal time? Do you not
understand, imbecile? Is there no one who understands?"
    I called Madame at this, as he was obviously delirious,
and, after some trouble, we got him quieted.

May 8th, 1789.

. . . My poor friend is gone, and peacefully enough at
the last. His death, oddly enough, coincided with the date
of the opening of the States-General at Versailles. The last
moments of life are always painful for the observer, but
his end was as relatively serene as might be hoped for,
considering his character. I was watching at one side of
the bed and a thunderstorm was raging at the time. No
doubt, to his expiring consciousness, the cracks of the
thunder sounded like artillery, for, while we were waiting
the death-struggle, he suddenly raised himself in the bed
and listened intently. His eyes glowed, a beatific expression passed over his features. "The army! Head of the
army!" he whispered ecstatically, and, when we caught
him, he was lifeless . . . I must say that, while it may not
be very Christian, I am glad that death brought him what
life could not, and that, in the very article of it, he saw
himself at the head of victorious troops. Ah, Fame—delusive spectre . . . (A page of disquisition by General
Estcourt on the vanities of human ambition is here
omitted.) . . . The face, after death, was composed, with
a certain majesty, even . . . one could see that he might
have been handsome as a youth. . . .

May 26th, 1789.

. . . I shall return to Paris by easy stages and reach
Stokely sometime in June. My health is quite restored
and all that has kept me here this long has been the dif-

ficulty I have met with in attempting to settle my poor friend, the major's affairs. For one thing, he apppears to have been originally a native of Corsica, not of Sardinia as I had thought, and while that explains much in his character, it has also given occupation to the lawyers. I have met his rapacious family, individually and in conclave, and, if there are further gray hairs on my head, you may put it down to them. . . . However, I have finally assured the major's relict of her legitimate rights in his estate, and that is something—my one ray of comfort in the matter being the behavior of her son by the former marriage, who seems an excellent and virtuous young man. . . .

. . . You will think me a very soft fellow, no doubt, for wasting so much time upon a chance acquaintance who was neither, in our English sense, a gentleman nor a man whose Christian virtues counterbalanced his lack of true breeding. Yet there was a tragedy about him beyond his station, and that verse of Gray's rings in my head. I wish I could forget the expression on his face when he spoke of it. Suppose a genius born in circumstances that made the development of that genius impossible—well, all this is the merest moonshine. . . .

. . . To revert to more practical matters, I discover that the major has left me his military memoirs, papers and commentaries, including his maps. Heaven knows what I shall do with them! I cannot, in courtesy, burn them *sur-le-champ,* and yet they fill two huge packing cases and the cost of transporting them to Stokely will be considerable. Perhaps I will take them to Paris and quietly dispose of them there to some waste-paper merchant. . . . In return for this unsought legacy, Madame has consulted me in regard to a stone and epitaph for her late husband, and, knowing that otherwise the family would squabble over the affair for weeks, I have drawn up a design which I hope meets with their approval. It appears that he particularly desired that the epitaph should be writ in English, saying that France had had enough of him, living—a freak of dying vanity for which one must pardon him. However, I have produced the following, which I hope will answer.

Here lies
NAPOLEONE BOUNAPARTE
Major of the Royal Artillery
of France.
Born August 15th, 1737
at Ajaccio, Corsica.
Died May 5th, 1789
at St. Philippe-des-Bains

"Rest, perturbed spirit . . ."

. . . I had thought, for some hours, of excerpting the lines of Gray's—the ones that still ring in my head. But, on reflection, though they suit well enough, they yet seem too cruel to the dust.

# BY THE WATERS OF BABYLON

The north and the west and the south are good hunting ground, but it is forbidden to go east. It is forbidden to go to any of the Dead Places except to search for metal and then he who touches the metal must be a priest or the son of a priest. Afterwards, both the man and the metal must be purified. These are the rules and the laws; they are well made. It is forbidden to cross the great river and look upon the place that was the Place of the Gods —this is most strictly forbidden. We do not even say its name though we know its name. It is there that spirits live, and demons—it is there that there are the ashes of the Great Burning. These things are forbidden—they have been forbidden since the beginning of time.

My father is a priest; I am the son of a priest. I have been in the Dead Places near us, with my father—at first, I was afraid. When my father went into the house to search for the metal, I stood by the door and my heart felt small and weak. It was a dead man's house, a spirit house. It did not have the smell of man, though there were old bones in a corner. But it is not fitting that a priest's son should show fear. I looked at the bones in the shadow and kept my voice still.

Then my father came out with the metal—a good, strong piece. He looked at me with both eyes but I had not run away. He gave me the metal to hold—I took it and did not die. So he knew that I was truly his son and would be a priest in my time. That was when I was very young—nevertheless, my brothers would not have done it, though they are good hunters. After that, they gave me the good piece of meat and the warm corner by the fire.

My father watched over me—he was glad that I should be a priest. But when I boasted or wept without a reason, he punished me more strictly than my brothers. That was right.

After a time, I myself was allowed to go into the dead houses and search for metal. So I learned the ways of those houses—and if I saw bones, I was no longer afraid. The bones are light and old—sometimes they will fall into dust if you touch them. But that is a great sin.

I was taught the chants and the spells—I was taught how to stop the running of blood from a wound and many secrets. A priest must know many secrets—that was what my father said. If the hunters think we do all things by chants and spells, they may believe so—it does not hurt them. I was taught how to read in the old books and how to make the old writings—that was hard and took a long time. My knowledge made me happy—it was like a fire in my heart. Most of all, I liked to hear of the Old Days and the stories of the gods.I asked myself many questions that I could not answer, but it was good to ask them. At night, I would lie awake and listen to the wind—it seemed to me that it was the voice of the gods as they flew through the air.

We are not ignorant like the Forest People—our women spin wool on the wheel, our priests wear a white robe. We do not eat grubs from the tree, we have not forgotten the old writings, although they are hard to understand. Nevertheless, my knowledge and my lack of knowledge burned in me—I wished to know more. When I was a man at last, I came to my father and said, "It is time for me to go on my journey. Give me your leave."

He looked at me for a long time, stroking his beard, then he said at last, "Yes. It is time." That night, in the house of the priesthood, I asked for and received purification. My body hurt but my spirit was a cool stone. It was my father himself who questioned me about my dreams.

He bade me look into the smoke of the fire and see—I saw and told what I saw. It was what I have always seen—a river, and, beyond it, a great Dead Place and in it the gods walking. I have always thought about that. His eyes were stern when I told him—he was no longer my father but a priest. He said, "This is a strong dream."

"It is mine," I said, while the smoke waved and my head felt light. They were singing the Star song in the outer chamber and it was like the buzzing of bees in my head.

He asked me how the gods were dressed and I told him how they were dressed. We know how they were dressed from the book, but I saw them as if they were before me. When I had finished, he threw the sticks three times and studied them as they fell.

"This is a very strong dream," he said. "It may eat you up."

"I am not afraid," I said and looked at him with both eyes. My voice sounded thin in my ears but that was because of the smoke.

He touched me on the breast and the forehead. He gave me the bow and the three arrows.

"Take them," he said. "It is forbidden to travel east. It is forbidden to cross the river. It is forbidden to go to the Place of the Gods. All these things are forbidden."

"All these things are forbidden," I said, but it was my voice that spoke and not my spirit. He looked at me again.

"My son," he said. "Once I had young dreams. If your dreams do not eat you up, you may be a great priest. If they eat you, you are still my son. Now go on your journey."

I went fasting, as is the law. My body hurt but not my heart. When the dawn came, I was out of sight of the village. I prayed and purified myself, waiting for a sign. The sign was an eagle. It flew east.

Sometimes signs are sent by bad spirits. I waited again on the flat rock, fasting, taking no food. I was very still— I could feel the sky above me and the earth beneath. I waited till the sun was beginning to sink. Then three deer passed in the valley, going east—they did not wind me or see me. There was a white fawn with them—a very great sign.

I followed them, at a distance, waiting for what would happen. My heart was troubled about going east, yet I knew that I must go. My head hummed with my fasting —I did not even see the panther spring upon the white fawn. But, before I knew it, the bow was in my hand. I shouted and the panther lifted his head from the fawn. It is not easy to kill a panther with one arrow but the arrow went through his eye and into his brain. He died as he tried to spring—he rolled over, tearing at the ground. Then I knew I was meant to go east—I knew that was my journey. When the night came, I made my fire and roasted meat.

It is eight suns journey to the east and a man passes by many Dead Places. The Forest People are afraid of them but I am not. Once I made my fire on the edge of a Dead Place at night and, next morning, in the dead house, I found a good knife, little rusted. That was small to what came afterward but it made my heart feel big. Always when I looked for game, it was in front of my arrow, and twice I passed hunting parties of the Forest People without their knowing. So I knew my magic was strong and my journey clean, in spite of the law.

Toward the setting of the eighth sun, I came to the banks of the great river. It was half-a-day's journey after I had left the god-road—we do not use the god-roads now for they are falling apart into great blocks of stone, and the forest is safer going. A long way off, I had seen the water through trees but the trees were thick. At last, I came out upon an open place at the top of a cliff. There was the great river below, like a giant in the sun. It is very long, very wide. It could eat all the streams we know and still be thirsty. Its name is Ou-dis-sun, the Sacred, the Long. No man of my tribe had seen it, not even my father, the priest. It was magic and I prayed.

Then I raised my eyes and looked south. It was there, the Place of the Gods.

How can I tell what it was like—you do not know. It was there, in the red light, and they were too big to be houses. It was there with the red light upon it, mighty and ruined. I knew that in another moment the gods would see me. I covered my eyes with my hands and crept back into the forest.

Surely, that was enough to do, and live. Surely it was enough to spend the night upon the cliff. The Forest People themselves do not come near. Yet, all through the night, I knew that I should have to cross the river and walk in the places of the gods, although the gods ate me up. My magic did not help me at all and yet there was a fire in my bowels, a fire in my mind. When the sun rose, I thought, "My journey has been clean. Now I will go home from my journey." But, even as I thought so, I knew I could not. If I went to the place of the gods, I would surely die, but, if I did not go, I could never be at peace with my spirit again. It is better to lose one's life than one's spirit, if one is a priest and the son of a priest.

Nevertheless, as I made the raft, the tears ran out of my eyes. The Forest People could have killed me without fight, if they had come upon me then, but they did not come. When the raft was made, I said the sayings for the dead and painted myself for death. My heart was cold as a frog and my knees like water, but the burning in my mind would not let me have peace. As I pushed the raft from the shore, I began my death song—I had the right. It was a fine song.

"I am John, son of John," I sang. "My people are the Hill People. They are the men.
I go into the Dead Places but I am not slain.
I take the metal from the Dead Places but I am not blasted.
I travel upon the god-roads and am not afraid. E-yah! I have killed the panther, I have killed the fawn!
E-yah! I have come to the great river. No man has come there before.

It is forbidden to go east, but I have gone, forbidden to go on the
    great river, but I am there.
Open your hearts, you spirits, and hear my song.
Now I go to the place of the gods, I shall not return.
My body is painted for death and my limbs weak, but my heart is
    big as I go to the place of the gods!"

All the same, when I came to the Place of the Gods, I
was afraid, afraid. The current of the great river is very
strong—it gripped my raft with its hands. That was magic,
for the river itself is wide and calm. I could feel evil
spirits about me, in the bright morning; I could feel their
breath on my neck as I was swept down the stream. Never
have I been so much alone—I tried to think of my knowledge, but it was a squirrel's heap of winter nuts. There
was no strength in my knowledge any more and I felt
small and naked as a new-hatched bird—alone upon the
great river, the servant of the gods.

Yet, after a while, my eyes were opened and I saw. I
saw both banks of the river—I saw that once there had
been god-roads across it, though now they were broken
and fallen like broken vines. Very great they were, and
wonderful and broken—broken in the time of the Great
Burning when the fire fell out of the sky. And always the
current took me nearer to the Place of the Gods, and the
huge ruins rose before my eyes.

I do not know the customs of rivers—we are the People of the Hills. I tried to guide my raft with the pole
but it spun around. I thought the river meant to take
me past the Place of the Gods and out into the Bitter
Water of the legends. I grew angry then—my heart felt
strong. I said aloud, "I am a priest and the son of a
priest!" The gods heard me—they showed me how to pad-
dle with the pole on one side of the raft. The current
changed itself—I drew near to the Place of the Gods.

When I was very near, my raft struck and turned over.
I can swim in our lakes—I swam to the shore. There was
a great spike of rusted metal sticking out into the river
—I hauled myself up upon it and sat there, panting. I

had saved my bow and two arrows and the knife I found in the Dead Place but that was all. My raft went whirling downstream toward the Bitter Water. I looked after it, and thought if it had trod me under, at least I would be safely dead. Nevertheless, when I had dried my bow-string and re-strung it, I walked forward to the Place of the Gods.

It felt like ground underfoot; it did not burn me. It is not true what some of the tales say, that the ground there burns forever, for I have been there. Here and there were the marks and stains of the Great Burning, on the ruins, that is true. But they were old marks and old stains. It is not true either, what some of our priests say, that it is an island covered with fogs and enchantments. It is not. It is a great Dead Place— greater than any Dead Place we know. Everywhere in it there are god-roads, though most are cracked and broken. Everywhere there are the ruins of the high towers of the gods.

How shall I tell what I saw? I went carefully, my strung bow in my hand, my skin ready for danger. There should have been the wailings of spirits and the shrieks of demons, but there were not. It was very silent and sunny where I had landed—the wind and the rain and the birds that drop seeds had done their work—the grass grew in the cracks of the broken stone. It is a fair island—no wonder the gods built there. If I had come there, a god, I also would have built.

How shall I tell what I saw? The towers are not all broken—here and there one still stands, like a great tree in a forest, and the birds nest high. But the towers themselves look blind, for the gods are gone. I saw a fish-hawk, catching fish in the river. I saw a little dance of white butterflies over a great heap of broken stones and columns. I went there and looked about me—there was a carved stone with cut-letters, broken in half. I can read letters but I could not understand these. They said UB-TREAS. There was also the shattered image of a man or a god. It had been made of white stone and he wore his hair tied back like a woman's. His name was ASHING, as I read on the cracked half of a stone. I thought it wise to pray to ASHING, though I do not know that god.

How shall I tell what I saw? There was no smell of man left, on stone or metal. Nor were there many trees in that wilderness of stone. There are many pigeons, nesting and dropping in the towers—the gods must have loved them, or, perhaps, they used them for sacrifices. There are wild cats that roam the god-roads, green-eyed, unafraid of man. At night they wail like demons but they are not demons. The wild dogs are more dangerous, for they hunt in a pack, but them I did not meet till later. Everywhere there are the carved stones, carved with magical numbers or words.

I went North—I did not try to hide myself. When a god or a demon saw me, then I would die, but meanwhile I was no longer afraid. My hunger for knowledge burned in me—there was so much that I could not understand. After awhile, I knew that my belly was hungry. I could have hunted for my meat, but I did not hunt. It is known that the gods did not hunt as we do—they got their food from enchanted boxes and jars. Sometimes these are still found in the Dead Places—once, when I was a child and foolish, I opened such a jar and tasted it and found the food sweet. But my father found out and punished me for it strictly, for, often, that food is death. Now, though, I had long gone past what was forbidden, and I entered the likeliest towers, looking for the food of the gods.

I found it at last in the ruins of a great temple in the mid-city. A mighty temple it must have been, for the roof was painted like the sky at night with its stars—that much I could see, though the colors were faint and dim. It went down into great caves and tunnels—perhaps they kept their slaves there. But when I started to climb down, I heard the squeaking of rats, so I did not go—rats are unclean, and there must have been many tribes of them, from the squeaking. But near there, I found food, in the heart of a ruin, behind a door that still opened. I ate only the fruits from the jars—they had a very sweet taste. There was drink, too, in bottles of glass—the drink of the gods was strong and made my head swim. After I had eaten and drunk, I slept on the top of a stone, my bow at my side.

When I woke, the sun was low. Looking down from where I lay, I saw a dog sitting on his haunches. His tongue was hanging out of his mouth; he looked as if he were laughing. He was a big dog, with a grey-brown coat, as big as a wolf. I sprang up and shouted at him but he did not move—he just sat there as if he were laughing. I did not like that. When I reached for a stone to throw, he moved swiftly out of the way of the stone. He was not afraid of me; he looked at me as if I were meat. No doubt I could have killed him with an arrow, but I did not know if there were others. Moreover, night was falling.

I looked about me—not far away there was a great, broken god-road, leading North. The towers were high enough, but not so high, and while many of the dead-houses were wrecked, there were some that stood. I went toward this god-road, keeping to the heights of the ruins, while the dog followed. When I had reached the god-road, I saw that there were others behind him. If I had slept later, they would have come upon me asleep and torn out my throat. As it was, they were sure enough of me; they did not hurry. When I went into the dead-house, they kept watch at the entrance—doubtless they thought they would have a fine hunt. But a dog cannot open a door and I knew, from the books, that the gods did not like to live on the ground but on high.

I had just found a door I could open when the dogs decided to rush. Ha! They were surprised when I shut the door in their faces—it was a good door, of strong metal. I could hear their foolish baying beyond it but I did not stop to answer them. I was in darkness—I found stairs and climbed. There were many stairs, turning around till my head was dizzy. At the top was another door—I found the knob and opened it. I was in a long small chamber —on one side of it was a bronze door that could not be opened, for it had no handle. Perhaps there was a magic word to open it but I did not have the word. I turned to the door in the opposite side of the wall. The lock of it was broken and I opened it and went in.

Within, there was a place of great riches. The god who lived there must have been a powerful god. The first room was a small ante-room—I waited there for some time, telling the spirits of the place that I came in peace and not as a robber. When it seemed to me that they had had time to hear me, I went on. Ah, what riches! Few, even, of the windows had been broken—it was all as it had been. The great windows that looked over the city had not been broken at all though they were dusty and streaked with many years. There were coverings on the floors, the colors not greatly faded, and the chairs were soft and deep. There were pictures upon the walls, very strange, very wonder- ful—I remember one of a bunch of flowers in a jar—if you came close to it, you could see nothing but bits of color, but if you stood away from it, the flowers might have been picked yesterday. It made my heart feel strange to look at this picture—and to look at the figure of a bird, in some hard clay, on a table and see it so like our birds. Everywhere there were books and writings, many in tongues that I could not read. The god who lived there must have been a wise god and full of knowledge. I felt I had right there, as I sought knowledge also.

Nevertheless, it was strange. There was a washing-place but no water—perhaps the gods washed in air. There was a cooking-place but no wood, and though there was a machine to cook food, there was no place to put fire in it. Nor were there candles or lamps—there were things that looked like lamps but they had neither oil nor wick. All these things were magic, but I touched them and lived— the magic had gone out of them. Let me tell one thing to show. In the washing-place, a thing said "Hot" but it was not hot to the touch—another thing said "Cold" but it was not cold. This must have been a strong magic but the magic was gone. I do not understand—they had ways—I wish that I knew.

It was close and dry and dusty in their house of the gods. I have said the magic was gone but that is not true —it had gone from the magic things but it had not gone from the place. I felt the spirits about me, weighing upon me. Nor had I ever slept in a Dead Place before—and yet, tonight, I must sleep there. When I thought of it, my tongue felt dry in my throat, in spite of my wish for knowledge. Almost I would have gone down again and faced the dogs, but I did not.

I had not gone through all the rooms when the darkness fell. When it fell, I went back to the big room looking over the city and made fire. There was a place to make fire and a box with wood in it, though I do not think they cooked there. I wrapped myself in a floor-covering and slept in front of the fire—I was very tired.

Now I tell what is very strong magic. I woke in the midst of the night. When I woke, the fire had gone out and I was cold. It seemed to me that all around me there were whisperings and voices. I closed my eyes to shut them out. Some will say that I slept again, but I do not think that I slept. I could feel the spirits drawing my spirit out of my body as a fish is drawn on a line.

Why should I lie about it? I am a priest and the son of a priest. If there are spirits, as they say, in the small Dead Places near us, what spirits must there not be in that great Place of the Gods? And would not they wish to speak? After such long years? I know that I felt myself drawn as a fish is drawn on a line. I had stepped out of my body—I could see my body asleep in front of the cold fire, but it was not I. I was drawn to look out upon the city of the gods.

It should have been dark, for it was night, but it was not dark. Everywhere there were lights—lines of light— circles and blurs of light—ten thousand torches would not have been the same. The sky itself was alight—you could barely see the stars for the glow in the sky. I thought to myself "This is strong magic" and trembled. There was a roaring in my ears like the rushing of rivers. Then my eyes grew used to the light and my ears to the sound. I knew that I was seeing the city as it had been when the gods were alive.

That was a sight indeed—yes, that was a sight: I could not have seen it in the body—my body would have died. Everywhere went the gods, on foot and in chariots—there were gods beyond number and counting and their chariots blocked the streets. They had turned night to day for their pleasure—they did not sleep with the sun. The noise of their coming and going was the noise of many waters. It was magic what they could do—it was magic what they did.

I looked out of another window—the great vines of their bridges were mended and the god-roads went East and West. Restless, restless, were the gods and always in motion! They burrowed tunnels under rivers—they flew in the air. With unbelievable tools they did giant works —no part of the earth was safe from them, for, if they wished for a thing, they summoned it from the other side of the world. And always, as they labored and rested, as they feasted and made love, there was a drum in their ears—the pulse of the giant city, beating and beating like a man's heart.

Were they happy? What is happiness to the gods? They were great, they were mighty, they were wonderful and terrible. As I looked upon them and their magic, I felt like a child—but a little more, it seemed to me, and they would pull down the moon from the sky. I saw them with wisdom beyond wisdom and knowledge beyond knowledge. And yet not all they did was well done—even I could see that—and yet their wisdom could not but grow until all was peace.

Then I saw their fate come upon them and that was

terrible past speech. It came upon them as they walked the streets of their city. I have been in the fights with the Forest People—I have seen men die. But this was not like that. When gods war with gods, they use weapons we do not know. It was fire falling out of the sky and a mist that poisoned. It was the time of the Great Burning and the Destruction. They ran about like ants in the streets of their city—poor gods, poor gods! Then the towers began to fall. A few escaped—yes, a few. The legends tell it. But, even after the city had become a Dead Place, for many years the poison was still in the ground. I saw it happen, I saw the last of them die. It was darkness over the broken city and I wept.

All this, I saw. I saw it as I have told it, though not in the body. When I woke in the morning, I was hungry, but I did not think first of my hunger for my heart was perplexed and confused. I knew the reason for the Dead Places but I did not see why it had happened. It seemed to me it should not have happened, with all the magic they had. I went through the house looking for an answer. There was so much in the house I could not understand— and yet I am a priest and the son of a priest. It was like being on one side of the great river, at night, with no light to show the way.

Then I saw the dead god. He was sitting in his chair, by the window, in a room I had not entered before and, for the first moment, I thought that he was alive. Then I saw the skin on the back of his hand—it was like dry leather. The room was shut, hot and dry—no doubt that had kept him as he was. At first I was afraid to approach him— then the fear left me. He was sitting looking out over the city—he was dressed in the clothes of the gods. His age was neither young nor old—I could not tell his age. But there was wisdom in his face and great sadness. You could see that he would have not run away. He had sat at his window, watching his city die—then he himself had died.

But it is better to lose one's life than one's spirit—and you could see from the face that his spirit had not been lost. I knew, that, if I touched him, he would fall into dust—and yet, there was something unconquered in the face.

That is all of my story, for then I knew he was a man —I knew then that they had been men, neither gods nor demons. It is a great knowledge, hard to tell and believe. They were men—they went a dark road, but they were men. I had no fear after that—I had no fear going home, though twice I fought off the dogs and once I was hunted for two days by the Forest People. When I saw my father again, I prayed and was purified. He touched my lips and my breast, he said, "You went away a boy. You come back a man and a priest." I said, "Father, they were men! I have been in the Place of the Gods and seen it! Now slay me, if it is the law—but still I know they were men."

He looked at me out of both eyes. He said, "The law is not always the same shape—you have done what you have done. I could not have done it my time, but you come after me. Tell!"

I told and he listened. After that, I wished to tell all the people but he showed me otherwise. He said, "Truth is a hard deer to hunt. If you eat too much truth at once, you may die of the truth. It was not idly that our fathers forbade the Dead Places." He was right—it is better the truth should come little by little. I have learned that, being a priest. Perhaps, in the old days, they ate knowledge too fast.

Nevertheless, we make a beginning. It is not for the metal alone we go to the Dead Places now—there are the books and the writings. They are hard to learn. And the magic tools are broken—but we can look at them and wonder. At least, we make a beginning. And, when I am chief priest we shall go beyond the great river. We shall

go to the Place of the Gods—the place newyork—not one
man but a company. We shall look for the images of the
gods and find the god ASHING and the others—the gods
Licoln and Biltmore and Moses. But they were men who
built the city, not gods or demons. They were men. I
remember the dead man's face. They were men who were
here before us. We must build again.

# THE LAST OF THE LEGIONS

The governor wanted to have everything go off as quietly as possible, but he couldn't keep the people from the windows or off the streets. After all, the legion had been at Deva ever since there was a town to speak of, and now we were going away. I don't want to say anything against the Sixth or the Second—there are good men under all the eagles. But we're not called the Valeria Victrix for nothing, and we've had the name some few centuries. It takes a legion with men in it to hold the northwest.

I think, at first, they intended to keep the news secret, but how could you do that, in a town? There's always someone who tells his girl in strict confidence, and then there are all the peddlers and astrologers and riffraff, and the sharp-faced boys with tips on the races or the games. I tell you, they knew about it as soon as the general or the governor—not to speak of the rumors before. As a matter of fact, there had been so many rumors that, when the orders came at last, it was rather a relief. You get tired of telling women that nothing will happen to them even if the legion does go, and being stopped five times in ten minutes whenever you go into town.

All the same, I had to sit up half the night with one recruit of ours. He had a girl in the town he was mad about, and a crazy notion of deserting. I had to point out to the young imbecile that even if the legion goes, Rome stays, and describe the two men I'd happened to see flogged to death, before he changed his mind. The girl was a pretty little weak-mouthed thing—she was crying in the crowd when we marched by, and he bit his lips to keep steady. But I couldn't have him deserting out of

231

our cohort—we haven't had a thing like that happen in twenty years.

It was queer, their not making more noise. They tried to cheer—governor's orders—when we turned the camp over to the native auxiliaries in the morning, but it wasn't much of a success. And yet, the auxiliaries looked well enough, for auxiliaries. I wouldn't give two cohorts of Egyptians for them myself, but they had their breast-plates shined and kept a fairly straight front. I imagined they'd dirty up our quarters—auxiliaries always do—and that wasn't pleasant to think of. But the next legion that came to Deva—us or another—would put things straight again. And it couldn't be long.

Then we had our own march past—through the town—and, as I say, it was queer. I'm a child of the camp—I was brought up in the legion. The tale is that the first of us came with Caesar—I don't put much stock in that—and of course we've married British ever since. Still, I know what I know, and I know what a crowd sounds like, on most occasions. There's the mutter of a hostile one, and the shouts when they throw flowers, and the sharp, fierce cheering when they know you're going out to fight for them. But this was different. There wasn't any heart or pith in it—just a queer sort of sobbing wail that went with us all the way to the gates. Oh, here and there, people shouted, "Come back with their heads!" or, "Bring us a Goth for a pet!" the way they do, but not as if they believed what they were saying. Too many of them were silent, and that queer sort of sobbing wail went with us all the way.

I march with the first cohort; it wasn't so bad for me. Though here and there, I saw faces in the crowd—old El-frida, who kept the wine shop, with the tears running down her fat cheeks, shouting like a good one, and Parme-sius, the usurer, biting his nails and not saying anything at all. He might have given us a cheer; he'd had enough of our money. But he stood there, looking scared. I expect he was thinking of his money bags and wondering if somebody would slip a knife in his ribs at night. We'd kept good order in the town.

It took a long time, at the gates, for the governor had to make a speech—like all that old British stock, he tries to be more Roman than the Romans. Our general listened to him, sitting his horse like a bear. He's a new general, one of Stilicho's men, and a good one in spite of his hairiness and his Vandal accent. I don't think he cared very much for the governor's speech—it was the usual one. The glorious Twentieth, you know, and our gallant deeds, and how glad they'd be to have us back again. Well, we knew that without his telling—we could read it in the white faces along the walls. They were very still, but you could feel them, looking. The whole town must have been at the walls. Then the speech ended, and our general nodded his bear head and we marched. I don't know how long they stayed at the walls—I couldn't look back.

But my recruit got away, after all, at the second halt, and that bothered me. He was a likely looking young fellow, though I'd always thought his neck was too long. Still, he was one of the children of the camp—you wouldn't have picked him to desert. After that, half a dozen others tried it—those things are like a disease— but our general caught two and made an example, and that stopped the rest. I don't care for torture, myself— it leaves a bad taste in your mouth—but there are times when you have to use a firm hand. They were talking too much about Deva and remembering too many things. Well, I could see, myself, that if we had to be marched half across Britain to take ship at Anderida, that meant the Northmen were strong again. And I wouldn't like to hold the northwest against Northmen and Scots with nothing but auxiliaries. But that was the empire's business—it wasn't mine.

After it was over, I was having a cup of wine and chatting with Agathocles—he's a small man, but clever with the legion accounts and very proud that his father was a

Greek. He has special privileges, and that's apt to get a man disliked, but I always got along well with him. If you're senior centurion, you have your own rights, and he didn't often try the nasty side of his tongue on me.

"Well, Death's-Head," I said—we call him that because of his bony face—"were you present at the ceremonies?"

"Oh, I was present," he said. He shivered a little. "I suppose you liked hearing them squeal," he said, with his black eyes full of malice.

"Can't say that I did," I said, "but it'll keep the recruits in order."

"For a while," he said, and laughed softly. But I wasn't really thinking of the men who had been caught—I was thinking of my own recruit who'd gotten away. I could see him, you know, quite plainly, with his long neck and his bright blue Northern eyes—a tiny, running figure, hiding in ditches and traveling by night. He'd started in full marching order, too, like an idiot. Pretty soon, he'd be throwing pieces of equipment away. And what would he do when he did get back to Deva—hide on one of the outlying farms? Our farmers were a rough lot—they'd turn him over to the governor, if they didn't cut his throat for the price of his armor. It's a bad feeling, being hunted—I've had it myself. You begin to hear noises in the bracken and feel the joints in your armor where an arrow could go through. He'd scream, too, if he were caught—scream like a hare. And all for a weak-faced girl and because he felt homesick! I couldn't understand it.

"Worried about your recruit?" said Agathocles, though I hadn't said a word.

"The young fool!" I said. "He should have known better."

"Perhaps he was wiser than you think," said Agathocles. "Perhaps he's a soothsayer and reads omens."

"Soothsayer!" I said. "He'll make a pretty-looking soothsayer if the governor catches him! Though I suppose he has friends in the town."

"Why, doubtless," said Agathocles. "And, after all, why should they waste a trained man? He might even change his name and join the auxiliaries. He might have a good story, you know."

I thought, for a moment. Of course they'd be slack, now we'd left, but I couldn't believe they'd be as slack as that.

"I should hope not, I'm sure," I said, rather stiffly. "After all, the man's a deserter."

"Old Faithful," said Agathocles, laughing softly. "Always Old Faithful. You like the boy, but you'd rather see him cut to ribbons like our friends today. Now, I'm a Greek and a philosopher—I look for causes and effects."

"All Greeks are eaters of wind," I said, not insultingly, you know, but just to show him where he stood. But he didn't seem to hear me.

"Yes," he said, "I look for causes and effects. You think the man a deserter, I think him a soothsayer—that is the difference between us. Would a child of the camp have deserted the legion a century ago, or two centuries ago, Old Faithful?"

"How can I tell what anyone would do a century ago?" I said, for it was a foolish question.

"Exactly," he said. "And a century ago they would not have withdrawn the Twentieth—not from that border— not unless Rome fell." He clapped me on the back with an odious familiarity. "Do not worry about your recruit, Old Faithful," he said. "Perhaps he will even go over to the other side, and, indeed, that might be wise of him."

"Talk treason to your accounts, Greek," I growled, "and take your hand off my shoulder. I am a Roman."

He looked at me with sad eyes.

"After three hundred years in Britain," he said. "And yet he says he is a Roman. Yes, it is a very strong law. And yet we had a law and states once, too, we Greeks. Be comforted, my British Roman. I am not talking treason. After all, I, too, have spent my life with the eagles. But I look for causes and effects."

He sighed in his wine cup and, in spite of his non
sense, I could not help but feel sorry for him. He was not
a healthy man and his chest troubled him at night.

"Forget them," I said, "and attend to your accounts.
You'll feel better when we're really on the march."

He sighed again. "Unfortunately, I am a philosopher,"
he said. "It takes more than exercise to cure that. I can
even hear a world cracking, when it is under my nose.
But you are not a philosopher, Old Faithful—do not let
it give you bad dreams."

I manage to get my sleep without dreams, as a rule, so
I told him that and left him. But, all the same, some of
his nonsense must have stuck in my head. For, all the
way down to Anderida, I kept noticing little things. Usually, on a long march, once you get into the swing of it,
you live in that swing. There's the back of the neck of
the man in front of you, and the weather, fine or wet, and
the hairy general, riding his horse like a bear, and the
dust kicked up by the column and the business of billets
for the night. The town life drops away from you like
the cloak you left behind in the pawnshop and, pretty
soon, you've never led any other kind of life. You have
to take care of your men and see the cooks are up to their
work and tell from the look on a man's face whether he's
the sort of fool who rubs his feet raw before he complains.
And all that's pleasant enough and so is the change in
the country, and the villages you go through, likely never
to see again, but there was good wine in one, and a landlord's daughter in another, and perhaps you washed your
feet in a third and joked with the old girl who came
down by the stream and told you you were a fine-looking soldier. It's all there, and nothing to remember, but
pleasant while it lasts. And, toward the end, there's the
little tightness at the back of the mind that makes you
know you're coming near the fighting. But, before that,
you hardly think at all.

This wasn't any different and yet I kept looking at
the country. I'd been south before, as far as Londinium,

but not for years, and there's no denying that it's a pleasant land. A little soft, as the people are, but very green,
very smiling, between the forests. You could see they took
care of their fields; you could see it was a rich place, compared to the north. There were sheep in the pastures,
whole flocks of them, fat and baaing, and the baths in
the towns we passed through got better all the way. And
yet I kept looking for places where a cohort or two could
make a stand without being cut off completely—now, why
should I do that? You can say it was my business, but Mid-
Britain has been safe for years. You have only to look at
the villas—we've got nothing like them in the northwest.
I couldn't help wondering what a crew of wild Scots or
long-haired Northmen would do to some of them. We'd
have blocked up half those windows where I come from—
once they start shooting fire arrows, big windows are a
nuisance, even in a fortified town.

And yet, in spite of the way Agathocles rode along like
a death's-head, it was reassuring too. For it showed you
how solid the empire was, a big solid block of empire,
green and smiling, with its magistrates and fine special
ladies and theaters and country houses, all the way from
Mid-Britain to Rome, and getting richer all the way. I
didn't feel jealous about it or particularly proud, but
there it was, and it meant civilized things. That's the difference between us and the barbarians—you may not
think of it often, but, when you see it, you know. I remember a young boy, oh, eight or nine. He'd been sent
down from the big house on his fat pony with his tutor,
to look at the soldiers, and there he sat, perfectly safe,
while his pony cropped the grass and the old man had a
hand in the pony's mane. He was clean out of bowshot of
the big house, and the hedges could have held a hundred
men, but you could see he'd never been afraid in his life,
or lived in disputed ground. Not even the old tutor was
afraid—he must have been a slave, but he grinned at us
like anything. Well, that shows you. I thought the worse
of Agathocles, after that.

And yet, there were other things—oh, normal enough. But, naturally, you can't move a legion without people asking questions, and civilians are like hens when they start to panic. Well, we knew there was trouble in Gaul— that was all we could say. Still, they'd follow you out of the town, and that would be unpleasant. But that didn't impress me nearly as much as the one old man.

We'd halted for half an hour and he came down from his fields, a countryman and a farmer. He had a speckled straw hat on, but it takes more than a dozen years' farming to get the look out of a man's back.

"The Twentieth," he said slowly, when he saw our badge of the boar, "the Valeria Victrix. Welcome, comrade!" so I knew at once that he'd served. I gave him the regulation salute and asked him a question, and his eyes glowed.

"Marcus Hostus," he said. "Centurion of the Third Cohort of the Second, twenty years ago." He pulled his tunic aside to show me the seamed scar.

"That was fighting the Welsh tribesmen," he said. "They were good fighters. After that, they gave me my land. But I still remember the taste of black beans in a helmet," and he laughed a high old man's laugh.

"Well," I said, "I wouldn't regret them. You've got a nice little place here." For he had.

He looked around at his fields. The woman had come to the door of the hut by then, with a half-grown girl beside her, and a couple of recruits were asking her for water.

"Yes," he said, "it's a nice little place and my sons are strong. There are two of them in the upper field. Are you halting for long, Centurion? I should like them to see the eagles before I die."

"Not for long," I said. "As a matter of fact, we're on our way to the seacoast. They seem to need us in Gaul."

"Oh," he said, "they need you in Gaul. But you'll be coming back."

"As Caesar wills it," I said. "You know what orders are, Centurion."

He looked at the eagles again.

"Yes," he said. "I know what orders are. The Valeria Victrix, the bulwark of the northwest. And you are marching to the ships—Oh, do not look at me, Centurion —I have been a centurion too. It must be a very great war that calls the Valeria Victrix from Britain."

"We have heard of such a war," I said, for he, too, had served with the eagles.

He nodded his old head once or twice. "Yes," he said, "a very great war. Even greater than the wars of Theodosius, for he did not take the Twentieth. Well, I can still use a sword."

I wanted to tell him that he would not have to use one, for there was the hut and the fields and the half-grown girl. But, looking at him, the words stuck in my throat. He nodded again.

"When the eagles go, Britain falls," he said, very quietly. "If I were twenty years younger, I would go back to the Second—that would be good fighting. Or, perhaps, to the Sixth, at Eboracum—they will not withdraw the Sixth till the last of all. As it is, I die here, with my sons." He straightened himself. "Hail, Centurion of the Valeria Victrix—and farewell," he said.

"Hail, Marcus Hostus, Centurion," I said, and they raised the eagles. I know that he watched us out of sight; though, again, I could not look back. It is true that he was an old man, and old men dream, but I was as glad that Agathocles had not heard his words.

For it seemed to me that Agathocles was always at my elbow and I grew very weary indeed of his company and his cough and what he called his philosophy. The march had done him no good—he was bonier than ever and his cheeks burned—but that did not stop his talkativeness. He was always pointing out to me little things I would hardly have noticed by myself—where a plowland had been left fallow or where a house or a barn still showed the scars of old burnings. By Hercules! As if a man couldn't plant wheat for a year without the empire's falling—but he'd point and nod his head. And then he'd keep talking —oh, about the states and the law they'd had in Greece, long before the city was founded. Well, I never argue with a man about the deeds of his ancestors—it only makes bad feeling. But I told him once, to shut him up, that I knew about Athens. A friend of mine had been stationed there once and said they had quite decent games for a provincial capital. His eyes flashed at that and he muttered something in his own tongue.

"Yes," he said. "They have decent games there. And buildings that make the sacred Forum at Rome—which I have seen, by the way, and which you have not seen— look like a child's playing with mud and rubble. That was when we had states and a law. Then we fought with each other, and it went—yes, even before the man from Macedon. And then you came and now, at last, it is your turn. Am I sorry or glad? I do not know. Sorry, I think, for the life is out of my people—they are clever and will always be clever, but the life is out of them. And I am not philosopher enough not to grieve when an end comes."

"Oh, talk as you like, Agathocles," I said, for I was resolved he shouldn't anger me again. "But you'd better not talk like that in front of the general."

"Thank you, Old Faithful," he said, and coughed till he nearly fell from his mule. "But I do not talk like that to the general—only to persons of rare intelligence, like yourself. The general does not like me very well, as it is, but I am still useful with the accounts. Perhaps, when we get to Gaul—if we go to Gaul—he will have me flayed or impaled. I believe those are Vandal customs. Yes, that is very probable, I think, if my cough does not kill me before. But, meanwhile, I must observe—we Greeks are so curious."

"Observe all you like," I said, "but the legion's shaking down very nicely, it seems to me."

"Yes, shaking down very nicely," he said. "Do you ever think of your deserter, who went back to Deva? No, I thought not. And yet he was the first effect of the cause I seek, and there have been others since." He chuckled quite cheerfully at that and went along reciting Greek poetry to himself till the cough took him again. The poetry was all about the fall of a city called Troy—he translated some of it to me, and it sounded quite well, if you care for that sort of thing, though, as I pointed out to him, our own Vergil had covered the same subjects, as I understand it.

We had turned toward the seacoast by then—we weren't going through Londinium after all. That disappointed our recruits, but of course the general was right about it. We'd kept excellent discipline so far, but it's a very different thing, letting the men loose in a capital. I was sorry not to see it again myself. I told the men that when they complained. This was southern country we passed through, very soft and gentle; though, on the coasts, there is danger. But, when we halted for the night, there had been no danger for years—it was a wide pocket of peace.

I remember the look of the big painted rooms of the villa, when I was summoned there. A very fine villa it was—it belonged to a rich man. They'd had Roman names so long, they'd forgotten their own stock, though the master looked British enough when you looked him full in the face. They had winged cupids painted on the walls of the dining room—they were sharpening arrows and driving little cars with doves—very pretty and bright. It must have been imported work—no Briton could paint like that. And the courtyard had orange trees in it, growing in tubs—I know what an orange tree costs, for my cousin was a gardener. A swarm of servants, too, better trained than our northern ones and sneakingly insolent, as rich men's servants are apt to be. But they were all honey to me, and sticky speeches—they knew better than to mock an officer on duty.

Well, I went into the room, and there was my general and the master of the house, both with wreaths around their heads in the old-fashioned way, and Agathocles making notes on his tablets in a corner and hiding his cough with his hand. My general had his wreath on crooked and he looked like a baited bear, though they must have had a good feed, and he liked wine. There were other people in the room—some sons and sons-in-law —all very well dressed, but a little shrill in their conversation, as that sort is apt to be, but the master of the house and my general were the ones I noticed.

My general called me in and told them who I was, while I stood at attention and Agathocles coughed. Then he said: "This is my senior centurion. . . . And how many leagues does the legion cover in a day, Centurion?"

I told him, though he knew well enough.

"Good," he said, in his thick Vandal accent. "And how many leagues would we cover in a day—let me see—accompanied by civilians, with litters and baggage?"

I told him; though, of course, he knew. It was less, of course; it made a decided difference. A legion does not march like the wind—that is not its business—but civilians slow everything up. Especially when there are women.

"As I thought," he said to the master of the villa. "As you see, it is quite impossible," and, in spite of his crooked wreath, his eyes were bleak and shrewd. Then arose a babble of talk and expostulation from the sons and the sons-in-law. I have heard such talk before—it is always the same. As I say, rich men are apt to think that all government, including the army, exists for their personal convenience. I stood at attention, waiting to be dismissed.

The master of the villa waited till the others had had their say. He was a strong man with a beaky nose, much stronger than his sons. He waited till the babble had ceased, his eyes calm, regarding our general. Then he said, in the smooth, careless voice of such men:

"The general forgets, perhaps, that I am a cousin of the legate. I merely ask protection for myself and my household. And we would be ready to move—well, within twenty-four hours. Yes, I can promise you, within twenty-four hours." There was such perfect assurance in his voice that I could have admired the man.

"I am sorry not to oblige a cousin of the legate," said my general, with his bear's eyes gleaming dully. "Unfortunately, I have my orders."

"And yet," said the master of the villa, charmingly, "a certain laxity—a certain interpretation, let us say. . . ."

He left his words in the air—you could see he had done this sort of thing before, and always successfully. You could see that, all his life, he had been accustomed to rules being broken for him because of his place and name. I have liked other generals better than this general—after all, the Vandals are different from us—but I liked the way he shook his head now.

"I have my orders," he said, and lay hunched like a bear on his couch.

"Let us hope you will never regret your strict interpretation of them, General," the master of the villa said without rancor, and a cool wind blew through the room. I felt the cool wind on my own cheek, though I am a senior centurion and my appeal is to Caesar. The man was strong enough for that.

"Let us hope not," said my general gruffly, and rose. "Your hospitality has been very enjoyable." I must say, for a Vandal, he made his manners well. On the way out, the master of the villa stopped me unobtrusively.

"And what would it be worth, Centurion," he said in a low voice, "to carry a single man on your rolls who was not on your rolls before? A single man—I do not ask for more."

"It would be worth my head," I said; for though my general did not seem to be looking at me, I knew that he was looking.

The master of the villa nodded, and a curious, dazed look came over his strong face. "I thought so," he said, as if to himself. "And, after all, what then? My nephew in

244   O'HALLORAN'S LUCK AND OTHER STORIES

Gaul writes me that Gaul is not safe; my bankers in Rome write me that Rome itself is not safe. Will you tell me what place is safe if Rome is not safe any more?" he said in a stronger voice, and caught at my arm. I did not know how to answer him, so I kept silent. He looked, suddenly, very much older than he had when I entered the room.

"A king's ransom out at loan and the interest of the interest," he muttered. "And yet, how is a man to be safe? And my cousin is the legate, too—I have first-hand information. They will not bring back the legions—blood does not flow back, once it is spilt. And yet, how can I leave my house here, with everything so uncertain?"

It seemed a fine house to me, though not very defensible; but, even as he spoke, I could see the rain beating through the walls. I could see the walls fallen, and the naked people, the barbarians, huddled around a dim fire. I had not believed that possible before, but now I believed it. There was ruin in the face of that man. I could feel Agathocles tugging at my elbow and I went away— out through the courtyard where the orange trees stood in their tubs, and the bright fish played in the pool.

When we were back in our billets, Agathocles spoke to me.

"The general is pleased with you," he said. "He saw that they tried to bribe you, but you were not bribed. If you had been bribed, he would have had your head."

"Do I care for that?" I said, a little wildly. "What matters one head or another? But if Rome falls, something ends."

He nodded soberly, without coughing. "It is true," he said. "You had nothing but an arch, a road, an army and a law. And yet a man might walk from the east to the west because of it—yes, and speak the same tongue all the way. I do not admire you, but you were a great people."

"But tell me," I said, "why does it end?"

He shook his head. "I do not know," he said. "Men build and they go on building. And then the dream is shaken—it is shaken to bits by the storm. Afterwards,

there follow darkness and the howling peoples. I think
that will be for a long time. I meant to be a historian,
when I first joined the eagles. I meant to write of the later
wars of Rome as Thucydides wrote of the Greek wars.
But now my ink is dry and I have nothing to say."

"But," I said, "it is there—it is solid—it will last," for I
thought of the country we had marched through, and the
boy, unafraid, on his pony.

"Oh," said Agathocles, "it takes time for the night to
fall—that is what people forget. Yes, even the master of
your villa may die in peace. But there are still the two
spirits in man—the spirit of building and the spirit of
destruction. And when the second drives the faster horse,
then the night comes on."

"You said you had a state and a law," I said. "Could you
not have kept them?"

"Why, we could," said Agathocles, "but we did not. We
had Pericles, but we shamed him. And now you and I—
both Romans"—and he laughed and coughed—"we follow a hairy general to an unknown battle. And, beyond
that, there is nothing."

"They say it is Alaric, the Goth," I said. "They say he
marches on Rome," for, till then, except in jest, we had
not spoken of these wars.

"Alaric, or another, what matters?" said Agathocles.
"Who was that western chieftain—he called himself Niall
of the Hundred Battles, did he not? And we put him
down, in the end, but there were more behind him. Always more. It is time itself we fight, and no man wins
against time. How long has the legion been in Britain,
Centurion?"

"Three hundred and fifty years and eight," I said, for
that is something that even children know.

"Yes," said Agathocles, "the Valeria Victrix. And who
remembers the legions that were lost in Parthia and Germany? Who remembers their names?"

But by then I had come back to myself and did not
wish to talk to him.

"All Greeks are eaters of wind," I said. "Caw like a crow, if you like; I do not listen."

"It does not matter to me," he said, with a shrug, and a cough. "I tell you, I shall be flayed before the ending, unless my cough ends it. No sensible general would let me live, after the notes I have taken tonight. But have it your own way."

I did not mean to let him see that he had shaken me, but he had. And when, six days later, we came to Anderida and the sea, I was shaken again. The ships should have been ready for us, but they were not, though our general raged like a bear, and we had to wait four days at Anderida. That was hard, for, in four days you get to know the look of a town. They had felt the strength of the sea pirates; they were not like Mid-Britain. I thought of my man at the villa and how he might die in peace, even as Agathocles had said. But all the time, the moss would be creeping on the stone and the rain beating at the door. Till, finally, the naked people gathered there, without knowledge—they would have forgotten the use of the furnace that kept the house warm in winter and the baths that made men clean. And the fields of my veteran centurion of the Second, would go back to witch grass and cockleburs because they were too busy with killing to plant the wheat in the field. I even thought back to my deserter and saw him living, on one side or the other, but with memory of order and law and civilized things. Then that, too, would go, and his children would not remember it, except as a tale. I wanted to ask Agathocles what a race should leave to its kind, but I did not, for I knew he would talk of Greece, and I am a Roman.

Then we sailed, on a very clear day, with little wind, but enough to get us out of harbor. It came suddenly, as those things do, and we did not have time to think. I was very busy—it was only when we were ready to embark that I thought at all. I am a child of the camp and the legion is my hearth. But I knew, as we stood there, waiting, what we were leaving—the whole green, rainy, smoky, windy island, with its seas on either hand and its deep graves in the earth. We had been there three hundred and fifty and eight—we had been the Valeria Victrix. Now we followed a hairy general to an unknown battle, over the rim of the world, and we would win fights and lose them, but our time was over.

I heard the speech for the last time—the British Latin. After that, it would only be the legion, wherever we went. Our general stood like a bear—he would take care of us as long as he could. Agathocles looked seasick already—his face was pinched and thin, and he coughed behind his hand. Before us lay the wide channel and the great darkness. And the Sixth still held Eboracum—I wished, for a moment, that I had been with the Sixth.

"Get your packs on board, you sons!" I shouted to the men.

As the crowd began to cheer, a little, I wanted to say to somebody, "Remember the Valeria Victrix! Remember our name!" But I could not have said it to anyone, and there was no time for those things.

www.ingramcontent.com/pod-product-compliance
Lightning Source LLC
Chambersburg PA
CBHW030810020726
47499CB00006B/1853